Welsh War

Book 5 in the Border Knight Series
By
Griff Hosker

Published by Sword Books Ltd 2018

SWORD
BOOKS

Contents

Prologue

My journey from Arsuf all those years ago had been a long one. I had fought as a mercenary. I had killed a Bishop and been declared an outlaw. I had lost all and yet after King John had died and after the Battle of Lincoln, we had rid our land of the French invader and my life had turned full circle. I had regained the lands of my father. I was now Earl of Cleveland as had been my great-grandsire, the Warlord. Sir Samuel had died a hero and his family rewarded with the loss of their lands. It was a hard-earned lesson. The Kings of England cared more for themselves than their people. We now had a boy king, Henry, who was the third to bear that name. My great grandfather and grandfather had served two of them. Would Henry turn out to be a king I could follow? He was just ten years old. My youngest son, William, was just a little younger and he had only just become a squire. Time would tell if the son of the great tyrant could become a good king.

The young boy king had inherited a land riven with dissension. Thanks to my family and my knights the Scots would not be a problem but Llewelyn, King of Gwynedd, was now beginning to encroach upon English lands. Worse, many lords wished more power. They had built adulterine castles. These had not been seen since the time of Stephen and Matilda. These were castles built without permission. The second King Henry and his son, King John, had pulled down all that had been built without their permission. There were lords who defied William Marshal. He was Regent of England.

4

I was now over forty years of age. There were few knights my age. William Marshal was the exception. He was old and he had been a knight when the Warlord had shaped England. He had assumed my great grandfather's mantle but his powers were slipping and I feared that when he passed away there would be no one left to assume his power. I had just knighted my son, Alfred. I had been honoured when he said he would prefer to be knighted by me than the aged Earl. Alfred had been my squire and now the position was taken by young William. With the ceremony over I could get back to being Earl of Cleveland. I could enjoy the valley I loved. I had lived away from it more time than I had spent there and I intended to make the most of it now that I was back from the wars. I knew that I would be called upon to serve my king and my country but for the moment I had peace and I would enjoy it. Once the King was crowned he was placed under the protection of William, Earl Marshal of England. He would ensure that the boy King came to no harm. Perhaps my work was done and I could just be Earl of Cleveland.

Chapter 1
The Evil Lord

My aunt, Ruth, had been a rock during my life. While I had been abroad she had kept me informed of all that went on in England and the valley. She had held on to Wulfestun and then managed to make Stockton her home once more. She was a survivor. She was now well over sixty years of age but remarkably hale and hearty. She had helped to raise my four children and now that Sir Geoffrey FitzUrse was courting my daughter Rebekah she was anticipating more babies for her to fuss.

It had been almost six months since Alfred had been knighted and I found her in the herb garden she had planted in the inner bailey. She waved me over, "Thomas, your daughter has a potential husband and he is a fine man. I approve but what of Alfred?"

I laughed, "You are ever blunt, aunt."

She smiled, "At my age, I do not have time to play with words and seek a diplomatic opening. Have you a bride in mind for him?"

"Have you forgotten, aunt, that in our family we do not have brides or bridegrooms chosen for us. We do the choosing."

She nodded, "True but you are his father. Point him in the right direction. There are many eligible girls who live close by. Alfred is the son of the most powerful baron in the north. He would be a great catch."

"He will find one when he is ready but, just to save my ears, I will speak with him."

She had been right to prick my conscience. It was not just the fact that he needed to sire an heir it was that I needed him married so that I could give him a manor. Bachelor knights did not have manors. I had many manors at my disposal. King John's reign had seen manors deprived of lords. Others had taken the cross. During my years abroad and as an outlaw I had learned that a knight needed power and coin if he was to survive. He also needed knightly skills and good men to follow him but coin and land gave a knight the opportunity to pay for good men. I had a large retinue. Henry Youngblood was the captain of my guard and I paid him and my men at arms well. They were equipped as well as knights. The only real difference was that they had a shorter hauberk and did not use spurs. I had not bought them destrier but we had been so successful that they all rode warhorses. They were good at what they did and captured many knights. Their war horses were the spoils of war. Alfred would need such men when he became a lord of the manor.

David of Wales, my captain of archers, saw me as I left my aunt. He had recently become a father. It was late in life for him. He no longer lived in my hall but he was the first to enter through the gates each morning and the last to leave before the watch was set. He was still industrious. He trained all my new archers and, each Sunday, would drill the men of the town at the green above St. John's Well.

"How goes the world, David?"

He smiled, "It is hard getting used to peace, especially with a baby who seems to spend each moment I am in my home wailing. I thought Cedric Warbow's snoring in a shared hovel was bad enough but a wailing child is a weapon we should use on the Scots!"

I smiled for I remembered Rebekah when she had been a baby. She had been a challenging child. Now a woman grown the problems of David of Wales' first baby brought the memories flooding back. "Well enjoy the peace. I fear it will not last." He cocked his head to one side. "A messenger came from York. William Marshal is unwell. There is talk of a Council of Regents who have been appointed to help

William Marshal guide our king. That may mean work for us."

"Will not the Earl Marshal be one of them?"

I shook my head, "He was invited but he claimed he was too old. He was not. My great grandfather was older still and held England for King Henry when he fought his sons."

"Who is on the council then, lord?"

"Pandulf, he is the Papal Legate. Peter des Roches, the Bishop of Winchester and Hubert de Burgh."

"Was he not the castellan of Prince Arthur?"

"Aye, and I have yet to forgive him for his part in the Prince's death."

"It was King John who had him murdered, lord."

"And Hubert closed a blind eye."

"He needs you, Sir Thomas."

"My valley needs me. My family needs me." I looked at my standard fluttering from my keep. I wanted it there as long as possible. "So, you came to speak to me?"

"Aye lord. I know we are at peace but, as you say, war could come at any time. I seek permission to ask Geoffrey Steward for funds. We need arrows."

"Of course, and how goes the training of new archers?"

"Well lord. Since the time of Dick, Sir Richard, Stockton has had a reputation for archers. Men seek training here. Even if we do not retain them then they can easily find employment when we have finished working with them." We both knew that few archers left our walls and those that did were not the best.

"I would have the best ten reserved for Alfred. He is not married yet but as my aunt reminded me he is eligible and he will seek a bride soon."

"Have you a manor in mind for him, lord?"

"Seamer has no castle and being situated south of the river would be a good place for him to learn how to be a knight. Do not say anything to him. I have yet to speak with him about becoming a lord of the manor."

Another of my knights, Sir Fótr, was Swedish and his people had been Vikings. He had the blood of Vikings in his veins. He often spoke of how seemingly inconsequential actions and conversations could be linked and set in motion events that seemed unconnected. So it was that those two conversations set in motion a trickle of rocks which became a landslide. I sought out William, my son and new squire. "Tomorrow we will ride abroad. Tell our squires to prepare our horses."

"Will we need guards?"

"The valley is at peace. If the earl and his son cannot ride without protection then it is a sorry day!"

That night when the four children had left us I sat with Margaret, my wife, in our chamber which faced west. She enjoyed the view, the solitude and the fact that the two of us were alone. "Aunt Ruth thinks that Alfred ought to be wed."

She squeezed my hand and sipped her wine, "She may be right but he is my eldest. I would have him as my boy a little longer."

"Rebekah is courted and is younger."

"And a fine catch she is. You will give her a good dowry and any knight would be a fool to ignore her. She is a girl and that is her future. Alfred is my son."

I nodded, "The money I have accrued is for one purpose, my children; all of my children. I would give Alfred a manor."

"Ah, now I see and understand. I hope it is not too far away."

"Seamer, just south of the river. We can be there in a couple of hours." I pointed to the river, "It is south of the river and he and his family will be safer there."

"Rebekah will be in the Palatinate."

"It may be worse than that. I believe the Bishop is considering Sir Geoffrey as the castellan at Norham."

"Norham! That is the border!"

"It may not be permanent. This is the best of times to be close to Scotland. They are weak and riven with internal dissension. He is a knight." I leaned over and kissed her. "You endured far worse when we were first wed."

"Aye but..." she laughed, "You are right. We survived. What does not kill you makes you strong. Look at your Aunt Ruth." I nodded. "Are there any suitable brides for him?"

"There are probably dozens but he must choose. I will not pick a bride for him. That is not our way!"

She leaned in and kissed me hard, "And that is why I love you so! You are the truest knight in Christendom." She took my hand and squeezed, "Come let us to our bed."

The next day the four of us mounted our palfreys and headed to the ferry. The river was busier these days. We had taken one of the loops out of the river and ships made the voyage from the sea half a day faster now. There were also many fishing boats supplying an increasingly large population. We had spread beyond our walls. At one time the tanneries to the north were as far as people lived. Now there were houses close to the cattle market which lay beyond the tanneries. We had not only farmers and tanners we had those who built and repaired ships. We had many smithies. In my grandfather's day we had begun to expand our production of iron. When King John and the Bishop of Durham had imposed their taxes, it had driven some people away. Now they had returned and my town prospered.

Seamer lay to the south of Yarm. I had a reason for choosing Seamer. In addition to Seamer, I had been given the manor of Northallerton which lay further south. It was too large for Alfred. He needed to learn how to be a lord at somewhere smaller and Seamer was perfect. There was rich farmland to the south and woods for hunting and timber to the north. I had said nothing to Alfred as we rode. I let him take in the land. I smiled when I saw him looking at how it might be defended. The village lay close to a stream. There was a green on which a few animals grazed. The ground rose but there was no hall there. Stokesley lay to the south and further south still lay Whorlton. Until Sir Ralph had been made Sheriff of York it had been his home. Now Sir Peter, who had been Petr son of Ridley the Giant, was lord of the manor.

We reined in at the green. There was a trough there for the animals. The reeve came over to speak with us. Edgar farmed the land and collected my taxes from me. He had often asked me for a lord. He did so again.

"My lord it is good to see you. It is a pleasant day for a ride. Have you chosen a lord of the manor for Seamer yet?"

"It is, Edgar, and all is well in the village?"

"We prosper but not as much as we might with a lord to live here. It is good that you exert your authority lord else we might starve."

I nodded. His wife came over with a jug of ale and her children carried four beakers. She poured us one each. "Thank you, gammer." I swallowed some ale and smacked my lips appreciatively. It satisfied Edgar's wife and she shooed her children back to their home. "A lord, Edgar, would mean you had less freedom. A lord would be watching you."

"I wouldn't mind that, lord. We don't get up to much that a lord might complain about. We have little disputes and a lord would be able to settle them. They are too trivial for the Stockton assizes." I nodded. "And we would be safer too!"

Alfred asked, "Is there a danger here?"

"Not any more, lord. But when your father was away then we had Scots and bandits to contend with. A lord would have been some protection. We do not even have a hall!"

I handed back the beaker. "I will think on this but I promise nothing." Mounting my horse, I said, "And you still keep up your archery each Sunday?"

His guilty face gave me the answer. "We try lord."

As we headed north, towards Thornaby Alfred asked, "Why did he say that it was good that you exerted your influence?"

My son had grown up in Stockton where I ran the manor as my father had. Others did not do so. "You know how in Stockton we allow men to gather wood from the forests and to graze their animals?"

"Aye, and you allow them to hunt when food is scarce."

"Well, it is not so in the rest of the country. Each lord guards his woods and forests jealously. They keep their people from the land which lies beyond their doorstep. My family has always believed that it is right for people to do so for they did it before the Normans came and my grandsire, Ridley, had grown up in such a world."

11

I saw him looking around at the land. He seemed to see, for the first time, the number of wooded areas. There were more woods than fields! "It would be an easy manor for a lord to manage but not profitable."

"Then you would not want it for your manor?"

He whipped his head around. "Of course, I would! I yearn for a manor."

"You are a bachelor knight. Until you are wed then you cannot have a manor."

His enthusiasm evaporated like morning mist. "But I have no one. Who would I marry?"

"That is your choice. Your mother and I care not save that you are happy. It is something for you to think about. I have David of Wales and Henry Youngblood choosing men at arms and archers for you but until you choose a bride then they will serve me."

He was silent on the way back to Stockton. I had planted the seed and I let it grow. He took to riding with his squire to speak to the other knights of the valley. He wished to seek their advice. To speak truthfully, I had much to occupy my mind in any case. Although we had scoured the land of rebellious lords and barons there were still some who were opposed to King Henry. They thought him too young. Others had ulterior motives. They sought land and power. I rode a month later to York with William. This time we were accompanied by men at arms and archers.

Sir Ralph had been my squire and was now Sheriff of York. His was a reassuring presence for I trusted him implicitly. He had married well and was related to a powerful Yorkshire baron. Part of the reason for my visit was to see if there were any suitable brides for Alfred. The ride from Stockton was a long one and we did not reach there until after dark. My name and standard were known and we were admitted quickly. Sir Ralph had rooms made up for us. Gone were the days when Sir Thomas would have to sneak around like a thief in the night and seek the most lowly of lodgings. I liked Ralph's wife. She was an open and honest lady. I hoped that Alfred would win as fair a bride. When she left us as soon as the food was finished I became wary. Sir Ralph sent his guards hence leaving me with my son and his squire. He had something to say. He filled my goblet, "You squires go and sit by the fire. Keep your ears closed and your eyes open. When our goblets are empty fill them!"

Sir Ralph had been a squire and knew how to speak to them. "Something is amiss, Ralph? You are acting strangely."

"I confess that I was on the cusp of paying you a visit lord. Your arrival was timely. You know that I take my role as Sheriff seriously?"

"Of course."

"I ride abroad. Often it is beyond my area of jurisdiction. I learned from you that a good knight watches for danger."

I could see that he was getting somewhere but it was a little too slow for me, "Come, Ralph, we have stood side by side and faced enemies with deadlier blades than the words which are stuck in your throat."

He nodded, "It is Lord Hugh of Craven. You have heard of him?" I frowned and shook my head. I knew the name but not the man. "He is a powerful baron who lives south-west of Barnard Castle." He took a drink and leaned back, "You know that the Sheriff of Northumberland is also Sheriff of Cumberland?" I nodded. "Craven lies just south of his jurisdiction and just west of mine. He has abused his position. He rules that part of England like a petty warlord. The Earl of Chester does not seem to bother with his northern manors." We both knew that the Earl of Chester was a politically minded knight. He sought power.

"I think I begin to see. That is why I do not know the man. He neither fought for us or against us. He sat and waited for a winner. Go on."

"It is said he was a favourite of King John who gave him Craven. He was a sword for hire. By all accounts he was a bad man even as a young knight. Some wonder if he was ever knighted at all. It is said that he did the King some service in France and was rewarded with Craven. He is a tyrant and the people there have no recourse. Chester is far away and the Earl is busy with the Welsh. I fear he has had those who would spread word of his tyranny imprisoned or murdered. He had fortified Skipton Castle so that he can laugh away any attempt to dislodge him. As I say it is not in my jurisdiction but I was trained by you and I cannot ignore such injustices."

I emptied my goblet, "And how did you learn of this?"

"Some of those fleeing the Lord of Craven did not head south but risked the high moors in winter. A handful managed to make the hamlet of Blubberhouses west of Harrogate and Ripon. When spring came they sent word to me and I rode to speak with them. There were four females and a boy. I had them brought back to York and gave them positions in my household. The news they brought saddened me and made me angry. You should hear it with your own ears for I fear my words would colour your judgement."

"I would speak with them tomorrow although I am not certain that I have any jurisdiction beyond my valley. It was my great grandfather who was Earl Marshal. He had power over every lord in the land. But, you are right, I must do something. I thought when we defeated de Percy and de Vesci we had ended all misrule and rebellion in the north and I can see that I was wrong. I would send a message to the Earl Marshal."

Ralph shook his head, "He is in Pembroke, lord, and there are Welsh twixt him and us."

"Then a ship. I will speak with these refugees and then return to Stockton to pick up my men. It may be that this Hugh of Craven listens to my advice and that will be the end of it."

"From what I have heard that is unlikely."

"In which case, I will send a ship to Pembroke and seek his advice and authority."

"And what of the King?"

"The King is a minor. It is his council that rules. They are based in the south and their eyes look either to France or the rebel barons who are still harboured there in the south of England. I fear I may have to resolve this myself."

We then spoke of our families. I told him of my sons and their progress and he told me of his children. "Seamer would be a good place for Alfred to learn to be a lord. Whorlton was the making of me, lord. I confess that I could not go back to such a small manor now."

"You have no need. I have the income of Northallerton but should you tire of the title of Sheriff then it is yours again."

"That is kind, lord. I confess that my wife yearns for the quieter life of lord of the manor. There are many demands upon my time. I will wait, however, until the King has attained his majority. I still remember King John!"

William held the candle which lighted our way to bed. Despite Sir Ralph's instructions to keep his ears closed he had not for he said, "Does this mean we go to war again?"

"Little mice have sharp ears eh? I hope not. As I recall Skipton Castle is well-situated and would not be easy to reduce. This Hugh of Craven may listen to reason. In any event, speculation is idle. I need to speak to these people on the morrow. Sir Ralph is not given to exaggeration. I fear that there is evil in the heart of Hugh of Craven."

I met the refugees in the Sheriff's chamber. It was less intimidating than the Great Hall. The four women and the boy were obviously from two families. The boy had not seen ten summers and a girl looked to be the same age. There was an older woman with strands of grey in her hair and what looked like her daughter for I saw a resemblance. The other woman looked to be the mother of the girl.

Ralph spoke gently to them, "This is Sir Thomas of Stockton, Earl of Cleveland. He is a good man and he would hear your story from your own lips."

As I expected it was the older woman with the flecks of grey who spoke, "We have heard of you, lord, and you give us hope for those who remain in the clutches of that monster. I am Sarah, wife of John. We had a farm east of Skipton. This is my daughter, Anne and her son John. We had heard of the evil perpetrated by Sir Hugh but as we lived far from Skipton we were able to live peacefully. The taxes we paid were too high but that is true of many who live in this land. All would have remained as it was but…"

15

The other woman, the dark-haired mother of the girl shook her head and spoke, "Until I brought disaster and ruin to you!"

"Mary, you did not! This is Mary, wife of Harold. Harold was my husband's younger brother. He served the lord of Gargrave, old Sir Henry. He was reeve to the old man. Old Sir Henry had lost his wife and brought up his daughter, Lady Matilda, alone. She had seen but fifteen summers and was a beauty." She looked at Mary, "You had better finish the tale, Mary."

The woman nodded, "Sir Hugh came to the hall of Sir Henry many times. He wished to court Lady Matilda. Lord, Sir Hugh had a wife!" There was real shock in her voice. "She disappeared. Folk said he had her killed for her money."

I nodded, "But there was no proof and it was just a rumour."

"Aye lord and the goings on of lords are not the business of those who work for them. Sir Henry was old but he stood up to Sir Hugh and told him that he would have to seek a wife elsewhere. Sir Hugh did not take it well. One night he and some men arrived at the hall to take Lady Matilda by force. My husband and Sir Henry joined with their other men to defend the girl. They were all killed. I fled lord. I am sorry but we could do nothing and I feared for my daughter. She has seen twelve summers. What if Sir Hugh had taken a fancy to her?"

Sarah patted Mary's hand, "She fled to us for we were her only family. We thought we had escaped. All of the manor knew that Sir Hugh had taken the manor of Gargrave and the Lady Matilda but could do nothing about it. When months had passed we thought we were forgotten."

"Why did you not seek help, Sarah?"

"We did and perhaps that was our downfall. Others had suffered at the hands of Sir Hugh. He had killed men and taken over farms. Each time help was sought from Chester but none came. My husband found a man who was travelling south and he gave him a letter for the Earl. My husband had been a soldier once and fought for the Earl against the

16

Welsh. The letter must have been intercepted. Riders came for my husband when he and my son were on the fells gathering sheep. My son escaped for he is quick but my husband was slain. We gathered what little we had and we fled."

I could see that she had told the tale so many times that her tears would come no more but I saw the sadness in her eyes. I was angry. The two families had been let down. I had to do something.

"And Lady Matilda?"

Sarah shrugged, "The last we heard she was in Skipton Castle. I know not if she lives or is dead."

"And what is it you would have of the Sheriff and myself?"

"Justice, lord, for our families, those of the manor and especially for poor Lady Matilda. She is innocent or was until she fell into Sir Hugh's clutches."

"And would you return to your farm?"

I saw them look at each other. They had not thought that far ahead. "To speak honestly I know not. We have yet to speak of that."

I smiled, "And it is unfair of me to ask you. I will deal with Sir Hugh first and then we can speak again." I stood.

The woman dropped to a knee and kissed the back of my hand, "Thank you, lord. We will have justice now!"

When they had gone I said, "Now I see why you wished it to be their words. I will pen a letter now. It should be sent by messenger to Chester. The Earl should know of this. I will write a second for you to send by ship. I will return to Stockton and I would have you and your men meet me at Ripon one week from now. Send to Whorlton for Sir Peter. I will call at East Harlsey and speak with Sir Richard. We will then go to Bolton Abbey. That is part of the manor of Skipton. Perhaps the Prior of the Abbey knows more than we do."

Sir Ralph smiled, "This will be like a crusade eh, lord?"

I shook my head, "I have been on a crusade and this is nothing like that. This is neither for gain nor for land. This is to bring hope and justice to those who have been abandoned."

Chapter 2
Castle Perilous

We left as soon as the letters were finished. We had a hard ride ahead of us. William was excited about the prospect of action. I was not. Skipton was a stone castle built upon a rock. It could not be mined and the land was not favourable for war machines. We reached our river at dark. Our horses were exhausted and we had walked the last mile to the ferry. Geoffrey, my steward, had grooms take away our horses and quickly organised food. I did not have time to tell my wife and my family of my news for Alfred suddenly burst out, "I have found a lady whom I could marry!"

I looked to my wife and she shrugged. I could see that she was not happy. "So soon? It is but a month since I spoke with you."

He nodded, "It was Sir Geoffrey who found her for me. She is a widow from Coxhoe in the Palatinate. The manor is not a rich one and she seeks a husband."

"You have seen her? Met with her?"

He shook his head, "She has no children and her husband died some years ago when the Scots raided."

"Some years ago? How old is she?"

"Does it matter?"

Rebekah said, quietly, "She is almost thirty, father."

"Which would make you twelve years her junior."

"Men often marry women who are little more than children. Queen Eleanor was fourteen years older than King Henry! Sir Geoffrey is older than my sister!"

Rebekah frowned, "By less than five years!"

"This is hasty and I have not time for it at the moment."
My son's face darkened. "You have not seen the lady. You
have not spoken to her and we have a war to fight."

All of them stopped to look at me. Margaret's hand went
to her cross. She liked not war. "The Scots?"

"No, my love. There is a lord in Skipton who has killed
some of his tenants and kidnapped a maid. Sir Ralph and I
will go to see if we can redress the situation."

"You said war."

"And it might come to that." I turned to Alfred, "So you
see that we put this matter to one side for a time. It may be
that this will be a suitable marriage although at the moment I
fail to see how it can be but there is no need for haste is
there?"

He smiled, "No, father." I think he was relieved.

The next morning, I sent riders out. I summoned the
knights who lived closest to the castle and my two captains,
Henry and David, to a counsel of war. There were just six of
them at the meeting. When they were gathered in my Great
Hall I told them all that we knew. They were all clever men
and I saw them take it all in. "Five days from now we march
to Ripon and thence to Bolton Abbey. We go as though we
travel to war but I will approach the castle with just the
Sheriff of York and some men at arms. If we can remedy the
situation by peaceful means then I would prefer to do so."

Sir Edward of Wulfestun said, "I have seen the castle. It
will be a hard nut to crack."

"I know and that is why I hope for peace. I have sent a
message to the Earl of Chester. This is his domain but time is
of the essence. Sir Hugh of Craven has a young girl in his
clutches and he appears to be a venal man. I would have you
bring all the men that you can. If we do not have to fight
then it will be a pleasant ride for our men but if we have to
fight then I wish the best that we have to do so."

They all knew the right questions to ask and left after an
hour. I sought out Tam, my hawker. He was also a good
scout. I sent him and two others to scout out Skipton. I
needed men who could be discreet. I had to know how many
men we faced. I would be busy from sunrise to sunset. A

campaign, even one as close to home as this, required planning. We were lucky in that we had many sumpters. All of my men at arms and archers were mounted as were those of my knights. Sir Peter had the fewest mounted men and he would bring the smallest retinue. When I visited the stables, I made certain the chief groom, Henry had enough horses for all of my men.

"Aye lord but Dragon is getting old."

"You mean I should not take her?"

"No, lord, she has more battles left in her but you need to consider a replacement. I would be happier if, when next you ride, you have a second warhorse to get them used to battle."

Henry was good with horses and I heeded his advice. I would seek a second horse. The blacksmith had checked over my armour. Now that we wore protective plates it was more important than ever that there were no weaknesses. He kept trying to persuade me to adopt a new helmet but I was comfortable with the old one. I was no longer the young warrior who was always seeking better mail, helmet and weapons. I knew that what I had would serve me well.

Two days before I left a rider came from York. I had had a message from London. I was summoned to a meeting with King Henry and the Earl Marshal. It was to be held at Windsor in three months' time. Of course, the council had not known of the problem of Sir Hugh. I did not like it but if the issue was not resolved then I might have to leave it in the hands of Sir Ralph. I was confident that I could leave him to handle the matter but it was not my way. We would cross that bridge when we came to it. We had left enough men to guard our walls and left to head upstream. We would not use the ferry, it would take too long. Instead, we would ride to Neasham and cross at the ford there. Had we men on foot it would have been difficult but we were all mounted. We had forty miles to go and we made it in one day.

The lord of Ripon was Sir Richard D'Omville. He was a good knight but I would use neither him nor his men. I preferred to use knights I knew and mine had all been my squires save for Sir William. I knew them like I knew myself. Sir Ralph and my other two knights had not arrived and so we camped. Sir Richard insisted that the knights and squires use his hall. It was large and rambling wooden walled hall. Sir Richard was childless and a widower. When he died I wondered who would inherit the estate.

As we drank some wine he said, "One of my ancestors, Robert de Romille, built the castle at Skipton you know."

"I did not."

"On my mother's side, of course. Lovely old castle. Robert de Romille's daughter, Cecilia, founded the abbey at Bolton. She married well too." He gave me a knowing look. "A hard castle to take, you know. I am not the warrior you are. I just rode my horse into battle and swung my sword a bit but it will be hard, even for you, to take with a frontal assault."

"I hope to talk him out."

He shook his head, "From what I hear he will not do that. When King John first gave him the manor I visited, as a good neighbour. I knew the castle and thought to give him advice about the grounds. I grew up there and played in every nook and cranny. He made it quite clear that he didn't want to socialize with me or any other of the nobles hereabouts. When I heard about some of the things he got up to, especially with the girls who had just become women then I was glad he had spurned my offer of friendship. If you want him out it would take a decree from the King and even then he might refuse to go."

It looked like it would be war. That would mean men dying. This would be a waste of my men's lives.

The old knight was in his cups and he had carried on talking. He laughed, "It was a wonderful castle for a lad to use as a playground. I remember as a lad how I used to scurry around the castle, hiding from the guards my mother sent to find me. I had too many places where I could hide." Shaking his head, he said, "There was even a passage I found out of the castle!"

My head whipped around and I saw that Alfred had heard the words too. "A passage?"

"Uhm, what? Ah yes, a passage. Not so much a passage as a cave I found. The castle is built upon a rock. It is what gives it its strength. There is a stream below the cliffs, Eller Beck it is called. There is a cave that comes out above the beck. If the river is full then you can drop into the water."

"Could you gain entry to the castle through it?"

"Not in mail you couldn't." He saw Ridley the Giant who was standing guard at the door. "He would be too big even without his mail." He pointed to Alfred and Fótr. "They could manage it." He had not taken a drink since he had begun the conversation and he suddenly saw what I was getting at. "Of course! You could use this as a means to sneak men into the castle." He sat upright. "I am not sure how you would get into the cave. I only ever used it to get out. Let me think backwards. If you were in the cave it would twist and turn as it climbed. It is dark. You can see nothing save at the beginning and the end. As a boy that was part of the excitement. It comes out in the beer cellar. As I recall it does not have a bolt on the castle side. One of the stewards managed to get himself locked in and he did so when the lord was away fighting for King Stephen. They found his body when they returned. The stink was such that they decided not to have a bolt any more. The steps take you to the other cellars and a second flight to the upper ward."

I patted him on the back. "You may just have given me the solution to my problem."

When Sir Ralph and my other two knights arrived, I told them what we had learned. We left the next morning our spirits boosted by the knowledge we had gleaned.

The Prior at Bolton Abbey was also happy that we were there to address the problem of Sir Hugh. "Thank you, Sir Thomas. The last years have been hard for us. Sir Hugh is not a lord who forgives what he perceives as mistakes. Even when they are not."

"Then why did you not seek help?"

He spread his arms, "From whom? He was the King's appointment! It is the poor people who have suffered the most. We helped those that we could but when Sir Hugh discovered two girls being sheltered by two of our friars he had them both whipped. After that we needed to be circumspect." He left much unsaid but the look in his eyes left me in no doubt about the baron's predilections.

The situation was getting worse the closer we got to Skipton. I left the bulk of the men there but I sent Mordaf and Gruffyd to the river to see if they could get into the cave. Both were agile and resourceful. I took Ridley the Giant with me as well as Henry Youngblood and ten of my biggest men at arms. Sir Ralph was the only knight I took. He brought ten of his own men too. It was enough to show we meant business without threatening the baron too much. The rest we left at the abbey. They would be just six miles away.

I had no doubt that the presence of such a large number of armed men would have been brought to the attention of the baron. As we passed through the village I saw doors were slammed shut as we approached. They were afraid. The gates to the castle were barred. It was as I remembered it. There was an imposing barbican and the castle rose high above it. Archers could make life difficult from both the keep and the gatehouse. William held my banner. It was well known. We halted beyond the range of bows and we waited. I knew we had been seen for men scurried away and then more men appeared along the wall and on the fighting platform of the double turreted gatehouse.

Neither of us had ever met Sir Hugh. When I saw him I saw a striking figure. The baron was a huge warrior. He had a long beard and looked to me, like the wild men of Estonia I had seen. The only difference was scale; he was larger. He roared, "What do you want here, Sir Thomas of Stockton? This is not your manor and you, Sheriff of York, also lack any power over me. I was given this castle by King John and you have no power to remove me!" I noticed that there was a slight accent to his words. Bizarrely he sounded Welsh.

I nodded, "You may be right Sir Hugh but we are here because of the privations you have brought upon your people. We are here because you have abducted the daughter of Sir Henry of Gargrave."

He was silent for a moment. How he thought to hide such a heinous act I do not know. "As her father died I have placed the daughter of Sir Henry under my protection. She will be my ward."

"Then we will leave but only when I have spoken to the maid and know that this is her decision and that she is not being held against her will."

He laughed, "You are pissing in the wind Earl! What I do in my manor is my business! I am lord here!"

"Perhaps but the Earl of Chester now knows of your actions as does the Earl of Pembroke. Either fetch the girl or a state of siege will exist until your liege lord, the Earl of Chester, arrives."

He must have already planned his attack for, without any warning, the gates were flung open and horsemen galloped out of the gate. I barely had time to don my helmet and pull my sword before they were upon us. I shouted, "William, get to the abbey! Fetch our men!"

I swung my sword in an arc at the two men at arms who had outstripped the others to reach me. My blade hit their spears and deflected them. As they pulled their arms back for a second thrust I reached down and pulled my shield up. When they struck again I managed to block one sword with my shield and my sword hacked through the shaft of the second. My men at arms were all veterans and they had quickly ridden to meet these horsemen and protect me. Sir Ralph had a mixture of veterans and new men. Some of his more inexperienced men paid the price for that lack of combat readiness.

The man at arms whose spear I had broken was reaching for his sword. I spurred Dragon and brought my sword around in an arc. I hit his coif so hard that I think I broke his neck. He tumbled from his horse. A spear is a good weapon to use when you charge. By the time you are in a mêlée, it is an encumbrance. The man at arms pulled his arm back. We were so close that the spearhead was less than an arm's length from my shield. He hit the shield. There was no power in the blow but the backhand strike with my sword across his chest had all of my strength behind it and the blade tore through his leather and into his chest. He fell from his horse. The losses we had sustained had come from Sir

Ralph's men. He and his squire were still battling but they were being forced back. My men, on the other hand, were fighting together. Ridley and Henry Youngblood were forcing back Sir Hugh's men at arms. Ridley's long arms and long sword outranged even the spears of the men he was fighting. I saw now an opportunity to exploit the situation. If William could get back quickly then we might force the gate. I spurred Dragon to join Ridley and Henry.

My war horse crashed into the side of a man at arms trying to get to the side of Henry. I stood in my stirrups and brought my sword down on his right arm. I laid him open to the bone and he used his left arm to wheel his horse away. Despite their overwhelming numbers the skill of my men, their armour and weapons meant that we were winning. It must have been obvious to Sir Hugh that he was losing too many men and I heard a horn sound. His men began to pour back through the gates. Instinct took over with me. I sensed the missile coming from the gatehouse and I raised my shield. The arrow thudded into it. Henry had been the target and, as he slew the man he was fighting he said, "Thank you, lord!"

I nodded, "Pull back beyond their range." We backed our horses away and I saw the extent of our losses. Sir Ralph had lost half of his men and two others were wounded. Will Red Leg had a crossbow bolt sticking from his leg. I saw that others had mail which was damaged. We had been lucky.

As we waited for William to bring up the rest of my men I examined the castle more closely. It would be hard to take but that strength also gave it a weakness. There was but one way in and one way out. We did not need to surround the castle we could just camp outside the front gate. They would have a well but they would not have laid in vast stocks of food. That would not worry Sir Hugh but it might demoralize his men. Of course, if my two archers could find a way in then perhaps we could dispense with the need for a siege.

Sir William brought my men at a gallop. They saw the dead. "We build a camp here. Sir Peter, have some men with shields advance and bring back our dead. I will not leave them there."

"And the enemy dead, lord?"

"Leave them where they lie."

I dismounted and handed my reins to William. Sir Ralph did the same. We both took off our helmets. He shook his head, "Does it always hurt to lose men, lord?"

"Always. I was lucky."

"Or perhaps your men were better trained." He looked at the gatehouse. Sir Hugh was still there. "He has signed his own death warrant."

"We will try him."

Sir Ralph laughed and waved a hand at my knights. "His peers will find him guilty!"

When the bodies were recovered Sir Ralph and his men returned to Bolton Abbey to bury them in the graveyard there. That left me with my knights. We had a line of sentries. So far, we had not used our archers. I intended to wait until the next day to show Sir Hugh just how good they were. I checked on Will Red Leg and discovered that the wound was not serious. We had a day or two before he would be needed.

"My plan is simple. We wait here unless Mordaf and Gruffyd can find a way in."

Sir William asked, "And if they can?"

"Then we send in our smallest men. We time it so that they sneak in during the hours of darkness. We will attack at dawn. As our archers are not yet returned we cannot attack tomorrow and so we spend the day building ladders. They will expect that and we will need them in any case." I waved over Dick and Henry Youngblood. "We may need small men to enter the castle. Choose the best twenty that we have."

"And who will lead them lord?" My son's voice was polite but I knew what he meant.

Sir Fótr stepped forward, "The two smallest knights are myself and Sir Alfred. I would say this task chooses us."

I felt my heart sink but he was right. Only Sir Peter was younger and he was a giant. He could not fit in a tunnel even if he was naked. "You know you will not be able to wear mail?" They both nodded. "It may be unnecessary. Perhaps Sir Richard misremembered."

My son smiled, "You do not think so, Earl. This is good. I am unafraid of the dark and of confined spaces. I am quick and without armour will be even quicker." I nodded and the two of them went with Henry and David to select the men. There was no question of them taking their squires.

The two archers slipped silently into the camp after dark. My knights and my two captains looked at them expectantly. They just grinned. Sometimes my two Welshmen could be infuriating. "Well?"

"Oh, there is a cave and we managed to climb up but others would need a ladder. We are both good climbers." Henry Youngblood snorted. Ignoring him Mordaf went on, "We went in until we found the beer cellar. We resisted the temptation to sample it but we tried the door. It does open."

I nodded and breathed a sigh of relief. "Then you have earned your ale this night. Rest for you will be leading our men tomorrow night. Sir Fótr and Sir Alfred will be leading you."

"It will be tight, lord. You will not be able to wear mail or a helmet."

Gruffyd grinned, "Although an arming cap and coif would save a few bumps!"

"Begin making the ladders tonight. We will need one by daylight."

As the men at arms and archers hurried off I sat with Fótr and Alfred. "You know that I would prefer it if I led?"

"Yes lord, but this task is appointed to us because of our size. Of course, if you do not think we can handle it…"

"Do not be foolish, Fótr! You are attempting something no one else has ever done. You will have to think on your feet. I know not what lies within. I do not know much save that there is an inner gate which will be held."

Alfred said, "Earl… father, we have the best of archers with us and our men at arms. We have surprise. We will take one gate and then the second. I will hold the inner gate with half of the men while Fótr takes the other gate. I am guessing

28

that David of Wales will have other archers clearing the walls. These men we fight have never faced us before. They are in for a shock." He was right but I would still worry. No man likes to lose a son.

I did not sleep well for I worried about my son. How could I go back to my wife and tell her that I had lost him underground and he would lie unburied? When dawn broke, those who would be attacking through the cave were left abed and David of Wales began to use his archers against the walls while ladders were built. Henry Youngblood and Ridley the Giant built them just beyond crossbow range but in clear sight of the castle. The ladders were made using the timber from the woods which lay close to the road. With luck we would not need them but as the task had to occupy my men all day they made a good attempt. We rose and went to view the castle.

We saw smoke rising from the inner bailey during the afternoon. That was as a result of my men laying out the ladders they had completed. The defenders were heating water or oil to pour upon the men who would climb the ladders. I summoned my knights. "We will keep men toiling all night. I want them to expect a nocturnal attack. We will all get some sleep but to the defenders it will be as though we have not slept and they will keep a good watch."

We had enough knights and men so that each knight and his retinue would just have an hour to work. I gave some of my men to Sir Peter. Mordaf led my son and Sir Fótr off before dark. They marched down the road as though heading for another camp. It would just undermine the confidence of those in the castle. They would wonder where my men went.

I slept but not well. I was listening for noises from the far side of the castle. My son and the others would be less than half a mile away as the crow flies but I knew that it would take them a good couple of hours to reach the river, cross it and then use the ladder they had built and taken with them. Mordaf was not certain if a light might be seen by someone using the beer cellar although they had discovered that the entrance to the tunnel was hidden by one of the barrels. I could not believe that the entrance had not been seen but as

29

Ridley the Giant had said, as we played out the game of building another ladder, "Sir Richard only knew it because he was a boy and played there. This new lord, Sir Hugh, does not know it. I cannot see one of his men investigating a dark hole. Men are afraid of confined spaces and the dark. I could not do what your son is doing. He is a brave man."

"I know."

I dozed and woke at every noise. It was in the last hours before dawn that I finally rose. It was Sir Peter who was toiling with his men. He pointed to the walls of the castle, "They have had men watching us all night. They must have burned all their brands."

Padraig the Wanderer said, "Aye lord and whatever they were heating has had to be refilled. What a terrible waste eh?"

We had taken our men into our confidence. They knew our plan. William came over. He had some stale bread, a hunk of cheese and weak ale. I ate but only because it gave me something to do. We woke all the men an hour before dawn. We would be ready to attack as soon as the dawn broke properly. I was able to watch the sun rise behind us. Our men, if all had gone well, would now be ascending the stairs. My archers would have their daggers and short swords ready to slit the throat of any unfortunate that they met. I hoped that they would only kill the warriors but we had to have silence and I knew that there might be some unfortunate accident. That was war. As I ate I said, "William you are too young to be a squire who fights. You are there to be used as my messenger. Keep your shield covering yourself and I do not expect you to have to draw your sword."

He nodded, "I am not a fool, lord. Alfred has told me that until I have seen a few more summers I am here to be used." He smiled, "One day I will draw a sword and defend your back!"

I had decided to attack when the gatehouse was illuminated. We were all ready. Men at arms held the ladders and our archers had their bows ready. They glanced at me. I would determine when to attack. I closed my eyes and I

30

listened. I hoped that I might hear, in my head, the sound of my son's thoughts. I heard something but it was not his voice. I drew my sword. As soon as I dropped it my men gave a mighty roar. That was to tell those inside that we were attacking and I shouted, "Charge!"

I held my shield before me as I ran and it proved to be a wise move as crossbow bolts clattered into it. Two stuck. Ridley the Giant and Padraig the Wanderer were with me. They held axes. We would try the gate. It was well made and was studded with iron but if Fótr and Alfred succeeded then I wanted to be the first one within the walls. The first of our men fell. I did not turn to see who it was but as the cry came from behind me I knew that it was one of our men. Sir William and Sir Edward were leading men to scale the walls.

We reached the gate and William and I held our shields above the heads of the two men at arms as they began to hack at the door. I heard ladders strike the walls. There was a cry and a thud as an arrow plucked a defender from the walls and dropped him ten paces from us. Then I heard the sound I had been praying for. It was the sound of fighting and was coming from inside the walls. My men had gained access. William glanced up and said, "Sir William has made the top of the walls!"

Despite their best efforts Ridley and Padraig were not going to damage the gate, "Hold, we will rely on our men gaining access." I had with me, my squire and ten men at arms. "Swing your shields around and when we gain entry we run for the inner gate, Sir Alfred will be hard-pressed to hold it." Even as I said it I did not know how many of my men had survived to reach the gates.

I heard the sound of heavy fighting on the other side of the gate. It seemed to be over quickly and then the bar was removed and the gate slid open. Sir William and Sir Fótr stood there. "Secure the gates! Well done Sir Fótr! My men, with me!" I led my men up the slope towards the other gate. I saw that the outer bailey had bodies upon it. I saw at least two of my men. The inner bailey could be seen through the opened gate. I saw Mordaf and his brother loosing arrows towards the hall. I saw that John the Archer was tending to

31

Henry, my son's squire, he had a wounded arm. The squire pointed his good arm. "Sir Alfred pursued Sir Hugh into the hall!"

The door to the keep was open and I threw myself through it. I heard the sounds of battle coming from the Great Hall. On the floor, just outside lay two of my men. As we burst in I saw Alfred with Thomas the Welshman and Sean Wild Eyes. The three of them were standing before a weeping girl. Sir Hugh and six men were trying to get at them. Even as we entered I saw Sean as he was stabbed in the leg. The Irishman fought on.

"Stockton!" I was angry but it was a cold anger. My son's life was in danger and these men who sought to hurt him and the girl were little more than savages. As the man at arms raised his sword to end Sean's life I rammed my sword deep within his guts and I twisted it out. Even as he fell I ran towards Sir Hugh. He was a big man and Sir Alfred had no armour. My son would have little chance. "Turn, you pathetic apology for a man, and face me!" I backhanded his squire away with my shield and exposed Sir Hugh's side. He had no choice. He had to face me.

He wore no helmet and his face was a mask of pure evil. "King John always hated you! Do you know he hired more than ten men to kill you?" If he said it to upset and shock me then he failed. I, of all people, knew the evil that had been within his breast.

"Then they failed! And now you will die. I will not save you for the executioner's block. You will die and your remains will be spread across this land. There will be no record of you so that men will wonder who it was who caused such pain and suffering."

I saw, in his eyes, the sign that he was about to strike and I took the blow on my shield. My men had disposed of the others and so I had room to swing. I put every ounce of strength I had in the blow and when it struck his shield I saw him wince. I stepped forward, pulled back my arm and raised it. The blow this time came down diagonally and he barely had time to swing his shield around. This time my strike must have completely numbed his arm. The shield dropped.

As I pulled back my right arm I punched with my shield and hit him in the face. He reeled. This was no warrior. This was a butcher, a killer. From what I had learned he was a predator who preyed on young girls. This was a knight who did not deserve the title. He abused his power and position on the weak and the innocent. He had been happy to attempt to slay my son for he had no mail but when he faced a real knight then all of his flaws were exposed. As he lay there I brought my sword from on high, "This is for Sir Henry and all the others whose lives you have ruined!" The sword tore through his throat and continued down to sever his head from his spinal cord. It rolled away and a lake of blood pooled around it.

There was silence in the hall save for the sobbing of the girl. I saw that my son had his arm around her and was giving her comfort. It was over.

Chapter 3
A Northern Welcome

I thought to speak to my son but saw that he was otherwise engaged. Ridley was tending to Sean. The only survivor in the hall was the knight's squire who was rising, groggily, to his feet. "Padraig, hold him. Ralph of Appleby search for any others who may have escaped us. Mordaf, come with me." As we headed upstairs I asked, "What was it like, Mordaf?"

He grinned, "As black as night lord! My grandfather worked in the copper mines and he had told me of the dark beneath the earth. I have seen it, lord, and I would not do as he did. He had more courage than I did. Your son and Sir Fótr were fearless. Sir Alfred showed no hesitation when the girl ran down the stairs. He stepped before her. That nasty piece of work, Sir Hugh, slew Jamie and Roger with two blows!"

When we reached the first floor we heard whimpering. Pushing open the door I saw two young girls and an older woman. The older woman had a bruised face yet she was comforting the two girls. She glared at me, "If you are one of his lordship's friends then you will have to kill me to get at these two!"

I sheathed my sword and took off my helmet. I spoke softly, "I am the Earl of Cleveland and Sir Hugh is dead. You are safe now, gammer."

In answer, she burst into tears and threw herself at my feet, "He is truly dead?"

"His blood is on my sword!"

"God has answered my prayers. And her ladyship?"

"She is safe. My son is giving her comfort." I turned to Mordaf, "Take these two downstairs."

"Aye lord. Come my little ones, let us see if we can find some food eh?" He had a gentle way about him and the two girls, who could not have been more than twelve summers' old went with him.

"Rise...?"

"Nanna, I am called Nanna. I am the maid and was the nurse to Lady Matilda. The two girls you saw were also her maids. They are Anya and Brigid." I sat her on the bed. There was a jug of ale and a beaker. I used the bed linen to wipe the rim of the beaker and poured her some. She drank it gratefully and I waited. She nodded at the bed. "This was the chamber of Sir Hugh. Those poor young things your man took away were abused by Sir Hugh and his squire." She shook her head. "The memory will haunt me until the day I die."

"And the Lady Matilda?"

"She was the reason that the two of them were hurt; the fey young things. He wanted her to marry him and she refused for he had killed her father. He seemed obsessed by her. He and his squire did what they did to make her agree but she would not. She knew that her maids would continue to suffer after she was wed. She prayed for someone to come but no one did. I tried to stop them but I was beaten. They were cruel, lord. Sometimes they would leave the girls alone and her ladyship and I would think that the ordeal was over but he was toying with them and giving them a little hope then when next he inflicted himself upon them it would be worse."

"You have cared for her a long time?"

"I was her wet nurse for her mother died in childbirth. Old Sir Henry and I brought her up on our own." It was as though she suddenly remembered him for she burst into tears. "He was murdered, lord! The two of them hacked him to pieces when he tried to stop them taking away his child!"

I took her arm, "Come let us reunite you. I killed him too quickly." As we descended the stairs I said, "Would she wish to return to Gargrave Manor?"

"No lord for that hall now has too many evil memories. The four of us are all that survived."

"Then until we decide what shall be done I will take you to Stockton." I smiled, "My Aunt Ruth is good with fey young things. She will heal your mistress." I patted her arm, "And you."

Sir Ralph was in the doorway as we descended. He gestured with his arm, "They all fought to the end. I think we had all of the rats but I confess I do not know. They fought hard. The castle is ours. Only the servants remain."

I nodded, "Dispose of the bodies and have the castle cleaned. We will stay here this night."

As we entered the hall I saw that Lady Matilda and Alfred were smiling at each other. Nanna said quietly, making the sign of the cross, "God be praised that is the first smile I have seen upon her lips since her father died."

"Amen to that Nanna. That is my son, Sir Alfred. Go and see to your lady while I deal with this." I walked over to Padraig and the squire of Sir Hugh. He was not a young squire. He was in his twenties and even though he was held he had an insolent look about him. "What is your name, squire?"

"Hubert of Garstang! What becomes of me, Earl? Will you let me take my horse and my goods and leave here? You have killed my lord and now I must seek another."

I smiled, "You think it is done now?"

"We defended our castle against an unwarranted attack; aye, of course, I think it done."

Mordaf brought the two young girls through the door and I saw them flinch when they saw that the squire was not yet dead. "And what of your sins? What about those unspeakable things that you and this animal did to those ladies?"

He made the mistake of laughing, "Ladies? We never touched Lady Matilda and they were just peasants. What else is their purpose?"

36

I smacked him so hard with the back of my hand that he tumbled to the ground, falling over his master's bloody body. "Padraig, find a rope and we will end this animal's life. Hold him!"

"Aye lord!"

"You cannot do this to me! I am noble born!"

"There is no nobility in you. Besides this is done legally. The Sheriff of York is here and he agrees with the death sentence!"

Sir Ralph had a dark look upon his face, "Aye lord and more if we could!"

The squire was held by Ridley the Giant and Henry Youngblood. He wriggled and squirmed but it did him no good. Our men all watched as we took him to the gatehouse. Padraig had slung a rope over the parapet and had a noose ready. There are two ways to hang a man. The humane way is to tie a noose and then drop him from a height with his hands tied so that he dies quickly when his neck breaks. We would use the other. While Ridley the Giant held him, Henry put the noose around his neck. They looked at me and I nodded.

"You will die unshriven. You will die slowly so that all of your sins will fill your head and then, when you are dead you and your master will be dismembered and your bodies spread so that no one will ever remember you. You will see your lord again but it will be with Lucifer for you will be in hell where you will burn until the end of time!" I nodded and my men hauled him up.

His hands went to the rope to stop the slow strangulation. When he was the height of a man from the ground the rope was tied off and my men watched as his legs kicked and he struggled. His eyes bulged as he tried to stop the rope from biting. He twisted and turned. His movements became slower. His hands dropped to his side and his eyes closed. It took longer than I would have thought and then it was over.

"Leave him there until sunset. Then cut him down and rid me of his body and that of Sir Hugh."

"Aye lord."

37

Our dead were buried by the chapel. I turned to Sir Ralph, "Until word comes from the Earl of Chester then you will have to leave men here. This manor will need help. Perhaps the Prior can help."

He shook his head, "How could a man do what he did? He was a knight!"

"Not all knights are like us. When I was in the Holy Land I saw that. Men like Sir Hugh enjoy power but I confess I do not know how they could have done what they did to those two girls. I fear that Aunt Ruth will be hard pressed to bring them back from the brink."

He nodded towards my son who was still speaking with Lady Matilda, "And those two? The girl has lost all. Your son..."

"Is a true knight and he will protect her until we can decide what we need to do. First, we get them to Stockton. I would have them all surrounded by kind people and there are none kinder than Lady Ruth and my wife."

We searched the hall and found much to disturb us. He had, in his chest, what appeared to be trophies and mementoes from women and girls he had abused. There were sacks of coins secreted in a chest and on his table, there was a half-finished letter. From the smudge, he had been writing it and then been disturbed.

Skipton
My son,
I confess that your sudden arrival came as a shock to me. I left your mother, my one true love, when she was carrying you. Perhaps that was a mistake. Now that I have had time to reflect I can see why you were sent to me. I hope the man I sent after you has given you my words but this letter will

That was all there was. He had a son? According to all those whom I had spoken to he had neither wife nor family. Would some son come to claim his father's inheritance? Had I found the letter before we had executed the squire I might have had an answer. I put the letter in my tunic. I could do nothing about it yet.

We left the next morning. The four women had all asked to share one room far from Sir Hugh's. Ridley and Padraig watched their door. By the time we left the sun was up and the women were in a wagon. It would take two days to get home. We stopped at Ripon where I was able to tell Sir Richard that his evil neighbour was gone. The old knight promised to watch over the manor until the Earl of Chester had appointed a new lord. I was unsure if it might not be the King who did so. When I travelled to London then I would ask further questions.

Alfred spent the whole journey north next to the wagon. Our wounded were also within and perhaps that was the excuse which Alfred gave himself for his squire rode within. I could see, however, that fate had intervened. This was like his mother and me. The two of them had not planned it but the collision of their lives had bound them to each other. I guessed that the widow from the Palatinate would now be a distant memory.

Sir Peter and Sir Richard rode directly east and I headed home with Sir Edward, Sir William, Sir Fótr and Sir Alfred. Sir Edward was quiet, "What is amiss Sir Edward? It is not like you to be so silent for so long."

"I feel as though I have not done enough in this campaign. Apart from climbing a wall, I did little. It was your son and Fótr here who did it all."

"Think of the times when it was Fótr and Alfred who stood behind us. This task was chosen for them and they acquitted themselves well. Make the most of your time at home. I fear that there will be more tasks for us and they will involve you and I putting ourselves in harm's way."

"It cannot be the Scots they are quiet and subdued."

"Oh they will rise again, of that I have no doubt. The problems lie further south. I have been summoned by the King's Council and I do not think they just want to tell me that we have done well in the north. I think there are problems with rebellious lords. And the Welsh, so I hear, are becoming more than a little aggressive. Make the most of your time here at home. I will have to leave soon. Our work is not yet done."

Surprisingly that seemed to brighten him, "That is the best news I have heard in a long time. We were not enriched by this action. Fighting the Welsh is always rewarding."

We had left the coin and treasure of the baron with Sir Ralph. We all agreed that it should be used for those who had suffered at the hands of the evil man. Those who had fled could return and the coin used for seed and animals. I hoped that Earl Ranulf would choose a better lord for the manor this time.

I sent Sir Edward and Sir Fótr ahead to warn my family of the new guests and they had already crossed on the ferry by the time we reached it. I knew that my wife and Aunt Ruth would want to make the castle welcoming for our guests. Fótr and Edward would have told them of the horror of Skipton. The two of them, Margaret and Aunt Ruth, along with Rebekah and Isabelle, were waiting at the wharf when the ferry landed. We had left the wagon on the Thornaby side. Aunt Ruth had a heart bigger than any I knew. She managed to embrace the three girls in one hug. I saw a smile on Nanna's face. It was the first time I had seen one and it gave me hope. Margaret hugged Alfred and I heard her say, "I am proud of you, son." She glanced up at me, "And you too!" She then shooed us all up to the castle.

Geoffrey, my steward, had servants waiting to take the girls to their new chamber. My wife had experience in these matters and knew that the last thing they would want would be to be separated on their first night in a new home.

I changed for the meal. I spoke with Geoffrey before I entered the hall for I would be away again within a few days. London called. He told me that there was no further news from the south and I took that to be a good thing. No news was good news.

I had not yet spoken to Matilda. My son had occupied her time. She did not seem to object. I, however, had to establish what she did wish. I waited until all had eaten and we had drunk enough for there to be a convivial atmosphere. There was a predominance of women for there were just my two sons at the table with me.

40

"Lady Matilda, in the next few days I will be leaving Stockton and before I leave I need to have it clear, in my mind, your views on your situation."

Aunt Ruth burst out laughing, "Thomas! So formal! You will frighten the girl to death! Speak plainly!"

I sighed for there was no arguing with my Aunt. "Matilda, you have a home here as long as you wish. If, on the other hand, you wish to return to Gargrave then I will understand. The third course of action would be to allow you to go a relative but I am not certain..."

She gave me a smile which lit up the room and she reached over to touch my hand with hers. "Sir Thomas, your aunt is correct, I do not need you to dance with words. I am so grateful to you that if I thanked you every day for the rest of my life then I could live to be a hundred and it would still not be enough. You and your family," she glanced and smiled at Alfred, "have put your lives in danger because of me. If you will allow me then I will stay here with my ladies and we will try to be of some use."

Aunt Ruth squeezed her hand, "You already serve a purpose for you bring life into this castle." She gave Alfred a sly look, "And I daresay you will improve the manners of certain young men here in the castle."

William laughed when his big brother blushed, "She means you, Alfred!"

Aunt Ruth shook her head, "It is a shame that you did not think that I might have meant you as well, William!"

Everyone laughed at my squire's embarrassment. The four females had a new start and I now knew that they would fit in easily. I could go to London knowing that there was naught for me to worry about in Stockton.

Travelling to London would be a major undertaking. I would need servants as well as men at arms and a couple of archers. We would need to have sumpters which would carry our clothes. We would need to stay in the homes of lords I knew, monasteries and priories or if all else failed then inns. Accommodation for twenty people was not easy to arrange. While we were north of Lincoln then it would not be a problem. My name and reputation were well known. I did not know what expenses would be involved and we would need coin. Once I reached Windsor then the King's Exchequer would deal with our subsistence. I did not think we would need war horses but we had to take four or five spare palfreys. It would not do to go afoot. The result of all this planning and preparation was that I did not get to see my son to speak to until the night before I left. I was in my office with Geoffrey. I had a good jug of wine and was just finalising the details of the trip and the matters I would deal with when I returned.

Alfred knocked on my door. Geoffrey was diplomatic, "I think that we have covered all and if not then I will shall see you in the morning. I will be up and about before you leave."

Alfred smiled, "Thank you, Geoffrey. You are a gentleman."

Alfred sat and poured himself some wine. He was steeling himself to speak with me. I smiled. My son had grown considerably but he still had some way to grow to be able to cut the strings to home. "Father, Earl, I am keen to have a manor. I like the idea of Seamer." I nodded. "You were right about the widow of Coxhoe. I can see now that she would have been an unsuitable bride for me. Your advice was sage."

"Good. Your father can be right, now and again."

"I like Matilda."

"I think we all saw that."

"How long should I wait before I begin to court her?"

"I am in a difficult position here, my son. She is my ward unless the King decides otherwise. To court her you would have to ask my permission."

He looked confused, "Then can I ask now?"

"I am worried about your motives. Do you do this simply to get a manor?"

"Of course not! I lov… I like Matilda and I believes she likes me."

"That is not the basis for a sound marriage. I will tell you what I will do. I say this as the guardian of Matilda and not your father. While I am away in London you have my permission to get to know Matilda. I will ask your mother, the Countess, to divine the girl's thoughts too. When I return I will speak with you both and give a decision."

I could see that he looked disappointed, "I thought you would be glad and say aye straight away!"

"You thought I would give a girl to a young man, a girl who has had to endure the horrors of Sir Hugh? I would be doing neither of you any favours. Matilda needs time to recover. She is young and scars will heal but they will need time. In any case I am not certain that you are ready yet. I have spoken to Geoffrey. You will deputize for me. I will see how you handle the duties of a lord of a manor. Mayhap you decide that it is not the life for you."

"But I know already!"

"Walk a mile in my boots and then tell me!"

That night I told my wife my decision and she hugged me, "You are getting wiser as you get older. This is a good thing that you do. I cannot begin to conceive how the young girl must feel. To have come so close to such abominations. The two girls, Anya and Brigid, are close to her. They must have told her what Sir Hugh and his squire did. You do not recover from that overnight."

I hugged her, "And FitzUrse and Rebekah?"

"Let us say that the stories from Skipton have made our daughter realise that she wants to be wed sooner rather than later. By the time you return Aunt Ruth and I will have made the necessary arrangements. There will have to be a dowry."

"I know. The manor of Elton is vacant and is still mine. How would that do?"

"They would both like that." We lay in a comfortable silence for a while. "Be careful when you are in London. It is a dangerous place."

"And I am a dangerous man. I confess that I will be happier when I have seen William Marshal. He is the one rock who remains in this land. The King's Council are not made of the same material and King Henry needs someone who can guide him."

"Then, husband, that must be you. You will have to do that which your great grandfather did. You will have to guide the King and save the Kingdom!"

Chapter 4
King's Council

I took my best men at arms and Mordaf and Gruffyd, two of my best archers. I rode a new palfrey, Bella. She was well schooled and named after my grandfather's old castle in the Holy Land. Alan the Horse Master thought the long ride might be good for her as we would have many hundreds of miles to get to know one another. Our first stop was at York. We rode hard so that I could spend time with Ralph. I was anxious to learn what had happened at Skipton after I had left.

"The Earl sent his nephew Gonville de Blondeville to deliver his message. It will not be a permanent appointment for he is a banneret but the young knight is keen to impress his uncle. It will suffice. I told him that Sir Geoffrey would visit as would I."

"Why not a more experienced knight?"

"The Welsh. They are threatening the borders of Shropshire and the Earl fears that they will move northwards. Cheshire has always been attractive to them." He sipped his wine. "Besides we know that the eyes of the Earl of Chester always look south and not north. I heard that Prince Louis offered him the crown when he invaded."

"That is true but the earl rejected the offer. Perhaps you are right. If the Welsh threaten Shropshire then the Earl Marshal would be concerned. That may be the reason for my London summons."

"From what young Gonville told me the Earl Marshal is dying. As the young man appeared prone to exaggeration I would think that it may be that the Earl is seriously ill but he is old."

I knew what he was thinking. "I could not do what my great grandfather did. It cost him too much. He may have owed the royal family a great deal but we do not. My father paid the ultimate price saving King Richard and that cost me my lands. I will fight for England and my King but I will not sacrifice all for either."

"It may be they just seek the advice of the most experienced knight in the land now that the Earl of Pembroke is ill."

The next seven days saw us travelling south and I was largely silent for I was listening as we stayed in castles, halls and monasteries. There was still much unrest. The King was young and no one trusted his Council. The rumours of the Earl Marshal's condition were well known. He had been the stability in the country and if he died then the unrest might flare into rebellion. The French were also seen as a threat. Prince Louis' invasion had failed but there were barons and lords with lands on both sides of the channel. They saw the opportunity to gain power with such a young King on the throne. By the time we reached Windsor, during the early afternoon, I felt I had the mood of the country. Now I had to gauge the mood of the King and his council. I approached the castle with dread in my heart. As we saw it in the distance I said, "Ridley, I want you and the men to keep your ears open. You know the difference between gossip, rumour and fact."

"Aye lord and how long do we stay?"

"That all depends. Why?"

"Southerners can't brew beer, lord and that's a fact. A long sojourn down here is like a punishment!"

The King's Steward greeted me. He had been there since the time of King Richard. He had seen many people come and go. He was calmness personified. "The King and his Council are meeting with the Earl Marshal. I will have you and your squire taken to your chambers. Your men can go to the warrior hall."

I nodded and handed my reins to Egbert. He was a servant but also a groom. He knew horses. At a pinch, he could fight too. My servants all had more than one skill. Travelling in Sweden, Outremer and Anjou had taught me that the more skills you had in servants the better. Our chamber befitted a senior baron who had already done great service for the King. There were cloths to wash and dry ourselves and bowls of water. It would do. Comfort was something I enjoyed at home. We changed from our travelling clothes into something befitting an audience with a King, even a boy king.

We headed down to the Great Hall where liveried retainers served us wine and gave us bread and cheese. When William had finished he said, "I will check on the horses and ensure that the men and servants have been accommodated." He saw my curious look and smiled, "Alfred told me that is what a good squire does and I would be a knight as soon as I can."

"Then you have made a promising start."

He had been gone but a short time when the door opened and William Marshal entered. He looked old. He looked thin. Perhaps the Earl of Chester's son was not exaggerating. The old earl held out an arm, "At last, a real warrior!" He waved a dismissive hand, "The Council are all politicians. Give me a warrior any time."

"Wine, my lord?"

He nodded at the servant. "They have told you I am dying?"

I had been taught well. You do not lie to another warrior, especially about death. "I had heard you were unwell."

"I will not see another spring. You are the hope for the future."

"What about your son?"

He shook his head, "We shall see. If you recall he sided with the rebels. I thought I had brought him up well. Perhaps I was away too long serving England." Then he looked at me. "And that is not true either. Your great grandfather was never at home and yet your grandfather and father turned out well. Your father was much younger than you when he led

46

the defence of London against the rebels. He told older lords what to do. Mind you he had the Warlord at his side but still, he had the stuff of greatness in him; as have you. You stood up to a Prince and then a King."

I cocked my head to one side, "For which, Earl, I was heavily criticised by you!"

He laughed, "Johnny Lackland was a nasty piece of work and I was trying to save England. I knew you would be all right. You have the Warlord's blood in you."

"Thank you."

"How did that business at Skipton turn out?" I told him and he poured himself more wine then he added, "There will be more like Sir Hugh out there. The King's father had poor judgement in almost everything. There are others like him and Falkes de Breauté. I will not be there to clean up the mess and help young Henry to sort out this land. That will be down to you! He is a good lad and has the makings of a king but he needs advice and before you say he has the Council I will tell you that they are incompetent at best and may be corrupt. It was I insisted that you be sent for. If I am not here then you are the next best thing. I need you to be his mentor. King John neglected his son or perhaps the Baron's War distracted him. Either way we need the King to know how to be a warrior and there is none better to show him than you. You shall do what your great grandfather did for Henry."

"Excuse me for saying so, Earl, but did you not appoint the Bishop and a prelate to be the King's guardian? Why not a warrior?"

"I did and before you say so de Burgh was responsible for defeating the French at Sandwich but while they helped to win the war they are not doing anything to win the peace. You should know that they are rivals. The three of them can run the country. My God the Steward of Windsor Castle could run the country but they would be a bad influence on the King. Take him away from here and make him a man. The people need someone they can follow. English knights need a leader to lead them. You are the one who can do this! The King's mother has gone to Poitou and married Hugh de Lusignan. She has abandoned her children. The Bishop is

47

backed by those lords in France. Hubert de Burgh is backed by the loyal barons of England. At the moment they get on but eventually there will be a clash and when there is it could cause a civil war or worse, a war where one is backed by France. Before they return let me tell you the problem. It is King John's legacy. The land is littered with men to whom he gave castles and power. They do not pay their taxes. They do not seek permission for marriage nor for wardships."

I suddenly felt guilty. I had made Lady Matilda a ward.

"These men must be ousted. I have here," he took from his tunic a parchment, "a list of the names of the barons appointed by King John. There are others who have not turned out to be poor lords. Their names are not on this piece of parchment but these are the worst. Keep it close. This is the only copy. Guard it well. I am the last of those who was close to King John. I was with him for many years and I have compiled the list without malice. None of these is my enemy. They are England's enemies. There is one name missing. That of my son. Although not appointed by King John I fear that he will need watching. I charge you with doing so."

The Earl's eyes were filled with regret. After what he had done for England it was sad that it had cost him his son. "And who is there for me to trust?"

He laughed, "Fewer than there should be. Chester of course so long as he gets what he wants might be an ally. York, Canterbury, Winchester and Westminster are all loyal prelates who wield power well. The rest? Those who fought with us at Lincoln are the only ones I would have at my back. The rest would as soon stick a dagger into it." There was a noise without. I secreted the parchment in my tunic. "One last thing, you need to be forceful with the King but do not treat him like a child." He smiled. "He does not like it!"

Each time I saw him I was amazed at the King's youth. He was approaching manhood and was filling out a little but there was no beard and he still looked like little more than a child. That boys his age went to war to sling stones and to fetch wood was not the point. They had been brought up that way. The King had been taught many things. He could read and write. He understood numbers. He could speak languages. He had skills with a weapon but he had never fought. He had lived within castles and fortresses where he was protected. I doubted that he had ever spoken to any who was not either a noble or one of the servants. When William, my son, went abroad in the town of Stockton then folks all spoke easily to him. He knew their business and their lives. When he led them in battle there would be a shared understanding of the world. King Henry's world and that of his people were entirely different.

The fact that his face lit up when he spied me made me feel pride. It contrasted with the neutral faces of his three councillors. "Earl, I am pleased that you have come! We need your help. With my two earls at my side we can make England safe again and then retake that which was lost in France!"

My heart sank. The last thing I needed was to go war in France. I smiled, "If I can help, my liege, then I will do so."

De Burgh coughed, "Earl, the country is still divided. The Earl Marshal has suggested that you may be the man to take the reins and guide us through this storm." His words sounded false. He gestured for us all to sit. He was the one with the power. I saw Peter des Roches give an irritated glance at de Burgh. He resented de Burgh. Pandulf, the papal prelate, was harder to read. He was the Pope's man but I had no doubt that he had his own ideas. As I sat I felt as though I had fallen in with thieves. Here the thieves were attempting to steal a kingdom. "You have travelled the length of the country. The Earl Marshal came from the west. He said that not only the lords but the ordinary people were unhappy. What do you say?"

"That he is right. I have just come from Skipton where a rogue lord acted like a bandit. I have rescued and made a ward the daughter of Sir Henry of Gargrave. Folk were driven from their land and over taxed. His majesty's tax collectors were not allowed to collect their taxes and they filled Sir Hugh's coffers!"

King Henry looked shocked, "And is this dealt with?"

"I slew Sir Hugh in combat and the others who perpetrated this evil have been dealt with. Such lords must be dealt with. I have made the lady my ward."

There were nods from all four of them. I saw William Marshall smile. "See, I told you he knew how to be decisive!"

I smiled at the old earl who was trying to be my advocate in what was clearly a hostile place. "Thank you, Earl, but it is easier said than done. Sir Hugh resisted the Sheriff of York and myself. If I was to go to every castle in the land and redress the wrongs I would need an army such as that which ousted Prince Louis."

Peter des Roches said, "We have no money in the Exchequer for such an undertaking."

I shook my head, "It could not be done in any case. We need the King to be present. If they resist then it is treason. We need to make every baron swear an oath to the King or risk losing their land."

"You would have me accompany you?" I saw the King brighten.

"So far as I can see lord that is the only way." I glanced at William Marshal. "I believe I know the lords who have flouted your authority. There are less than fifty who have enough land to cause trouble. We begin with those. Give me half a year and we might be able to reassert your authority."

I saw that the Council was happy about that. The responsibility of guarding the King would be mine. Hubert de Burgh nodded, "But how does that help us with the people?"

I had given thought to this. "Your majesty, when your father signed the Great Charter the barons were mollified for they had rights. Certain rights were also given to the ordinary people but they were dependent upon their lords of the manors behaving reasonably. Some lords chose to select the parts of the charter which suited them. The ordinary folk need their own charter."

"Charter? For ordinary men?"

I nodded, "The right to graze in the forests. The right to forage in the forests. We do so in Cleveland and the people there are content and prosperous." I looked at the Bishop. "They happily pay taxes."

Peter des Roches nodded, "Perhaps Pandulf and I might draft such a document. It would cost us little and if it made the land safer then it would be a price that the barons might happily pay."

Unwittingly I had said something which did not threaten the position of the three men. They saw it as a way to weaken the power of the barons. We spent the hour until the food was made ready going through what might constitute a fair charter. King Henry came up with the name, Charter of the Forest. We then spoke of how many men would need to accompany the King on our journey through England. Despite the warning from the Earl Marshal, the three men seemed remarkably positive. The Bishop and Pandulf would draft a charter and Hubert de Burgh would select the men. The Earl caught my eye as we headed for the food which had been prepared for us. The Council was putting on an act. They were trying to impress me. I was under no illusions. It was my military prowess and record which had prompted their eagerness. It would not last. However, I had the King and that was all that I wanted. My great grandfather had done the same for young Henry. I had trained enough knights to know how to do it. I had promised the Earl Marshal six months and I would try to spend most of that time in Stockton. I could make the King a warrior and yet still be close to my family.

William returned. Although younger than the King he was as tall and slightly broader. It reflected the training he had undergone with my men at arms. When the King saw him, he smiled. He had someone with whom he could speak. He had someone who was not trying to tell him what to do. He insisted that my son sit next to him at the feast. As the Bishop sat on the other side it meant I could not speak with the King as I had intended. Instead, I spoke with the Earl Marshal. In light of what happened when we eventually went to war with the Welsh, it was useful for the Earl died soon after leaving London. Had my son not been seated with the

51

King I might not have discovered all that lay in William Marshal's head.

The old earl knew Wales well. His land lay in the southwestern corner and he had Welsh between him and England. He had good ports and Bristol was just across the Severn Estuary but he had to have a good understanding of his neighbours. It became clear what the problem was. He had to fight to stop his animals being stolen and his people robbed. It sounded like Scotland before we had dealt with the situation. The north of Wales, from what he told me, appeared to be a dangerous place for the Welsh archers had the advantage there and heavy, mailed knights were at a disadvantage. When that war came I would have to come up with a new strategy. The Marcher Lords had built castles but the Earl was sure that they could be strengthened. "That is the way to deal with the Welsh. Build strong castles and control their valleys."

It was late into the meal when the King leaned over William, "When will we leave, Earl? I am anxious to reclaim my kingdom. I know I have much to heal in this land."

I nodded to the three members of the council, "When your lords have secured the men and I have ensured that they are the right ones it will be then."

"Will they not be the right men if they are chosen by my council?"

I lowered my voice, "With respect, lord, my men and I have fought for the last twenty years. We know what makes a good warrior. Do you have a squire? Servants?"

"I have no squire yet but there are eight servants who accompany me."

"Then we shall meet them on the morrow and assess their suitability."

I saw him frown, "They are my servants."

"Can they ride? We shall be in the saddle more than we are not. Can they defend themselves? We will not have enough men to watch over servants." He smiled when he understood. "And horses. We will need good horses."

"There is more to do than I thought. I wondered if we would just have a pleasant ride around my realm."

52

"In a perfect world we would but we will visit those who do not wish you to be King. Do not expect smiles and good wishes. You are just as likely to receive frowns and scowls."

"Will we have to fight?"

"I intend to ride first to Stockton and we will gather my knights and men at arms. If we have to fight then we will. You will need a knight to carry your standard."

William Marshal said, "I have one ready for you. He is one of my knights. He is a bachelor knight from Pembroke. He will be landless. If the King makes him his standard-bearer then it may help his name to become known." He smiled, "Who knows Earl, he may become one of your knights. His name is Robert de Ventadour. I have not seen him fight in war but he has won tourneys."

"I will meet him and then decide!" King Henry nodded forcefully.

I smiled, "Well done your majesty! I would expect nothing else from one descended from King Henry!"

The Earl said, "He will be ready to meet you in the morning."

That night as we prepared for bed I asked William about his conversation with Henry. It turned out that the young king was petrified of making a mistake and losing his land. He was well read and knew of the horrors of the first civil war. He did not wish it repeated. He also missed his mother. I confess that I had thought it a cold act to leave for France and marry as soon as he was crowned. As I recall from my grandfather Empress Matilda had stayed in England to ensure that her son's reign went smoothly.

"I would have you stay near to the King."

"But I am your squire!"

"I have servants and the best men at arms. Fear not. I will be safe but we need a confident King and a happy one. Become his friend. I have treacherous sands to negotiate."

"Where do we go first?"

"When the men are assembled we will head up the Great North Road. When we were in Lincoln, the Lady of Lincoln, Nichola de la Haie, told me that Newark, the place where King John died, was filled with those who wished the King and his family ill. There may be other castles and towns which deserve a visit but that one is the closest and on our route home. It will serve as a warning for others. Until we have all of our men I dare not risk a major battle."

As I lay, trying to sleep, I ran through the list of troublesome knights which William Marshal had given me. London had many lords who sought to change the way the King ruled but that had always been true. My father had put down a Templar inspired rebellion. The first thing I would do, while we awaited the King's men, would be to ride with the King to the Tower. It had fallen when Prince Louis had invaded. I needed to ensure that it had a good castellan and was well defended. Then we could head north and deal with de Vesci and de Percy. Both had been opponents of King John and had yet to acknowledge his son as King. I would make them do so. After my northern border was secured I would be able to leave the north and bring the majority of my men south. It was in the castles and the manors of the south coast where the greatest danger lay. Only Dover and Windsor had failed to fall to the rebels. I hoped that the other barons and lords opposed just King John and not the crown itself. I had not liked him either. Perhaps his young son could convince them that the crown was on the right head!

I did not sleep well and I was up before dawn. William Marshal was also up. He gave me a sad smile, "I hope the reason for your poor night's sleep was not the same as mine. I have to make water so often that I am sure I could fill a moat!"

"No Earl. I have much on my mind. You have not given me an easy task."

"You are appointed to the task by your blood." He waved me over to the table. "There were other matters I did not mention last night for they were intended for your ears alone. King John angered the Lusignan faction in Poitou when he married Isabelle, Henry's father. They rebelled. The son of Hugh de Lusignan has had his revenge for the queen has married him. The young Hugh plots to take the throne. I have no doubt that marrying the Queen was an attempt to give him legitimacy. Bourgogne de Rancon, Maurice de

Craon and Aimer Taillefier are three Poitevin lords who have sworn to end Henry's life. There may well be assassins who have been hired to kill the boy before he becomes a man."

"They are in England?"

"They could be. Any of those knights on the list I gave you could be giving them sanctuary. Had the Good Lord given me more time or a son on whom I could depend then I would have sought them myself. I have given you one task already but you should beware these lords. They are ruthless. All are young and unmarried. All are skilled in war for they have fought as hired swords and in tourneys. Do not make the mistake of underestimating them. I am afraid that you do not have the power which I enjoy. I fear I have given you an impossible task but the blood of the Warlord is within you and if any can do this then it is you."

I nodded. "I will try."

He sighed, "I pray you do better than I. When King Henry the Second made his son joint King I was given the task of making him a king. I failed and he rebelled against his father and almost plunged England and Normandy into a second civil war. Your father and grandfather stopped that happening."

I had had little sleep and after William Marshal's words I could not see me enjoying sleep for some time to come.

"I will go and pack. I will bid you and the King farewell before I go. I do not think we will meet again."

"Despite what you say I know that you have served England well. You will be remembered as England's hero."

"Kind of you to say so but looking back I can only see my mistakes." He looked like a sad and broken man as he left me.

William came rushing into the room. He had obviously woken and realised that I had risen. He was still keen to impress me. "You have time to eat and then we will go to speak with our men and have the horses prepared. Egbert will advise me if any of the other horses in the King's stable are suitable. Has Alan been to the room?" Alan was our personal servant. He had waited in our room to light us to

55

bed and to tidy away our clothes when we had retired the previous night.

"He was the one woke me when he discovered you had risen."

"Good then we will be in a position to ride when the King is risen."

Ridley the Giant and Henry Youngblood had not been idle. They had been speaking with the men in the warrior hall. By the time they had reported to me I knew as much about the garrison as any man and probably more than the King's council and the King himself. "One more task for you. Some of these men will know London. I need to know who runs the city. Which inns can be trusted? Where do the bandits and outlaws gather?"

They nodded but William asked, "Outlaws?"

Ridley the Giant said, "They live inside the city walls. They have great power. Your father is right to find where are their haunts. If we can then we use them and if not, we destroy them. Leave it with us lord."

"If I can persuade him then we will travel to London today."

When I returned to the hall I saw the Earl speaking with a young knight. He was older than Alfred. I liked Robert de Ventadour as soon as I met him. He was both earnest and honest. "Sir Robert, this is the Earl of Cleveland."

"I am honoured, Earl. I have heard of you and your exploits." He gave me a shy smile, "You are my inspiration for I know that you began with nothing and was a sword for hire. When I learned that my father would give his land to my brother I knew that if I could do half as well as you then I would become a great lord."

"You are kind. You know what we seek?"

"You need someone to carry the King's standard."

"We need more than that. We need a knight who can defend the King. He has no retinue as yet. There are no household knights. His men, at the moment, are mine. You will be there when it grows. You will need to be the eyes who watch him when I am not there."

"And I am happy to do so."

"First you have a king to impress."

"Have you a squire?"

"Aye, a likely lad, Walter."

We spoke, while we waited for the King to rise and join us, of the task ahead. William Marshal added to what he had told me the night before. He told me of London and the problems we would face. When the King joined us, I watched him appraising Sir Robert. When he was introduced the King asked pertinent questions. I hid a smile for many of them had come from my son and I.

Eventually, a smile broke on the King's face. "Then I am happy Sir Robert. I have begun, Earl, to gather my men. A small start but a step in the right direction."

While we waited for the King and his new knight to mount I spoke at length with Ridley and Henry Youngblood. What we had learned about London had disturbed me and I had decided to act sooner rather than later.

"You are certain of the information?"

They both nodded, "It was not just one man who told us, lord. *'The Trip to Jerusalem'* is the centre of the gangs who run London. One Eyed Waller is the man who runs the gangs and that is where he lives."

Henry nodded, "From what we can gather, lord, he served a knight in the Holy Land. He was a sergeant and is handy with a sword."

"Then today we end his reign of terror."

Chapter 5
The Tower of London

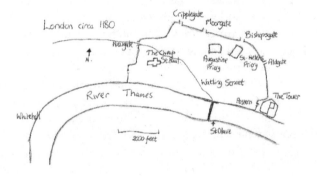

When I first saw the White Tower, I was disappointed.
Firstly, it was not white for it had been burned in the
rebellion. The white painted stone was blackened and peeled.
Secondly, all the work which had been done when my great
grandfather and father had held it had been allowed to fall
into disrepair. Young Henry had seen it before and did not
appear dismayed. We paused on London Bridge so that I
could point out what was wrong with it. "See, Your Majesty,
the ditch which should carry the water around the western
side of the curtain wall has not been maintained. It is no
longer a barrier. Two of the towers have been damaged in
the rebellion and not repaired."

"But this is London!"

"And London is as fickle as the wind. The populace can turn in an instant. You need a stronghold which can control the city and, more importantly, be held for you."

He was a thoughtful youth and he nodded, "I would value your advice, Earl."

"It will not be a quick task, your majesty. The repairs and the cleaning will not take long but you need two more towers building at each corner of the inner bailey. We will have a better idea once we are within its walls."

We were riding without standards and with plain cloaks covering our surcoats. I wanted to gauge the mood of the city and this was the best way. The streets were thronged. People were going to and from the Cheap, London's market. They looked happy. There appeared to be plenty to buy and people looked to have coin. That was good for it meant the people of London would be less likely to rebel. The Tower had depressed me but my hopes were raised by the city. We left through the Aldgate for I wished to see the northern side of the Tower. The ditch which led from the river was a muddy morass rather than a trapped filled moat. It would merely slow an attacker down and not stop them. There were just two sentries who lounged at the gate which also looked as though it had been battered and then hastily repaired.

"Yes, lord, what can we do for you?"

The words were insolent enough for a bachelor knight but for an earl and a king they were tantamount to treason. I nudged my horse closer to him, "This is King Henry of England and I am the Earl of Cleveland. Choose both your words and your manner of speaking carefully lest I have to draw my sword to remove your tongue!"

The two men leapt to attention, "Sorry my lord! Your Majesty! Open the gate!"

The gate opened. Not only had it not been properly repaired it had been badly repaired and it scraped on the cobbles. We ducked our heads beneath the gateway and entered the outer bailey. I glanced and saw that King Henry was not happy at what he saw. He was used to castles and he saw that this one was not well looked after. "There is much work here, King Henry, and the work will cost coin."

"I know."

We were seen from the gate which led to the inner bailey and when we passed through the constable awaited us. He was not a young man. As we dismounted I turned and said, "Mordaf, Gruffyd, go into the city. Ridley will tell you where." I tossed them a purse. "He will tell you what to do! Buy ale and learn what you can!"

They grinned, "Aye lord."

I saw the disappointment on Ridley's face, "I am sorry my friend but you stand out just a little too much! Tell them where they need to look. This is a scouting expedition."

"Aye lord."

Leaving the rest of my men with the horses I turned and climbed the steep steps which led to the entrance. I knew every lord of the north but not those in the south. It worked both ways. My surcoat was hidden by my cloak. I swept it back as I climbed and then I was recognised.

"Earl! I am honoured to have the hero of Lincoln here! I am Sir Ralph Tancraville the constable of the Tower."

I nodded, "This is King Henry!"

The knight bowed, "I am doubly honoured."

As we stepped inside the keep King Henry said, "My castle looks like it is in need of repair and the men you employ to guard it do not look capable."

I was delighted with his words. He had taken charge. Freed from his three wet nurses he was beginning to learn to be King!

"I am sorry, Your Majesty, we have not been paid regularly and I cannot find the funds for the repairs to the castle."

I gestured with my arm, "Then show the King its strengths and its weaknesses. The Kingdom is in a parlous state." He led us inside the keep and up the stairs. We came out at a doorway which led to a fighting platform. He led us on a circuit around the walls. There was a tower and a turret at the northeast corner. There was one man within. I saw the partly demolished old Roman wall leading north. The Romans had enclosed more of the city than we did. Heading south along the fighting platform we passed through another tower and I saw a more substantial one by the river.

I turned to the King, "You need more towers lord. There are none on the north wall and the ditch has been allowed to become overgrown."

"Towers are expensive to man, lord."

I stopped, "When King John took his crown jewels to war, castellan, why was that?"

I could see that he had not given that any thought. "I know not. Perhaps he wanted to wear them to battle!"

Henry was cleverer than his constable. "He had nowhere safe to keep them! That was why he took them. They should have been safe here but even I can see that they would not be safe here!"

I nodded and we continued our progress. "This keep is the most powerful I have ever seen save for Karak des Chevaliers in the Holy Land. With a deep ditch and solid towers on the walls then this could be a stronghold which could be held against any number of enemies."

It took two hours for us to examine the walls and see what could be done. We returned to the Great Hall to eat, drink and to use a wax tablet to plan the improvements. The King had many good ideas and I was able to give him my practical experience.

The Constable looked shocked at the extent of the work which would be needed, "But majesty, where will you get the coin?"

Henry looked at me and I answered. "You have a chancellor. He will find the money but there may be a way to augment your own coin. Come, my liege. Let us shed these cloaks and go into the city. I think that you should speak with the mayor and the merchants who make up the men who really run London. You have a rich city and I think that we could use its prosperity to our advantage."

As we rode across the outer bailey with our banners unfurled we rode through the Aldgate into the city. Sir Robert and his squire, Walter, rode just behind the King. I rode next to the King and William carried my banner behind Sir Robert. As soon as the King and his banner were seen

61

and recognised there was a cheer. It rippled along the roads and it gave me hope. There might be barons who did not want a king but the people did. I knew that London was not England. Here they did not need to forage in the forests. These were well off compared with the rest of the country but it was a start.

We reached the Guildhall. The noise and acclamation had drawn the mayor and his council to the door. The standards told them that they had important guests and I saw the mayor turn and give orders.

"Your Majesty, I am at your service. I am Serio de Mercer, mayor of London. This is an honour."

"I am sorry to call unannounced but the Earl and I were at the Tower and thought we would have conference with you."

Already King Henry was growing into his role. Each moment away from the Council was helping him to evolve into a real king.

We were taken into the Guildhall. Servants hurried and scurried to fetch us food and drink. The King and I had spoken in the Tower and on the ride through the streets. I was confident that he would know what to say.

"Mayor, my castle is in need of repair."

"It is, majesty."

"I have a proposal for you. I would have you share in the cost of repair. You pay half and I will find the other half." I saw the mayor begin to open his mouth but the King hurried on. "You may ask why should you do this. It is simple. The Tower will offer protection for the city. You have, I believe, gangs who operate in the city. From what I have learned they extract money from honest businesses."

The Mayor looked surprised at the knowledge the King had and he nodded, "We are powerless to stop them. Many are ex-soldiers."

"Then we will rid you of them. The money the businesses used to give to them can be used to build new towers and repair walls. The men who will be paid to build the walls will be those in the city who have no employment. As we rode through the streets I saw healthy looking men begging. They can labour for you. A man who is paid to work values himself more than a beggar. Your guilds will all be rewarded. Your craftsmen will be employed in the building work. London will benefit for it will be prosperous."

I could see that the idea appealed. "I will have to speak with the rest of the leaders of the guilds but if you can rid us of these gangs then…"

The King smiled and waved a hand in my direction, "The Earl will begin that this day. Is that not right, Earl?"

"It will be a pleasure."

Ridley knew the alehouse they used as a base and Mordaf and his brother were busy looking for the ways out of the rat holes of the alehouse.

Serio de Mercer turned and said to the guildsmen, "We have business to discuss, for the Earl of Cleveland will snuff out these villains who plague us."

I saw a man rise and head for the rear door. I shouted, "Sir Robert, hold that man!"

The King's knight raced to apprehend the man. He grabbed him and the man complained, "I have done nothing!"

"Then why do you flee?" The mayor looked at me in confusion. I explained, "Sir, you did not think that all of your guild masters were working for the common good! You cannot have such gangs operating in your city lest they are receiving information from someone in power. I am wagering that you have tried to stop these gangs before?"

"Aye lord, but when we reached their dens they were fled."

"And there is your reason. That is why we strike with haste. The longer we delay the more likely it is that they will get word of what we intend. I charge you to hold this man until we return. I would have words with him." The mayor nodded. "Sir Robert, William, leave the standards here. We need to move quickly."

My men were already waiting outside. Their shields were on their horses as were their helmets. This would not be like fighting men at arms. Henry Youngblood said, "Ridley the Giant, William of Lincoln and two others are lounging close to their back door. They will find and join Mordaf."

"And the hidden passages?"

"Gruffyd is inside." He grinned, "He is with a whore. He is spreading your coin around, lord."

My men knew their business, even business such as this. We strode through the crowded streets towards the Bishop's gate. From what we had learned the inn lay close to the northern wall and backed on to St. Helen's Priory. In a perfect world we would have spent a day or two watching the building to identify all the entrances and exits but we did not have the time. From what we had learned One Eyed Waller was gaining power. The mayor had almost confirmed that even though he did not know the identity of the criminal who ran his city. That was not a surprise. If this man had come from the Holy Land then he would have learned to deceive and to hide behind others. The name made my senses tingle for there had been a knight, Fitzwaller, who had been in the Holy Land and who had served Robert of Blois, another evil man. Perhaps this sergeant had been one of his men. If so there was a connection to my past.

Backed by my two largest men at arms I walked as though we were going to the Bishop's gate. The rest approached from other directions in pairs. I saw the man they had lounging outside. He was the lookout and he stiffened as we neared the alehouse. As we neared the door Henry Youngblood said, loudly, "I hope they still have those horses! I do not relish a long walk north of the wall if they are gone!"

Ridley laughed, "If they have sold them to another they will have a broken coxcomb for their dishonesty."

I joined in the laughter. Our pace was such that it would have appeared as though we were rushing for the gate and I saw the lookout relax a little. I took out a gold coin and when I was a pace away let it slip from my fingers. It hit the ground and rolled a little before it stopped close to the wall of the alehouse. I saw the lookout glance down at it. He was already distracted. I passed him and he smiled at me. I kept on walking. Ridley and Henry made to follow me and when the man stooped to pick up the coin Ridley's fist smashed into the side of his head and knocked him against the wall.

He fell unconscious. Ridley picked up the coin and flicked it to me. I caught it and, as we entered the alehouse flipped it once more in the air. The light from the outside and the tallow lights from within made the gold sparkle. As I had expected it drew attention to me so that my two men could slip inside unnoticed. The alehouse was full. There were girls and women seated on men's knees. They were working girls. They would be tempting the men to go with them to their beds and part with hard earned coin. Not all of the men in the inn would be criminals; most would be but not all. I saw the men drinking in pairs examining me. I looked like a visiting noble with too much money looking for a whore. Most went back to their drinking. I saw one girl try to disengage herself from a potential client. I was a much more lucrative prospect. I had a gold coin. I would not smell as bad as the man who grappled with her to pull her back to his knee.

I smiled and continued to flip my coin. I spied Gruffyd who was in the corner. He gave a slight nod of acknowledgement. His hand was on his short sword. I saw one of the whores go to a back room and call to someone. I continued to walk slowly towards the trestle table where the beer barrel stood. Two men came out of the back room. From the eye patch, I guessed that one was One Eye Waller. He had grey hair but he moved like a soldier. The other was simply muscle. The only man in the room who was bigger, Ridley the Giant, had slipped into the inn behind me and now hid in the shadows. One Eye Waller was smaller but still well-muscled. I saw he had a short sword at his side while his muscle held a wicked looking cudgel. The criminal Lord of London smiled and, as he approached, gave me an exaggerated bow. I saw the muscle out of the corner of my eye. He was moving behind me. I was confident that, by now, most of my men would be in the alehouse and I did not worry about my back. That was protected.

"My lord, what an honour to serve a knight! How may we be of service? Ale or a girl perhaps? More than one? We have young girls if that is what you desire or more

65

comfortable older ladies who have learned the art of love and know how to please a man."

My spurs, good armour and sword all marked me as a knight. The fact that I had entered such a low establishment told them that I was seeking female company."

I flicked the coin high in the air and his eye followed it. I was able to draw my dagger unseen. I smiled as I watched his eye follow the coin. I caught it and slipped it into my purse. "You are One Eye Waller?"

Suddenly he was a different man. I saw a sergeant at arms. His hand went to his sword and my dagger came up to prick his neck. As his muscle stepped forward Ridley and Henry pinioned his arms.

I said, quietly, "As you can see I am not alone! You have one eye and look to be the man who runs this alehouse so let us dispense with the dissembling. You are One Eye Waller! And, my friend, I would like your hands up in the air so that I can see them. I will not lose a moment's sleep if my hand slips and I slit your throat."

He swallowed and blinked his eyes. "You have the advantage of me, my lord. You appear to know my name yet I do not know you nor understand why you threaten a poor innkeeper." The whore who had fetched him linked her arm in his and hugged him.

From behind me I heard a sound like a piece of wood hitting another and then Padraig's voice, "My lord did not say you could leave so wait until he does before you try to move."

One Eye Waller's one eye flicked from side to side as he took in the men who had suddenly appeared. He raised his head, "My lord, you do not know what you do here. If you wish to live then withdraw!"

"You misunderstand me, I am Thomas, Earl of Cleveland, and I need to stay here for I am the rat catcher who will cleanse London of the disease that is…"

I got no further for the whore had drawn a dagger and lunged at me. I was wearing mail and a gambeson. The tip caught in the mail links but her intervention was enough to make my left arm move away from Waller's neck. He

wriggled away, pushing the whore towards me. I pushed her
out of my way for Waller had drawn a sword. The inn
erupted as his gang rose, almost as one, to draw swords and
try to get to me. This was not an even fight. Although they
outnumbered us my men wore mail. Even so the brigands
went for faces and hands which were unprotected by metal.

Waller swung his sword at my side. I fended it off with
my dagger as I brought my sword in a sweep. It was the
wrong strike for the alehouse was filled with bodies and my
sword caught on the leg of a table. Waller reached into his
boot to pull a second dagger. I did the only thing I could do.
I kicked hard and my boot connected with his groin. His face
showed that I had hurt him. His doxy rose and clung to my
leg. One Eye Waller turned and began to push his way
through the mêlée. Sheathing my dagger, I knocked the
whore from me and hurried after Waller. I held my sword
before me and that saved my life. As I stepped through the
door which led to the back an axe swung towards my middle.
I punched with my sword and took the force from the axe
which merely rasped against my mail.

I stepped into the back room. Behind me were the sounds
of sword on sword and the cries of those wounded or dying.
My men would be ruthless. They would not risk their lives
for brigands. As I did so I saw that there were piles of coins
there. Waller pulled back his arm to swing at me again. I saw
that he was an old soldier for he held the axe as a weapon
and not a tool. He was balanced and it would not do to
underestimate him. As the axe came towards me I picked up
a handful of the coins and threw them at his face. He
continued his swing but there was not enough force behind
it. I leaned back and the head tore through my surcoat. This
had to end. I rammed my sword hard towards him. It slid
through his tunic and into his side. I felt the metal scrape
along his ribs. Had this been a battle I would have torn the
sword sideways but there was not enough room in the tiny
chamber and so I pulled the sword out. I grabbed the axe
with my left hand and ripped it free from his hands. I threw
the weapon behind me.

"I would not have you cheat the hangman!"

67

Blood was pouring from his side and he sank to his knees. "You have done for me!" His one eye glared hatred at me. "You were lucky to leave the Holy Land alive! Have you made a pact with the devil that you have survived?"

I saw, from the pooling blood, that he would not live to see trial and hanging. "You will be able to ask him yourself soon enough." I suddenly saw, beneath his tunic, the sign of the Templars. "We have fought before!"

He could not hold himself up any longer and he lay on the floor. He was smiling, "You and that Swede were lucky then too. You will not enjoy your life, hero of Arsuf, for there are men in this land who are sworn to end your life! There is a bounty on your head." Before I could ask him more he sighed and died.

The back door of the inn opened and Mordaf entered. He had a bloody sword. "We have five men here, lord who tried to flee. Three of them surrendered."

"Hold them." I turned as Gruffyd entered. He looked down at the dead man. "Gruffyd, gather all the coin. The King has his first contribution to the funds to rebuild his castle."

Picking up the axe I stepped back into the alehouse. Most of the fighting had already ended but there were men who were still engaged in combat. I swung the axe and it thudded into one of the beams which held up the roof. It must have struck a nail for it rang and sparks flew. Dust fell from the ceiling. I roared, "Hold! Your leader is dead!"

The whore who had tried to save him dropped to her knees and began to weep.

I turned to my men. "Henry Youngblood, bind the men who fought against us and take them back to the Guildhall." I pointed to the whore, "Fetch her too! Ridley, I would have those who did not fight lined up here so that I may question them."

Even as they began to obey me the whore leapt to her feet and, after spitting in my face, brought her knee up into Henry Youngblood's groin and then darted out into the street. Henry shouted, "Bitch!" I hoped that my men outside would stop her. They did not! That proved to be a costly mistake.

As I questioned the supposedly innocent customers I realised that we would not be able to return to Windsor. I waved Mordaf over, "Ride back to Windsor and tell them that the King will stay this night in London."

"Aye lord. Gruffyd says that there is much gold in the back room. We found, beneath the floor, a chest with even more."

I nodded, "Do not rush back, Mordaf. We will return to Windsor tomorrow."

"Aye, Lord." We emptied the inn of all that was of value. I had six men left with me. "Padraig, demolish this inn. I will speak with the mayor and see what can be done with the site."

"What about the ale and the food lord?"

"Take what you want and then give the rest to the people."

By the time I reached the Guildhall the prisoners had all been lined up. The mayor, Serio, the King and Sir Robert were speaking with Henry Youngblood. The man who had tried to flee was lined up with them. When they saw me the three men turned expectantly. "Well, my liege, we have the coin to pay for the stone you need. If the mayor can find us the masons then we can begin work."

"Are they all captured, Earl?"

"One escaped." I walked over to one of the prisoners. "You, what was the name of the whore who escaped?" I saw hesitation. "We will judge you soon. Are you so keen to die that you will not cooperate?"

"Her name is Morag. She is Welsh. You will not find her. She knows every alley in London."

"We will see." I turned back to the King. "I have sent word that we will stay the night in the Tower. We have much to discuss." He nodded. "Mayor, these men need to be secured and I fear that this Guildhall is not the place. I would suggest that we retire to the Tower. There we can determine the fate of these prisoners and plan the improvements to the castle."

The King showed his increasing maturity. He turned to Serio de Mercer, "The Earl has made a good suggestion. We will fetch the prisoners and you and your council will follow."

"Yes, Your Majesty."

In that moment a precedent was set. The King was no longer a boy. He had become the King. The council of guild masters accepted it and all those around did. The word spread so that the actions of my men were attributed to King Henry. I did not mind for if London was secure and, more importantly, loyal, then that was one less problem to worry about.

As we rode back to the Tower Sir Robert asked, "Why did your men not suffer wounds?"

"They did but not serious ones. My men all have a short hauberk. It costs me coin to equip them thus but it is worth it. A new hauberk is cheaper than training a good man and mine are the best." I saw that the King nodded. He was learning. We headed back slowly for we had a line of men who were roped together. Some had wounds. As we neared the walls of the castle I began to formulate an idea.

The King asked, "What will we do with the men?"

"Your father, quite rightly, gave all Englishmen rights. These men have committed crimes but we cannot punish them without a trial. Their punishment? That will be up to you." I would speak to him privately about my idea.

The Tower had large cellars. Thanks to the damage done in the rebellion there were two empty ones. I had the men secured there while we set up a court. Sir Ralph Tancraville the constable of the Tower, was keen to make up for the poor state of the walls and he had the servants do all that was required. The King sat in the centre of the table with Serio de Mercer on one side. He gestured for me to sit on his right. He said quietly, "I have never done this, Earl."

I smiled, "Nor had I until I became a lord of the manor. You should know that all of your lords have to administer justice on your behalf. If you wish I can advise you."

"I would appreciate that."

We had the prisoners brought up one by one. We began with the spy in the Guildhall. The King said, "What is your name?"

"I protest my innocence, Your Majesty!"

I interrupted, "Do you have impaired hearing? Answer the King! Your name!"

"Aymer of Bexley. I am a member of the locksmith's guild."

I nodded to the King who said, "Why were you passing information to One Eye Waller?"

There was a slight hesitation which I knew meant his next words were a lie. Would the King realise that? "Who, my lord?"

The King jabbed a finger out, "Address me as majesty and do not lie to me! We will have all the other prisoners brought forth and they will confirm that you were his spy. Do not lie!"

I was impressed. The King had used the voice of authority. He might have looked like a boy but he spoke like a man.

I saw the man's shoulders sag and his voice was no longer belligerent. "Your Majesty, he paid me to tell him if there was danger to him. I was forced to do so for he was a violent man."

I leaned forward, "And as a Master Locksmith you could also help him to break into houses and chests!"

He looked at me as though I was a witch, "How did…?"

We went through all the prisoners in the same manner and a picture emerged. One Eye Waller was a clever man. He suborned servants or threatened their families. It explained why he had been able to operate for so long and yet remain unprotected. I saw the Mayor and his council shake their heads in disbelief. The lack of taxes was now explained. Local businesses had to pay protection to Waller and that meant less money for taxes.

The King turned to me, "Now what do I do?"

"You punish them."

"And what is the punishment?"

I said, "That is up to you. If you pronounce them guilty then you can determine their fate. They can be executed if you wish."

King Henry was not yet a warrior. He had not killed any in battle. He had fifteen men before him. Could he order their deaths?

"And if I wish them to live, what then?"

"They would be branded on the chest with an M for malefactor."

"And…?"

"They could be imprisoned but then you would have to feed them. I have another suggestion."

I leaned in and whispered in his ear. I saw him smile. He stood, "You are all guilty of many crimes. You attempted to kill my Earl and his men. I could have you all executed." Their heads fell forward. "However, the Earl has made a suggestion and it is one which shows a degree of clemency." They all lifted their faces as one. "You will all be branded to show that you have committed a crime and you will be put to work here in the tower. The Master Mason and the constable will ensure that you work and do not escape. I will return here in one year. I may release you to return to live your own lives. If you have not shown that you can work then you will continue to labour for me. Escape will be punished by death. Constable have them taken away and branded. Have the farrier fit shackles to their legs. Take them away."

"Yes, Your Majesty!" I could hear the respect in Sir Ralph's voice.

The King turned to the Mayor, "I have provided the labour and given you the method to increase the number. You have authority in the city use it! Have the vagabonds employed to work on my walls. You and your council will feed the ones who build and you will provide the stone and the Master Mason. The money we collected from Waller will provide most of the stone. I expect all of the rest to be supplied by you. When the remainder of you leave the Earl and I will tell the mason of our needs."

He did not request he commanded and I saw the council all nod. That one moment in the Tower saw the beginnings of a King.

Chapter 6
The Road North

We left Windsor a week later. Hubert de Burgh had
managed to hire some men at arms. He brought more than a
hundred but after I had examined them sixty were dismissed
as being unsuitable. The King showed his new-found
maturity by supporting me against the King's Council. I
knew that I had made three enemies but that did not bother
me. When I told them that I would take him north their
reaction was a mixture of pleasure that they could act as they
saw fit but jaundiced by the worry that I might change their
young charge. The King showed that he had been listening
and told them that they had three months to draft the Charter
of the Forests. That told them how long he would be away.

One of the names supplied to me by William Marshal was
Roger de Hauteville. He had a strategically placed manor
close to the Great North Road. Sawtry had been three
manors in the time of the Saxons but William the Conqueror
had made it into one. Roger de Hauteville was another
favoured by King John. When the French had invaded he
had changed sides. Once they had been defeated he had
reverted to allegedly supporting King Henry. William
Marshal told me that Roger de Hauteville was plotting with
other dissident lords to usurp the King. He had shaken his
head sadly when he had pointed to the baron's name. "I was
one who supported this knight, as I supported you. He let me
down and deceived me. If I could fight one more battle it
would be against him." That alone might have helped me
make the decision to confront the baron. My other reason

was more pragmatic. Sawtry had just a fortified hall. We would not have to besiege it. I was aware that I had less than a hundred men to enforce the King's will.

As we headed into Cambridgeshire I confided in Sir Robert and the King. Ridley the Giant, William and Henry Youngblood rode behind us so that we would not be overheard. "We need to make other potentially rebellious lords know that we will brook no opposition to your rule."

"I am still in my minority!"

"Yes, my liege but the longer we allow the Council to rule England the more likely it is that rebel barons will think they can get away with flouting your authority. William Marshal told me that Sir Roger has begun to build a keep. He has not sought permission to do so. You cannot allow your enemies to have homes which can be defended against you."

"How will we approach this, Earl?"

"Simple. We ride to the hall and speak with the baron. He has two choices: he can meet and speak with us or he can fight."

Sir Robert said, "Fight the King?"

"Others have done that. As the King says he is in his minority. We will see."

"And do we have enough men, Earl?"

"We could use a few more but it will do. I am guessing we will outnumber his garrison." I saw the doubt on his young face and I understood it but I had been given the responsibility of making him a king. The three lords who were advising him were just trying to run a country. When Henry reached his majority then he would have to rule without a crutch. "You need to have strong castles, my liege. You have made a good start with the Tower but Windsor could be improved. When we reach Stockton then you will see what we have done." I had the nettle to grasp and I did. "Your father pulled down my castle when I was in the Holy Land. I have had to rebuild."

"Yet you now support me."

"I would have supported your father if he had let me but he did not. That is water under the bridge. As they say in Normandy, '*the carrot is out of the ground*'." He frowned.

"It means, lord, that what has been done cannot be undone and a wise man learns to live with the past and make a better future."

"I see. Castles cost coin, Earl."

"And you can defend them with a few men. Less than forty men could hold Stockton for me. So long as there is a well and you have high, well-made walls then you can hold out for a long time." I did not mind his questions. They were a mark of his increasing maturity.

We stayed that night, at the small manor of Sir William d'Urberville. He had a manor at Knebworth. It was just a fortified hall but I noticed that the King paid a great deal of attention to it. He was looking for the weaknesses. Sir William was in his thirties and had a couple of sons. His manor had been ransacked by the retreating French and I had known of his views before I suggested staying with him.

After we had eaten his wife took the boys away so that we could talk. "What do you know of Baron de Hauteville?"

I asked the question deliberately and I saw the knight hesitate. I said nothing but allowed him to make up his mind first. I looked in his eyes. One thing I had learned while travelling the world, was how to recognise a lie. The lessons had been expensive. Men had died because I had not always seen the signs. Now I could. When he spoke, I saw no lie in his eyes.

"I confess that I do not like him. Until the French came we served together in King John's army. When he deserted it cost us dear for he knew the back ways of this land and he led French warriors as well as his own to pillage. I was lucky that my wife was staying with her father, the Earl of Bedford. The French besieged the Earl and the old man died. My wife, as you might understand is bitter. Many of our people were made homeless." I saw him glance at King Henry. If he thought the King could have done anything then he was a fool. From the look I saw on the boy king's face, he was also unhappy about the actions of this rogue knight. "He has received no punishment."

The King said, "I knew not about this until you spoke. Earl, are there many such knights who have caused pain and mischief in my land?"

"There are, my liege. While your father was fighting rebels and the French some lords took advantage of the situation. Some sought power and others sought land. I know the names of some of them. I hope that a few lessons might bring most of them to heel. They are testing the waters, my liege. They want to know how you will respond." I turned to Sir William. "We go to speak with this knight on the morrow. You are more than welcome to join us. Justice will be done."

"Justice?"

The King nodded, "I will make him swear an oath and I will demand that he makes reparation. Which other manors did he damage?"

The knight gave us a list of four manors. Two were now without lords because de Hauteville had slain them. The King looked at me. "I know not the full extent of my powers yet, Sir William, but I am certain that the Earl will guide me."

When we left, the next day, Sir William did not accompany us. I knew why. He feared to leave his wife alone and he saw how few men we had. He feared we would fail and did not wish to risk the wrath of a vengeful neighbour. I did not blame him but, as we headed north, I saw the doubt begin to creep across the King's countenance. It was a lesson he would have to learn. There were no certainties in life. Roger de Hauteville had been a companion of King John who had played both sides. He had survived because the Pope had demanded that there be no retribution after the civil war. De Hauteville had reaped the benefit.

When we were less than a mile from Sawtry I said, "Sir Robert, William, unfurl the banners. We will let them know who approaches."

The land was flat and the hall only stood out because it had two floors I guessed that the baron lived on the first floor and kept his animals beneath him. There was a fighting platform around the roof. I spied a warrior hall. It was almost as big as the hall save that it had just one floor.

We did not gallop up the road. We kept a steady pace. I watched men come from the warrior hall and then enter the hall. I saw mailed men appear on the fighting platform. Sir Robert asked, "Does that mean there will be a problem, Earl?"

"I think the baron will be taking precautions. He knows not why we approach. Keep your hand from your weapon, Sir Robert. I have two archers with me and they will ensure that there is no treachery."

As we neared the hall I saw a knight accompanied by two others leave the hall. I had never met the Baron de Hauteville but I recognised his livery. When we reined in he bowed, "King Henry, this is an honour! I served your father for many years and was rewarded by this manor and two others."

Had we not stopped at Knebworth then the King might have been taken in by the baron's smooth words. The King did not dismount. He was learning. If he had dismounted he would have had to look up at the baron. This way the baron stared up at the King and into the sun. "And yet, Sir Roger, you sided with the French. More you took advantage of the confusion to take more land and to help the French to ransack manors."

"That is a lie, Your Majesty!!"

I leaned forward, "And are you calling the King a liar?"

He glared up at me, "The King, as you well know, Cleveland, has no powers yet for there are three men who are Regent. I do not call the King a liar for he is young and does not know yet how to judge a man properly. It is my belief that he heard the lie from your lips and is merely repeating it."

I heard my men begin to murmur, "Peace!" I dismounted and, handing my reins to William, walked forward. I took off my leather gauntlet. "Sir Roger, I am unaccustomed to being called a liar. Know you that the Earl Marshal of England told me of your pernicious acts. You will now apologise; first to the King and then to me. We will then come to the meat of our visit."

The knight was just slightly taller than I was and I saw that he was broad too. He smiled at the King as he gave him a slight bow.

"King Henry, I am sorry. I am sorry that you have been duped by this murderer of clergymen!"

I took my glove and struck him across the face. Out of the corner of my eye, I saw a crossbow appear over the parapet. There was the snap of an arrow and the crossbow fell to the ground with a clatter. The crossbowman had an arrow in his hand.

"It seems your men are as treacherous as you. I take it you accept my challenge?"

"Of course. I choose the sword and we fight on foot."

"As you wish."

I turned and walked back to my horse. I saw that while William looked confident, the King and Sir Robert looked apprehensive. "William, my helmet and shield." He dismounted and handed the reins of both horses to Ridley. Ridley the Giant also looked confident. I took off my cloak and hung it over my saddle.

"Are you sure about this, Earl?"

"Yes, my liege, there was no way of avoiding it once he called you a liar. It was a deliberate provocation. Had we done nothing then it would have encouraged others to be as insolent."

Sir Robert said, "I should have challenged him."

"And you would have lost, Sir Robert."

"I protest, lord! I have fought in tourneys."

"And this is a fight to the death. How many of those have you fought?"

There was an eloquent silence. William returned with my helmet. He held my shield until I had donned my arming cap and pulled up my coif. I did not need a ventail as the coif left just my nose and eyes exposed. The helmet was well made and I had good vision. Many knights preferred one with narrower eye holes. A lance or a spear could penetrate my eye holes. It was a risk I was willing to take. I held out my arm and William slid the shield onto it. He also slipped a dagger into my left hand and then he tightened the straps around my arm. The Warlord's father had fought with a bigger shield which he held in his fist. In the one hundred and fifty years since then, shields and styles of fighting had changed.

"Ready, Cleveland?"

I turned. He had a full helm such as I wore but he had narrower eye holes. His sword looked to be a good one although it did not have a tip. His surcoat covered most of his mail as did mine but I saw that he had metal disks on his shoulders and elbows. He probably had them on his knees too. "I am ready. Do you not wish to speak with a priest and confess?"

"No, for when this is over it is your soul which will be wandering in purgatory!" The baron was confident.

I smiled for he was not as well versed in such matters as I was. "To the death?"

He nodded, "To the death!"

He had great belief in his own chances of victory for he was slightly younger than I was. I now had some grey hairs. In a few years, I would be over fifty. He launched himself at me. Stepping forward on his right leg he swung his sword in a wide sweep. He was going for my neck. I brought up my shield and put my weight on my left leg. The blow was hard but he made the mistake of using the edge of the blade. It would rip the leather of my shield but also begin to blunt his sword. Even as I stepped forward I swung my own sword. My blow would be delivered with the flat of the sword and I deliberately aimed for his shield. I would not blunt my edge. In particular, I went for the place he held his shield. The crack as my sword hit his shield made one of the horses whinny and he had to step back. Full helmets meant that you could not see your opponent's face. I did not need to see it to know that he had been hurt for he took two steps backwards. My men cheered.

I had time on my side and I did not follow up. I was more than happy to fight a defensive battle. When he shuffled his shield, I knew that he was trying to get the feeling back into his arm. My shield had padding on the inside. I had learned that from the Swedes. He came at me and this time he feinted. He wanted me to lift my shield but I did not for I saw that, unlike his first strike, he did not raise his arm as high. I feigned moving my shield up and he changed his swing to strike at my thigh. He had quick hands and I barely managed to bring the shield down to block the blow. The sword slid down the shield and struck the metal plate on my knee. It rang and this time the knight's men cheered. I lunged with my sword. I did have a tip. It was unlikely that I would break a mail link but I hoped to weaken it. He was not expecting the blow and his shield did not rise in time. Perhaps his arm was still numb. My sword hit his left shoulder. The blow was a hard one and he took another step back. I had not broken the link but I had widened it. I could see it. He could not.

He changed his tactics. He suddenly held up his shield and ran at me. He tried to strike me with his shield and his sword at the same time. He was bigger and heavier than me. I pirouetted on my left foot. As I did I brought the flat of my sword around. He struck at my sword with his own. The difference was he hit the flat of my sword with the edge of his. Sparks flew. He swung his head around and his helmet caught me on the side of the head. He punched at me with the pommel of his sword. My shield came up to take the blow. The strike to my helmet had made me see stars. I think he sensed victory for he launched a furious attack on me. He was almost like a Viking who had gone berserk. He swung shield and sword at me in as a succession of quick blows. My instincts and training saved me and he began to tire. When a tired and lazy blow came at my shield I turned the shield and then swung my left arm down towards his thigh. I still held the wickedly pointed dagger in my shield hand. The tip was narrow enough to penetrate the mail links and to make a hole in the gambeson. I hit flesh and blood was on my dagger when I withdrew it.

He stepped back. I felt as though I could read his mind. He was running through the last tricks that he had left. I felt less dizzy but the constant attacks had tired me. I needed to end this. When he brought his sword from on high I did not meet it with my shield but the flat of my blade. I intended not only to blunt his blade but, if I could, bend it. The metal rang together and sparks flew. He struck again and expected my shield. I met his sword with mine and then punched with my shield. The move took him by surprise. The top of my shield caught him under the chin. He swung again at my head but this time he punched with his shield at my head at the same time. He caught my helmet a glancing blow and I stepped back. As I did so I saw that his sword was no longer straight. When he held it against the light I saw the slight kink in it. The next time he swung the arc was not as true and when I met it with the edge of my shield the sword bent a little more. He had hacked wood from my shield but that was a small price to pay.

"Sir Roger, yield. Your sword is no longer true!"

"What and be put on trial? I will take my chances. Lay on!" As he raised his sword I did something totally unexpected. I spun around. His sword came where I had stood and my sword, the edge this time, swung around to hit his back. It was a powerful blow. When I had weakened his mail at his shoulder the integrity of it all was affected. My sword hurt him. I heard something crack beneath his skin. It may have been ribs. I spun the other way and this time brought my sword down diagonally. I hit his neck hard. Before he could recover I lifted my left arm and plunged my dagger into his throat. Blood spurted and he slowly sank to his knees. My men cheered. I lifted the mask from the lower half of my face for I was hot beyond words.

As William took my dagger and shield from me Sir Robert said, "I see what you mean, Earl. Had I fought then I would now be lying in the widening pool of blood."

I sheathed my sword and took off my helmet. "Aye, he was a fool for I gave him the chance of life."

The King said, "And he fought on?"

"He knew that a trial of his peers would have seen him lose everything and possibly his life."

I looked at the two knights and three squires who had watched their lord die. "Do you yield or will there be more bloodshed this day?"

They looked at each other and held their swords, hilt first, to the King, "We yield, your majesty. We are your men to command!"

I saw the King nod, "Then you do yield to the Earl. He has the power of life and death over you now! We will decide on your punishment later." He shouted to the men on the roof, "Come down and open the doors. This is now my manor!"

The heads disappeared and then the garrison, all twenty of them trooped out. I waved for Henry Youngblood to take my men inside. I did not trust that all would have obeyed. There would be a treasure in the hall and some of them might have thought to take it.

"William and Walter, take the horses to the stable."

Even as we entered the hall we heard the clash of steel on steel and then a cry. Henry was wiping his sword on the surcoat of one of the two sergeants at arms who had tried to take some treasure. Henry pointed at the five cowering girls. "It seems, lord, that the Lord of Skipton is not the only knight with venal habits."

"Care for them, Henry."

"Aye lord. Come my little chicks. Don some clothes. Your trials are over now. The Earl of Cleveland will see that you come to no harm."

We spent some time at Sawtry for there was, like Skipton, much evil to be undone. The King had not been at Skipton. He knew the term rebel and he understood dissident lords. The reality was manors like Sawtry. As soon as Sir Roger was dead then the farmers and folk who worked in the village came to us and dropped to their knees in thanks. The fact that the priest fled before we could speak with him told us a great deal. Many priests would have gone to a lord who was doing wrong and intervened but this one had turned his head and allowed the suffering.

"Why did the Sheriff of Cambridge not intervene?"

The King asked a good question, "He may not have known. Do not forget King Henry, the war ended only recently. I am not exonerating him, he may be palpable but do not judge. That is partly the purpose of this progress. You do not know your land nor your people. This is your opportunity to do so."

Sir William d'Urberville had impressed the King. We sent one of King Henry's new men back to Knebworth to ask the young knight to come to Sawtry and put its affairs in order. We waited until we returned before we left. While the King and his baron were closeted I spoke with the Captain of the King's Guard.

James of Corfe should have been a knight. He had been a squire and he had been trained as a knight. He had gone on crusade with his father and his brothers. We had much in common for his brothers and father had been killed. James had had to fight for pay. He had honed his trade and returned to England towards the end of King John's life. The family manor had been given to another and so James had had to fight for pay once more.

"I have been trying to speak with you in private for some time, James."

"Aye lord."

"Our stories are similar and so I hope you will not object to my bluntness. Like you, I lost my family lands and I resented King John. Although I did not fight against him directly I opposed him. What are your feelings towards the King?"

"Thank you for your honesty, my lord. My father was a deeply religious man. We went on crusade when my mother died. I hated King John when I found that our lands had been given to another but the deaths of my family were not his fault. I was in the Holy Land and the manor needed a lord."

It was a plausible answer but I detected that there was more to it. He had an honest face. It was like a map showing his life. There were scars and there were signs of the sun. Flecks of grey were in his beard but his eyes showed that he was hiding something. "What did the King say when you made representation to him?"

84

His head dropped, "That I was not a knight and could not be lord of the manor." I remained silent. "When I heard that you were in London then I headed for the city. I hoped to join your men for all have heard of the hero of Arsuf. Then, when the news was spread that the King sought men at arms it seemed to me that it was a sign from God. You fought for your land and I will fight for my knighthood. I am a gentleman by birth and it is in the hands of you and the King to knight me. I will try to impress you."

I shook my head. "James, the King and I need you to be the leader of these men. These are early days. Thankfully none have had to draw sword yet. That will come. I am pleased that you were honest with me for I have to trust you as I trust my men."

"They are good men, my lord. I have spoken to them. They are very loyal to you."

"And that is because they have been with me for a long time. Some fought alongside me in the Holy Land and Sweden as well as Poitou and Anjou. The bonds were sealed in blood and with steel. You know how hard they are to break."

"Then I will attempt to do the same with the men I lead."

"Until we have fought alongside them and know their mettle you will be the one to speak to me of any flaws you find in them. The Baron of Sawtry had flaws in his metal and it cost him his life."

"I will lord."

"And when there is time we need more men to be hired as the King's Guard. We have too few at the moment."

"I will seek more men. Like you, lord, I have seen deception and know how to recognise it. I will choose good men only."

We left for Lincoln. Sawtry was the first decision the King made without the advice of the Bishop, de Burgh or the Cardinal's man. In the greater scheme of things, it was not particularly important but the boy king made a good decision and bound a knight and two manors to him. In lieu of the losses incurred by Sir William, the King allowed Sir William to have the income from both manors until such time as a new lord of the manor was appointed. The knight was charged with protecting the land and ensuring that a new priest was appointed so that the people could have God's grace once more. We were all in a more confident mood as we neared Lincoln.

Chapter 7
Newark

Lincoln was a joy for Nichola de la Haie was a strong woman and a good constable. Even the King's father had been impressed by her. She liked the young King. I had to smile for she did not treat him as King but as a favoured nephew come to visit. The only sour note was introduced by one of the guests at the feast. Hugh of Wells was Bishop of Lincoln and he was a good man. I knew he had something on his mind for he was quiet during the early part of the celebration of the King's visit.

While the King was being entertained by the Lady of Lincoln's stories of the war I said, "Bishop you know who I am and that I can be trusted. I beg of you to say that which is on your mind."

"I would, Earl, but when we heard the King came north I hoped for a larger force of men."

"There is trouble?"

He nodded, "Newark."

"The Lady Nichola told me last time that it was filled with those who wished the King harm. I thought to visit there on our way north."

"The Lady does not have the whole of it, Earl. There is a mercenary, Robert de Gaugny. He holds the castle and the town. It is my manor and he refuses to hand it over to me. He is like an old-fashioned warlord. Newark Castle is well built and hard to take."

I nodded. He was right. I knew the castle having visited it before the Battle of Lincoln. The river bounded one side and the town the other. King John had died there. "How many knights can you raise, Bishop?"

"No more than twenty and that would take some days."

"Men at arms, archers, fyrd?"

"I believe that there are sixty men at arms who serve my knights. We have about the same number of archers. The fyrd? If we mustered all who owe service then almost a thousand."

I nodded and stared at the fire for I was thinking. This de Gaugny had a town with a wall around it. That would be his first line of defence. If we could take the town quickly then we might catch many of his men in the town. I knew that there was limited accommodation within Newark Castle's walls. He would not have supplies for a lengthy siege.

"How many men does he have?"

"I confess that I do not have an exact number but I would say no more than one hundred and fifty. That is still enough to hold the castle against attack."

"The castle and town are less than twenty miles from here. If you summon your knights, men at arms and archers then I have a plan which might gain us the town and, possibly the castle."

The King suddenly laughed at something the Lady of Lincoln had said and the Bishop said, "And the King?"

"I will speak with the King. Do not worry about him, Bishop. He may be young but he is learning well. The Earl Marshal has asked me to take him under my wing and help him to become a better king than his father."

The Bishop made the sign of the cross and said, "Amen to that."

I excused myself from the table and sought James of Corfe and Henry Youngblood. They were in the warrior hall where the Lady of Lincoln, who appreciated men at arms more than most, had provided them with a good feast and fine ale. As I would have expected the two of them had not indulged as much as many of the others. Henry knew me well, "Yes lord? Is aught amiss?"

"We have to take Newark. I want six men, including Mordaf and Gruffyd, to be ready to go to Newark in disguise tomorrow. I will give them the details in the morning." I smiled for Mordaf was walking along the table using his hands and the rest were banging the table. "I am not sure that he is in any condition tonight."

Henry nodded, "Yet in the morning this night's excesses will not impair him."

"That I know. I need to know how many horses we can muster."

"Aye lord."

James said, "And will we be taking part, Earl, or guarding the King?"

I smiled, "Both!"

I did not speak with the King that night but, after he had gone to bed, I spoke with Sir Robert. He needed to know my thoughts. I went to bed happy that I had a plan. There was risk involved and the King might be in danger but only by being in danger and risked could the King learn to be a leader. I knew that the Council would frown upon my actions. I had been given my instructions by the Earl Marshal and his word was sacrosanct. I would do as I always had. I would serve England and its King.

I was one of the first to rise and I met Nichola de la Haie as she came from the chapel. She was one of the cleverest women I had ever met. Only my wife and Aunt Ruth were more intelligent. "Earl you and the Bishop were in conspiratorial mood last night."

"It is Newark, my lady. I intend to take it back for the Bishop."

"Good. Is there anything I can do?"

"The Bishop has twenty knights how many can you spare?"

"If you are leading then as many as you need. I have six knights, twenty men at arms and forty archers. I have learned the value of such men."

"And horses?"

"We can mount half of the men."

"Good. I thank you and now I will speak with the King."

"He is a good boy. He has potential but he is like a piece of raw clay, Earl. Firing may reveal flaws. Be careful that you do not press too hard."

"I know, my lady, but this task was given to me by William Marshal. It will be a test of my skills. I shall do my best."

The King was late to rise for he had enjoyed the food and the ale which was not the small beer he had once enjoyed. I met with my chosen men. James of Corfe, Sir Robert, Henry Youngblood and Ridley the Giant attended, "I would have you go to Newark. John, you will wait a mile from the town with horses. I want you to go in on foot and from different directions." I placed a purse on the table. "Do not wear surcoats. You go as men heading south to London. The coin I give you means that you will not be treated as vagabonds. I will bring the rest of the men on the morrow soon after dawn. You have a simple task. I need to be able to bring our men quickly into the town. We can hide for part of the way but we will be seen when we are half a mile from the gates. You will ensure that the gates remain open. If you can find weaknesses in the defence of the castle then so much the better."

I saw the amazement on the faces of Sir Robert and James of Corfe when my men nodded, took the purse and left. Sir Robert said, "And that is all you need to say? They will know what they do?

Henry Youngblood and I smiled. "Aye Sir Robert and they will think I said too much. They know their business and that business is war."

I spent longer explaining my plan to the King. When he heard that a mercenary held an English town he was furious. I had to counsel him, "Your Majesty, I will have men watching you closely tomorrow. These men we fight care not that you are King. You are not their King."

"But I want to fight!"

I stared at him, "And are you ready to fight, my liege? Could you stand and face a man at arms and win?"

His shoulders sagged, "No but I wish to learn. Sir Robert, from now on you teach me!"

"Aye my liege, with pleasure."

By noon the knights summoned by the Bishop began to arrive. The ones who lived the closest were first. I had learned a lesson in London and we told none our destination. I did not know if there were spies in the town. All that they knew was that the Bishop of Lincoln, the Earl of Cleveland and the King of England needed their swords. We would not be taking our servants and so we would use their horses to mount men at arms and archers. I wanted to strike as quickly as we could. I was pleased that the King was never further than earshot from me. He was attentive and noticed how much trouble I took to get the details right.

As we ate our evening meal he said, "War is harder than it looks, Sir Thomas."

I cocked an eye, "War, my liege? We have not yet begun to fight. This is preparation."

"Yet there is much preparation involved. I am impressed."

I shrugged, "Some lords are lucky enough to have a man to do the organizing. When I am at home I could leave the order of horses, supplies, weapons and the like to my Steward, Captain of arms and Captain of archers. Here I do not have that luxury and some knights do not take kindly to instructions from a man at arms, no matter how skilled."

I had the men roused an hour after midnight. This would be a night ride. The journey would take just two hours at the most for the horsemen but more than half of our men were afoot. They would only be in place as dawn was breaking. After Collingham, the road ran close to the river and I sent twenty men ahead under the command of Ridley the Giant. There was a sally port on that side of the castle and with luck, my men might gain entry. We waited just six hundred paces from the walls. There was a convenient wood with a farm behind which we could shelter. When I led the knights to the gate I needed to be as quick as I could. There were perilously few men trying to hold the gate for me. I left Sir Robert with the King and ten handpicked guards. They would only follow when the gate was secure.

As we waited by the woods I gathered the knights around me. I had spoken to them in Lincoln but I did not know them and I wanted them to be sure that they understood my plans and orders. There were twenty-six of them. Our squires would follow but they would be behind my men at arms and those of the King. "When we enter the town gates we ride hard for the castle. Stop for nothing. If someone falls from his horse then let the squires help them. If we can gain access to the castle then we save time and, more importantly, men's lives." I looked at each of them. It was dark but none of us had yet donned arming cap or coif. I could see their eyes by the light of the moon. "We are mailed and I doubt that any we meet will be mailed. I am told that many of the garrison spend the night in the town for the accommodation in the castle is meagre. If so we have a chance. When the alarm is given they will rush to return to the safety of the walls. This is one of the largest towns in England. The Bishop tells me that there are more than a thousand people who live within its walls. There will be more innocent civilians than warriors. Remember that. The cry is 'King Henry'!"

William nudged his horse next to mine. "Sir Robert says to tell you that he can see the first hint of dawn in the east."

"Good. Arm yourselves. We have no banner. Follow me and if I fall then it is up to all of you to take Newark."

They murmured, "Aye, lord." Noise carried at night and soon the town would begin to wake.

I fastened my arming cap beneath my chin and slipped my coif above it. When I donned my helmet, I did not lower the visor. I would not need to. If we faced mailed men then I would. Until then I would be cooler and, more importantly, able to see better. I nudged my horse forward until he was in the eaves of the wood. It was a risk. When the sun rose, it might glint off my helmet. I would have to take that risk for as soon as the gates were open then we would move. There would be neither horn nor shout. Our hooves would give us away but by then, hopefully, we would be almost at the gates. I knew that I was relying heavily on the men I had sent into the town but they were the best that I had. It soon became clear that it would be a grey day for there was no sudden flaring of light. Instead, it was a slow lightening of

92

the sky. When I heard the town bell sound then I knew that they were opening the gates.

I turned, "Ready. There will be no command. When I ride then you follow."

The town walls were a dark shadow so that when the gate opened I could see movement. I spurred Bella and she responded instantly. She opened her legs and began to create a lead. For once I did not mind. I was not charging to meet a line of mailed men. This was a race to a gate. I was seen when I was two hundred paces from the gate. The darkness to the north of Newark helped me. I heard shouts and then the town bell tolled. I was just a hundred paces from the gate when they began to close. I saw two men pitch from the gatehouse and then the gates stopped closing. I drew my sword. I could hear the clash of metal and the shouts of combat. As I galloped through I saw Padraig fighting two men. I leaned from my saddle and brought my sword into the side of the head of one of them. I took the top of his skull like a gammer eating a boiled egg. I did not pause. I dug my spurs into Bella who galloped over the cobbles of Newark's streets. I had a moment of doubt. I was not leading my own men. I found myself laughing. This would be the ultimate joke if I reached the gates of the castle, found them open and then discovered that I was alone!

Even though Bella was a big horse, she was almost war horse size and the streets were so crowded with people leaving their homes and fleeing to the castle that I was slowing. I still had my visor up and I shouted, "Out of the way in the name of the King!"

My words had an immediate effect. I think some of the burghers were fleeing because the civil war and the French invasion had made them wary. They stopped and obeyed. The ones who did not were obviously no friends of the King and I used the flat of my sword to strike them in the back. Their shouts and the sound of their bodies hitting the stalls which lined the street made more people get out of my way.

The sun was now high enough to shed light in the streets and I saw that there were armed men before me. Armed men meant they served de Gaugny. They did not deserve mercy.

One warrior emerged from a whorehouse with his breeks around his ankles. He held a sword in his hand and he was trying to pull up his breeks. He succeeded in tripping himself up. I swerved to ride around him but when I heard a sickening crunch then I knew that I had knights behind me and they could not avoid the body. Ahead of me, I saw the gate. The castle had a moat. It fed from the Trent. There were men on the drawbridge and I could hear the cries of those within as they shouted for people to get off the bridge so that they could raise it. Human nature put self-preservation ahead of any thought of their fellow men and they continued to pour across. It spelt their doom.

Bella and I ploughed into the back of them. Those on the side fell into the moat. Two men who stood just inside the gatehouse raised spears to prevent my entry. The press of men made it hard for them but one did manage to stab at me. My shield was still hanging over my left leg. His spear struck my leg but did me no damage. The second sentry's spear came for my face. I lowered my head. The spear slid off the side of the helmet and as Bella galloped beneath the gatehouse I swung my sword across his throat. I was inside the gatehouse. The castle was not yet ours for they could retreat to the keep but I had a toehold and so I pulled up my shield and looked for enemies.

Maurice of Branston was an older knight yet he had managed to keep up with me and he reined in next to me. Like me he had his visor up. He grinned. I could see the light of battle in his eyes. "You have the luck of the devil my lord! Long may it continue."

"As soon as the rest are within the gates we ride to the keep."

He turned in his saddle, "We have twelve men now, lord."

"That will have to do!" I pulled back on Bella's stirrups and raising my sword shouted, "King Henry!"

This time the knights cheered and I raced towards the gate to the keep. The keep was attached to the walls and I knew that my men at arms would dismount and gain access to the keep along the fighting platform. We had breached the outer wall and the men we faced had little confidence in their ability to defeat mounted knights. They ran. This time the gate to the keep was up a staircase. I would not be able to ride Bella but the gate was still open as we approached. I threw myself from the saddle and ran up the stairs. They were filled with men but I had the advantage of a shield, mail and a helmet. Those on the outside fell to the ground as I pushed up through them. Some tried to strike at me with swords and daggers but we were too close for them to have any power and they did not penetrate my mail. I saw the door slowly closing against the press of men. Two arrows flew and the men before me both fell. My archers were on the walls. Using the two bodies to help me spring upwards I threw myself at the closing gate, using my shield and my shoulder as a human battering ram. The gate sprang open and I fell to the ground. My life would have been ended there if Maurice of Branston had not lunged with his sword and ended my would-be killer's life. Another spear plunged down at my chest. I managed to bring my shield around. The spear blow was a hard one. I swung my foot and the rowel on my spur raked across the chaussee of the man at arms. He reeled backwards for the spikes had drawn blood. Maurice of Branston had wounded his opponent and he held his hand out to help me up.

The stairs above us leading to the main hall were narrow and suited the defender. Behind us, our knights and men at arms were fighting the men attempting to get in. I could hear the shouts of, 'I yield!"

We now had the difficult task of ascending the stairs. It had been many years since I had done this. I could not wield my sword because of the stone to my right while the knight who retreated before me could bring his sword down with great force. I sheathed my sword and took out my dagger. Behind me, the sounds of battle were fading as more men surrendered. I heard more knights enter behind me. Maurice of Branston had just said, "Why the dagger?" when one of the Bishop's young knights leapt between us and ran to tackle the knight on the stairs. He swung the sword and the blade hit the top of the stairs. Gaugny's knight swung his sword and almost decapitated the foolish young warrior.

"Hold! Sir Maurice and I will advance. The rest will follow! Slowly!" I turned to Sir Maurice. "Keep to my left and use your shield to protect my side." I held my shield above my head and stepped on the stair. The knight above me fetched me a mighty blow with his sword. I was expecting it but even so, it shook me. I lifted the shield and then, raising my dagger, drove it through the mail and foot of the knight. Sir Maurice rammed his blade through the knee of the knight. Blood spurted and he began to fall forward. We had not planned it but the two of us angled our shields and the body slipped behind us. I quickly climbed three slippery blood-covered steps. Another knight was waiting. He had not seen what had happened because of the curve in the stairs. He had an axe and this time, when he struck, he made my shield crack and numbed my arm. He was a shorter knight and I lunged up and under his hauberk. My dagger entered his thigh and then his groin. He squealed like a pig. Blood and entrails flooded from his body. He slipped backwards. I could see that we were almost at the hall and so, while I had the chance I leapt over his body. A man at arms hurried down the stairs towards me. I did not hesitate but used my shield as a weapon and even as he was slashing down at me I was hitting him in the jaw with my shield. My dagger was the key for as he fell backwards I tore it across his throat. Slipping my dagger into my left hand I drew my sword and stepped into the corridor before the Great Hall.

It was obvious now that the purpose of the three men they had sent was to slow us down so that they could organize their defence. I had had enough solo heroics and I waited for the knights to join me. Sir Maurice said, "My lord you are too reckless!"

I nodded, "It is not in my nature to allow others to risk their lives for me. We now fight as one." I could see that they had knights in the Great Hall and they were flanked by men at arms. They were just four paces from the door and the doors would only accommodate four men at a time. When we entered we would be outnumbered. I turned and pointed to the two largest knights who had just joined us. "You, Sir John, to my right and you, Sir Gilles, to the left of

Sir Maurice. Hold your swords over your shields and lock the shields. The next four I want your swords pointing over our shoulders. We step onto our right feet."

"Aye, lord!"

"King Henry!"

"King Henry!" The words echoed down the stairs and along the corridor. It made it sound like there were more of us than there actually were.

I shouted, "Now!" We moved forward and entered the room. Gaugny and his men had been waiting for the move. They were outnumbered in the castle but not in the hall. If they could kill or capture enough of us they might escape. These were desperate men. I had chosen big knights for it gave us an advantage. Swords, axes and spears rattled off our shields and helmets. The hall had a high ceiling and they could swing their swords easily. I lunged forward with my sword. As luck would have it the man at arms I faced had a helmet with a nasal. I drove the tip of my sword through his eye. It takes a brave man to fight with a sword in his skull. I pushed and my tip entered his brain. He slumped to the ground and my sword was freed. I swung it sideways and it clattered off the side of the helmet of the knight next to him. The sound of the ringing helmet was loud to us and it must have deafened the knight. A sword came over my shoulder and struck the knight's shoulder. Sir John had suffered many blows and his retaliation came when he brought his sword over his head to smash into the knight's helm. Two of their front rank were dead and Sir John and I stepped into the gap their deaths created. As soon as we did so the whole of the enemy line disintegrated for men had warriors on both sides of them.

I found myself facing Robert de Gaugny. I recognised his device. "De Gaugny, surrender. Save men's lives for you cannot win."

"Yield and then what?"

"A trial."

"And we both know what the outcome of that will be. I will try a bout with you lord. Who knows if I win I may buy my freedom with your life."

97

"Do not count on that, my friend!"

I had been watching his eyes. I saw the movement there before he made it and my shield smashed into the sword which came for my head. I had been fighting for some time and I was his first opponent; he and his blade were fresher. He was younger. I deliberately took a step back to give him confidence. I feinted with my sword and he laughed. "Earl, I expected more. You disappoint me."

I took another step back aware that the hall was now filled with men fighting each other. So long as de Gaugny lived they would fight on. He began to swing harder. I kept blunting his blade with my shield but I was aware that there was a crack in the shield and it would split. When I felt the wall at my back I had nowhere else to go. He sensed his opportunity and he brought his hand over to shatter my shield with his sword. I chose that moment to hack down at his thigh. As my shield broke he shouted in pain as my shield split but I held a dagger in my hand and I put the tip at his throat. "Yield!" I pushed and the narrow tip went into one of the mail links and pricked his chin.

"I yield!" His sword clattered to the floor of the Great Hall.

The battle was over and the Bishop had Newark but I had been lucky. If I had not had the dagger in my left hand then I would now be dead.

Chapter 8
The Homecoming

The King learned about justice when the mercenary and his men went on trial. He saw now the leniency of my justice in London. The men who were not executed were branded or maimed. As all of them had been warriors they could not continue to ply their trade. As we headed for York he asked me what their future held for them.

"If they are lucky then they might be taken on as a labourer. Warriors, even one missing fingers or hands, are strong men. However, farmers would fear for their families for warriors who fight for pay are dangerous men too. If they have family they could return thence and, perhaps, learn a trade but that is unlikely. Most warriors fight because that is the only trade they enjoy. If I was to be brutally honest, King Henry, then I would guess that most of them will end up as brigands and bandits in forests such as this one." We were passing through the huge forest which covered most of Nottinghamshire and Yorkshire. "They will live a frugal life and probably a short one but they will be free and they will be doing that which they know."

He was silent for a while. "Why do men choose to be warriors? Knights choose a warrior's life for it is noble but what of the men who follow?" He lowered his voice and looked over his shoulder, "Men such as those who follow me?"

"Lord, I began, after Arsuf, as a sword for hire. If I had not been lucky enough to be knighted by King Richard then I would have had to fight for a master in Outremer. I hope that

I would have been as James of Corfe and chosen a good master to follow but sometimes beggars cannot be choosers. Fate can throw you into places you would not normally go." He was silent as he reflected upon my words.

We halted at a small village that had been carved out of part of the forest. There was a water trough and so we watered our horses. The folk there had little and we were offered nothing more. William had been listening, as he rode behind us. When he had watered and fed our horses he said, "Father, tell him the tale of Dick and Harold. I used to love that story when I was growing up."

I smiled. William and Alfred had both been told the stories of the Warlord and his father for without them our family would have had nothing. King Henry said, "I pray you do so. When I was growing up I had no stories. I listened to the conversations of adults and I rarely saw my father." He shook his head, "When I did see him then he had little time for me. I suppose he was trying to save a kingdom."

The boy king had shown me that he was growing but it was easy to miss the fact that growing up as a prince was not a happy experience. I nodded and we mounted our horses and headed up the Great North Road. "Dick and Harold were both outlaws. When my great grandfather and his father were travelling up the road they were attacked and the outlaws saved them. Harold was a young outlaw, a little older than your majesty and William. He became my father's squire. Eventually, he became a knight and he saved my father's life in London when your grandfather's realm was threatened. He died a hero."

"An outlaw became a knight? That sounds like the stuff of ballads."

"I never met him but my great grandfather was the man who helped to reclaim England from King Stephen. You owe your throne to him and he was not an ordinary man. He sacrificed his life and family to make England safe. His blood runs through my veins. I try to live up to the standards he, my grandfather and my father set."

"I heard that your father died saving my uncle."

"He did, I was there." The memory of that hot and dusty day came rushing back to me. The sound of neighing horses and the thundering hooves of the Seljuk Turk. Had I really survived? Was this all a dream of death?

I realised that I must have been silent for some time as the King said, quietly, "And this Dick?"

I nodded, "In many ways his story is even more remarkable. When we reach my home, I will show you his grave for he has a monument the equal of the Warlord."

"An outlaw?"

"He redeemed his past and atoned for whatever sins he had committed. He became an outlaw through no fault of his own. He became the Warlord's Captain of Archers. In the battles to end the civil war he and his well-trained men won back the kingdom. My father was in no doubt about that. Mordaf and Gruffyd are just two of my archers but I have many and they are the finest in the land. They are the legacy of Dick. He was knighted. As far as I know he was the only knighted archer. He never had a manor and, so far as I can tell, rarely if ever used his title. When he died the great and the good came to pay their respects. Outlaws can be redeemed, King Henry, and my son was right to have me tell you the tale for it is too easy to forget those who are not noble born. Without them you would have no kingdom."

He turned to look at Ridley the Giant and Henry Youngblood who were chatting easily to Sir Robert. Once more I saw the King changing. He had been brought up the son of a King he rarely saw. The servants and those responsible for raising him had done so looking over their shoulders for they feared that King John would lose and they would have to seek a new master. His upbringing must have been lonely. He had not enjoyed, as I had, the company of men such as Edward and Edgar, my grandfather's hawkers. He had not watched Alf's grandson make his first mail hauberk. He had not ridden through Hartburn woods to hunt and to share food with the pig farmer, Osweyn. He had lived apart. His life had been that of a monk in luxury. I saw envy in his eyes. He wanted to be able to talk as Sir Robert did.

"Your Majesty, your honour and your position are not threatened if you are familiar with those who are around you. Even if lower born in death we are all the same. If you get to know them then they will fight harder for you and you will not be profligate with their lives. De Gaugny could have saved men's lives if he had surrendered just a few moments before he did. Sir Maurice, Sir John and the others all killed men who might otherwise had survived."

"And possibly received the sentence of death!"

I laughed, not in a cruel way but in remembrance of my own life. "So long as a man lives there is a chance for another life. In the Holy Land, Sweden and Anjou there were many times I might have died but I sought life."

"You mean they could have escaped?"

"Would you await death? Would you not do all that you could to live?"

We rode in silence. That day was many years ago but my words must have affected the King for his son showed that he had learned to be resourceful and to do all that he could to survive. That would be the future for Henry had neither a wife nor a son. I had thrown a stone into the pond and the ripples, once started, would continue for a long time.

When we reached York, he heard from the Archbishop and Sir Ralph of the state of the land. The ones who had fled the evil of the Lord of Skipton spoke to him. He heard first hand of their privations. It hardened him to lords of the manor who did not look after their tenants.

We had been away far longer than I had expected. I was looking forward to seeing my family again. The King and William were chattering away like magpies behind me. William was pointing out features, such as the priory at Mount Grace and the ancient white horse carved upon the hills. Since our talk in the forest he had begun to enjoy the company of others and was easier with them. I put my mind to the task ahead. I knew, from our journey north that Newark had been a warning to others who thought to flout the King and his lords. We had been greeted warmly in each town through which we had passed. De Vesci and de Percy still remained a problem north of my river and north of the

Palatinate. We would need to visit with them. I had a mind to ride to Norham. It would be a long ride and autumn was upon us but it would serve to show the Scots that we had a new king and it would bolster the resolve of that northern outpost of England. If we could leave the north at peace then I could return the King to London knowing that his hands were firmly upon the reins. Already the harvest was in and the animals gathered for their cull. This was the perfect time for the Scots to raid.

He was impressed by my castle. We awaited the ferry and he commented upon it. "The river is wide here, Earl. You have strong walls."

"They were stronger, King Henry, but your father and Bishop destroyed them. They will do. So long as the Scots are at peace then they will be adequate enough."

My wife and family were waiting to greet us. The day, which had begun cold at East Harlsey, had warmed up but there would be another chill in the air come evening. My wife and my daughters were well wrapped. The King had a riding cloak wrapped around him as did William. He did not look like a king. My wife rushed to me as I stepped ashore and hugged me, "I have missed you husband!" She kissed me hard and I saw my daughters grin.

"And I have missed you too, my love." I gestured with my arm, "May I introduce King Henry of England and his knight Sir Robert. They will be our guests for a while."

My wife glowered at me and then curtsied, "Your Majesty, this is an honour." She rose and said, more to me than the King, "Had I been warned of your imminent arrival then I could have prepared rooms."

"I do not need to be pampered, my lady. Your husband has been teaching me to be a warrior."

I suddenly realised who was missing, "Where is Aunt Ruth? She is not ill, is she?"

"No, my husband, she is with Lady Matilda. Your Aunt is teaching her. The two get on. We have much to tell you but that can wait until we have made our guest comfortable."

103

She and my daughters scurried ahead. Alfred clasped my arm and bowed to the King, "You are in such trouble now, father! You should have sent a rider to warn us!"

I knew he was right, "I know but we have had much to occupy us since we left London."

King Henry was confused and it showed upon his face, "You are Earl. You should not have to worry about such trivia."

"King Henry you will learn that I may be master of the valley but like all husbands I am not master of my own home."

"My father did not worry what my mother thought!"

I said nothing but, in my mind, I reflected on the fact that the Queen had wasted no time in quitting England and remarrying. It spoke volumes for the marriage. Mine was built on firmer foundations and I would not change my wife for the world. We headed through the gate into the inner ward. I pointed out the defensive features. I compared my castle with the Tower and the other castles through which we had passed. King Henry later forgot many of the lessons I taught him but he never forgot the strength of a castle. He was mightily interested and we spent some time in the inner ward. My wife had gone through like a whirlwind. People scurried hither and thither. She was a clever woman and knew that the King would have men and servants with him. It was not just accommodation for the King which she needed.

Geoffrey, my Steward, was waiting for us in the Great Hall. "My lady has given me instructions, lord, I am to take the King and his knight to his chambers so that he may cleanse himself after his journey. Until his servants are ferried across I have men who will wait upon him."

"Thank you, Geoffrey." I turned, "William go with Geoffrey and the King. When you get to the chamber see if your mother has forgotten anything."

He nodded and laughed, "Unlikely but I will do so. I can continue to show the King our home!" My son was easy in the King's company. It would be good for them both.

I could see that Alfred was desperate to speak with me. I poured us both a goblet of wine. "Go on then, speak that which is on your mind and about to flood from your mouth."

"I am to be wed! Matilda will have me as her husband." I nodded and sipped my wine. His face clouded over. "Are you not happy? Mother is happy as are my sisters. Rebekah... I will let her tell you."

"Alfred, Matilda is my ward and I have certain responsibilities. You cannot decide that you wish to marry her and then just do so. There are laws and there are conventions."

His voice became hard, "You would stop this? I..."

I held up my hand and my voice became the voice I used on the battlefield, "Hold there and do not say anything that you may regret. I did not say that I would prevent the marriage but I am disappointed that you did not do as I asked before I left. I said to speak with me when I returned. You should have asked my permission. Now, calmly, speak with me." I nodded, encouragingly.

He seemed confused then realisation dawned, "My lord, I would wed the Lady Matilda."

I smiled, "That is better. First I will speak with the King and then with Lady Matilda." I saw him flush again. "The King is the one who ultimately decides what happens to the wards."

"But he is not even a knight!"

"Yet he is King and we will do this properly." I pointed to the walls. "My great grandfather did not ask permission to build this castle. When a new King came to the throne then it was pulled down. Now do you understand? We have to do things properly or risk the wrath of a monarch. If not this one then another."

"I think I understand." He finally drank some wine. "What is the King's business here in the north, my lord?"

"He comes with me on a progress. There are lords who oppose him. We defeated one at Newark and I am hoping that the example will make the others fall in line. We go north to see de Vesci and de Percy. They bear grudges."

He shook his head, "Eustace de Vesci was killed at Barnard Castle. The news only reached us two weeks since. His son is a minor and has been placed with William Longespée, Earl of Salisbury. There is now just Thomas de Percy and I think that he will be less belligerent now that his ally is no longer with us."

"And all else is well?"

He smiled, "All else is well and I am sorry for my temper. I am eager to be wed."

"For the manor?"

He shook his head, "I care not if we have to live here so long as we are married." I nodded. He added, "But I would like a manor!"

"We will be riding tomorrow. You can come with us. Go and tell David of Wales and Henry Youngblood to prepare for a ten-day journey.

I spoke with the King when he descended and he, of course, agreed immediately. We both spoke with Lady Matilda while my aunt looked on. It was clear to me that Lady Matilda was smitten by my son and that made me happy. I knew of many loveless marriages. Sometimes they endured. The people in them were wracked with torment. Lady Matilda hurried off to speak with Alfred and my wife.

Aunt Ruth looked the King up and down. She put her hands on her hips, "And are you going to be a good king like your namesake or will you be a tyrant like your father?"

Poor King Henry did not know what to say. He almost cowered before my Aunt's gaze.

I said, hurriedly, "Your Majesty must excuse my aunt. She thinks that because she rules this roost she rules England too!"

She shook her head, "Thomas, I have lived too long to worry about upsetting little boys, even if they are King of England. I knew your father when he was your age. He was spoiled and unpleasant. I am hoping that you are different. Is he, Thomas?"

She was digging a hole not only for herself but for me too. "I did not know King John as a child but as William Marshal has asked me to mould King Henry into a monarch then I believe that you can trust me to do so. He will be a good man and he is learning."

Having seen me bear the brunt of my aunt's tongue King Henry gained confidence. "And I will continue to learn but know this, my lady, I will be King and I will rule this land. Some may not like the way I rule. If I could please everyone then I would be pleasing no one for my land and people are all different. I have seen that in my progress north."

She beamed, "Good! Stand up to the old witch! Your father would have run away crying for his mother! She spoiled him. I have high hopes for you. Now come Thomas, give your aunt a hug and a kiss. I have missed you and such reunions will be fewer in future."

Geoffrey came in, "My lord, the food will be ready in less than an hour." He looked pointedly at my dust covered clothes.

Aunt Ruth said, "You may leave the King with me. I shall not devour him!" The King smiled.

I felt exhausted as I headed to my chamber. It would be a relief not to have someone badgering me. I commanded everywhere, it seemed, save my own home. I had not even reached the door when Rebekah and my wife met me. My wife pushed my daughter towards me. "It is good to see you, father."

I hugged her. She smelled of rosemary. "This is the first real welcome I have had since I walked from the ferry."

"And whose fault is that, Thomas? All you had to do was to send Mordaf to warn me. That is all. Come let me kiss you for I have missed you!" It was a heartfelt kiss and hug. When she pulled away she said, "Now ask you, father so that he may bathe and change. He smells of sweat and horses!"

"Perhaps later?"

"Now, young lady!"

She sighed, "Father, Geoffrey FitzUrse has asked me to be his bride."

I was about to say that he should have asked me first but I saw the fire in my wife's eyes and so I smiled, "And that is good news. I have a dowry already picked out!"

"I know! Mother told me! Elton! I shall need to rebuild it. The manor has lain vacant for a generation!"

I shook my head and went into my chamber. My daughter's plans would involve more expense. At least I might have a little peace. My wife came in and shook her head. "Sometimes, husband I wonder about you. Alfred was more than a little taken aback by your response. He was happy!"

"And I am pleased that they are both happy but there are ways of doing things. King Henry is not far down the road from being a child. I have managed to take him away from the three men who rule him so that I may shape the King into one who is more like Henry and less like John. I have been charged to do so by William Marshal."

"And why cannot he do it?"

"He has served England and served her well. Besides, he is dying."

Her hand went to her mouth. "I am sorry, I did not know. Does this mean you will be away?"

"Possibly but I thought to keep him here for as long as we could. The three members of the Council are more than capable of running England."

"But will they do a good job?"

"I doubt it but set me one task at a time."

"Come, you are a good man still and I will be the servant who prepares you for the feast." She shook her head as she began to unfasten the mail. "I hope the King approves of the food we have prepared for him."

"He will because it is new to him. He has lived at court. Thanks to his father and, I suspect, his mother, he knows little of the real world. William has been good for him. They get on well."

She took the mail from me and then slipped the gambeson from me. When she removed my undershirt, she saw the bruises from my combats. "You have been fighting!"

"I am a warrior and we won."

"I thought when Louis was defeated and King Alexander crept back to Scotland that we would have peace."

108

"Lady Matilda is an example of what happens should we cease to be vigilant." I was naked and I pulled her to my lap, "And I am pleased that she is safe and will be happy with my son. If he has half the wife I have…"

She looked down for I had been aroused, "Or half the man of his father. Come, I have missed you!"

When we finally dressed we had but bare moments to reach the Great Hall. Aunt Ruth gave me a wry smile. I wondered if she had some magical powers for she knew all that went on in my castle. The feast was a joyous one for we celebrated two engagements. Sir Geoffrey was not present but my family were and I saw the envy on the face of King Henry as he saw my four children all getting on so well. His family, like that of his father, had always bickered and fought. As I retired I was hopeful that the internal strife which had beset the family of the King since the second King Henry might have been expunged with his father's death.

Chapter 9
The settling of the north

When I left for the north I almost stripped Stockton of its defences. I left a skeleton garrison. The men I left, however, would be able to defend the castle if trouble flared and the King's person was far more important. We went first to Durham. Richard Marsh was the Bishop. He was one of Prince John's appointments. After the Bishop, I had been forced to slay all others seemed good men. Richard Marsh was no exception. When I told him of the dowry I would be giving FitzUrse and my son he seemed quite happy. He did not fear me. He respected me for he knew that I was the knight who had defeated the Scots and kept his land safe. "I had planned on giving FitzUrse, Norham. Elton is good. You have my approval."

The King got on well with him and the Bishop explained Carucage to him. Carucage was a medieval English land tax introduced by King Richard in eleven ninety-four. The young King turned to me, "Why did not Hubert de Burgh explain that to me? It was used in my name and yet I knew not what it was. When we were at Windsor one of the local lords asked me about it and I must have looked like some sort of village fool for I knew nothing."

My daughter's future husband, Sir Geoffrey, was amongst the knights who followed my banner. He wisely rode at the rear of the column. There were many reasons for that. He did not wish to inflame jealousy in his brother knights and he did not want to do anything foolish which might jeopardise the wedding.

Alfred rode behind King Henry and explained to King Henry why he thought de Burgh had not told him all that he should have. "I fear, my lord, that there are many men such as that. I know for when we campaigned there were knights who took delight in seeing a squire confused and dismayed. I always preferred campaigning with knights of the valley. They did not try to humiliate me." I looked in surprise at my son. He had never spoken of that.

King Henry said, "I envy you your spurs, Sir Alfred. Would that I had my own and like yours that they were earned."

Every day saw a change in Henry. As we headed further north I grew more hopeful about England's future. The Bishop gave us an escort of twenty of his knights for the journey to Prudhoe. William de Percy had acquired the castle and I felt it important that the King establish his authority. Prudhoe was a magnificent castle and had held out against the Scots twice. It guarded the Tyne. I would have been happier with another lord of the manor for I did not trust the Percys. The Bishop had told us that Sir Richard de Percy, the head of the family, had fought against King John but made his peace before the King died. He had had his manors returned to him and now lived in Topcliffe. If Sir Richard represented the past then his nephew, William, represented the future.

He gave us a warm greeting and that made me suspicious. He showed the King around the castle, pointing out the damage inflicted by the Scots. He had not been there. It had been in that campaign that Aunt Ruth's husband had been killed. The young noble seemed to take credit for the sieges. I said nothing although the King looked impressed. On the journey north, we had spoken of how King Henry might approach the meeting. When we sat in his Great Hall I knew that I could say nothing for that would undermine the King's authority.

"You have a fine castle here, Baron."

"Thank you, majesty."

"You have a noble tradition to uphold. The lords who defended the river from the Scots did so to preserve England."

"Just so." De Percy was almost preening himself.

"Your family, however, along with the de Vesci clan, sought to profit from the French invasion and joined forces to fight against my father." I saw the look of shock on the face of de Percy. He looked as though the King had slapped him in the face. "If it had not been for the Earl of Cleveland and the Bishop of Durham then who knows what the result might have been."

"I am sorry, lord! Put it down to a misjudgement of youth."

"Yet your uncle and de Vesci were not young."

"I was led astray!"

"I am young and I know that I have much to learn but I would hope that I would not be so weak as to be easily led astray. I will watch you, baron, for any signs of disloyalty and rebellion. I expect your taxes to be paid promptly and I expect a summons for muster to be greeted with joy that you can serve England."

"I swear that it shall be so."

We left the next day. I complimented the King as we rode north for Norham. He shrugged, "I did what you advised but I confess that it was easier to speak your words than those put in my mouth by the Council. They mean well and they have England at their hearts but they are not you. You are England." I nodded at the compliment. "So, what will we see in the north?"

"No rebels remain. De Vesci and de Percy were the last two. The Scots are ever close and my family has ensured that they do not risk our wrath. The purpose is for you to see the northern outpost of your land. It is as far north as you rule. London is so many leagues away as to be almost in another country. When you sit in the Great Hall at Windsor I would have you remember the men who defend your land."

"That is a sobering thought."

"Your standard flying from Norham's keep will remind the Scots that the King of England regards the north as his land and that he has not forgotten it."

We stayed at the mighty fortress that was Bamburgh. Impregnable and majestic it was now a royal castle with a constable. Sir James Redvers was delighted to be hosting his king. The castle rose above the sea and the sand on a solid rock. As far as I knew it had never been taken and that was why it was now a royal residence. It might be rare for a King of England to visit but it would not be in the hands of a potential rebel. I asked Sir James about the Scots.

"They appear to be behaving themselves, lord. Merchants can travel the roads and there have been far fewer cattle raids. However..." He hesitated.

The King said, "Go on. Speak. Do not stop because you fear you might offend me. This is my castle and you are my castellan. I expect the same honesty from you as I receive from the Earl of Cleveland."

Sir James inclined his head, "You are right, majesty. The truth is they have not dismantled their castles. Their knights are frequently seen by the Tweed. Sir Richard at Norham can give you a better idea for he is the closest knight to the Scots but the merchants who travel the roads are uneasy and there are now far fewer of them."

The King looked at me for clarification. "That means, King Henry, that they fear something will happen and they will stay away until it is safe. Merchants are cautious men and think in terms of facts and figures, profit and loss. When the threat of a loss looms, they stay away from danger. Of course, it may be that there is little for them to trade."

Sir James shook his head, "The contrary, lord. I have heard that the merchants can make great profit in Jedburgh and Berwick. They do not even need to travel to Edinburgh."

That had me puzzled. I had intended this progress to show the King his land. Now it looked as though I had brought him into danger. "How many men can you spare for a journey to Norham?"

113

"I have five knights and ten men at arms who are mounted." He smiled. "It is widely known, Earl, that you prefer your men mounted."

"That I do. I would have them accompany us to Norham. We will return them when we head south." After I had escorted the King to his chamber and Sir Richard had set the watch I went, with Alfred, to David of Wales. "Send two good men north of the Tweed tomorrow. I would like to know if there is danger."

"Aye lord. I think you are wise."

"Have you heard something?"

"Cedric Warbow often visits an alehouse in the village when we are here." He smiled, "The alewife who runs it and Cedric are both of an age. When he was there he was talking with some of those who fish along the coast. They speak of more mailed men than they have seen in a long time. They are suspicious of the Scots."

"They are always suspicious of the Scots!" My son's tone was scornful.

"Aye but you are right to send men north, lord. I believe there is something amiss. I will send Cedric and Will son of Robin. They are both familiar with the Tweed."

"But why would they come now?"

"Because, my son, it is harvest time. These border lords are lazy men. Why raise your own crops and animals when you can steal them? Their clans have been doing it for generations. It is why the Romans built a wall."

We left after dawn. With the men from the Bishop, the King's men, my own men and those from Bamburgh I had almost two hundred men. It was not an army but if we had to fight then it would take a much larger force of Scots to defeat us. Once we had climbed the rise from Bamburgh the land was largely flat. We headed up the old Roman road which led to Norham. I had fought at Norham more than once. It was a well-made castle. Hugh Puiset had allowed it to become prey to the predatory Scots but since then it had been much improved. Even when the outer wall fell it was hard to take. A natural gorge forced an attacker to the bridge which could be raised. The well had never run dry and I knew that the Bishop of Durham kept it well supplied. Only a fool would try to take Norham but the Scots might well be contemplating crossing the river to raid.

King Henry was puzzled, "Everyone, you included, Earl, said that the Scots were finished. Is there a threat?"

"You have to understand, my lord, that there are two Scottish threats. The first is the King and his army. They are not a threat for there is trouble in Caithness and the King's eye is drawn thither. The second type of Scot is the beast which is the border lord. In times past, they had land on both sides of the Tweed and down as far as the New Castle. They still try to claim Carlisle even though it was theirs for but a couple of years during the time of Stephen and Matilda. These Scots would like another war. If they cannot have another war then they will take the riches of England for Scotland is a poor and desolate country. You father defeated them and I have beaten them."

"Yet they rise again."

"And that is why we have such strong castles."

Norham was built of red stone and stood high above the Tweed. The small village which had grown up nearby lay closer to the river and below the castle. The walls of Norham represented sanctuary for the villagers. Sir Richard Scoop knew me and he recognised my banner alongside that of the King. He was cautious. The Scots were tricky and ruses were often employed. The fact that my coif lay around my shoulders and he could see my face helped. He greeted us close to his keep.

Recognising the King's livery, he bowed, "Welcome Your Majesty. Earl, it is good to see you again. Does your visit presage problems?" He was looking at me as he spoke.

"We thought not when we set out. The King has never seen the northern extremities of his land. The Earl Marshal asked me to watch over the King." Sir Richard was an old soldier and he read the message beneath my words. I saw it in his eyes. "However, Sir James and the villagers of Bamburgh were uneasy. They thought that the Scots might be up to something. You keep men watching the river?"

"The river? Yes. Beyond the river? No, for I did not wish to prompt another war."

Sir Richard was letting sleeping dogs lie and that was always a mistake. It would not do to berate him for he had a difficult task. I nodded, "No matter. I have sent two scouts north of the border. They will return later this night. We would stay a day or two before returning to Stockton."

"Of course, although you may find the accommodation a little basic. The hall is a little small for such a host."

Alfred nodded, "No matter, my lord. We will make do. We are warriors, after all." My son was young but he was putting the King's knight to shame. I saw the King's knight look at Alfred in a new light. It was not his fault. I had had to concentrate upon the King and I had neglected the instruction for the man who would lead King Henry's household knights. The Earl Marshal had set me a mighty task.

While the King was settled into his quarters I went with Sir Richard Scoop and William down to the river to view the other side. The path down to the river was steep and an enemy would struggle to assault the castle from that side. The undergrowth, however, on both sides of the river was thick. "Sir Richard why have you not removed the undergrowth from the far side of the river?"

"The Scottish side?"

"Yes, Sir Richard. How do you know if there are enemies there?"

"They could not scale this side of the defences."

"That is not the point. They could move downstream and cross by the village. You could be cut off from the south."

"They have never done so yet."

I sighed. The castellan felt safe in his castle and had not thought through the implications of an attack on the hinterland. "We will help your men to fell the trees and clear the undergrowth. At the very least it will give you firewood and kindling for the winter."

He laughed, "Aye lord and up here the winters are long and grim."

"I know for I have often fought here in winter. Come we will follow the path to the village."

The path was not an easy one and that was a good thing. It was little used. The village was a huddle of perhaps seven dwellings. I guessed that they owed their livelihood to the castle. Although Sir Richard had his own bakehouse and alehouse those in the village would supply them with river fish and vegetables. There would be women and girls there who would satisfy the needs of a garrison of men who had need of them. I had seen old Roman forts where the same settlements had grown up. The villagers bowed as we passed.

"Do they practise their archery on Sundays?"

"Sometimes but there are less than fifteen men in the village."

"And if you were attacked then those fifteen men could add to your defence. Make it so."

We began the steep climb to the castle. The constable said, "My lord have I disappointed you?"

I shook my head, "You have become complacent is all. I have learned both here and abroad that the moment you cease to be vigilant is when an enemy can strike. I do not envy you your position but it is your appointed duty. You have no wife?"

"She and my children died when the pestilence visited my home in Durham. It is why I accepted this position."

Now it became clear to me that the castellan had come here to die. He was like a monk and Norham was his cell. I would have to speak with the Bishop. Norham needed someone who looked out and not within.

That evening, as we ate, I smiled for Norham's food was basic. It was plainer fare than he was used to and there was no wine. For myself, it was good honest food. The King was learning about his people.

Cedric and Will arrived late in the evening. David of Wales brought them to me as soon as they arrived. "The Scots are up to something, lord. There are armed camps just two miles from where we crossed the river downstream from the village."

The castellan said, "I knew nothing of this." I said nothing for he had been remiss in his duties.

"We crept close enough to their camp to hear their words, lord. It is why we were so tardy returning. Three days from now is when they plan to cross the river. There will be no moon that night. We heard them joking about leaving just twenty men to watch the castle while the rest would disport themselves in the land hereabouts. They said that no word would reach the castle and the constable would think that the fairies had spirited the people and animals away."

I looked at Sir Richard, "And they would be right. Sir James in Bamburgh has men riding but not as far as this part of England." I turned back to my men. "How far south are the camps?"

"As we said, lord, there is one just two miles from here, one at Kelso and one at Jedburgh."

I turned to the King. "We need to act."

For the first time in a few days he looked anxious. "We will be breaking the peace."

"Aye to save the lives of your people. Your majesty, I will take it upon myself to lead volunteers and rid the border of these camps. I have been outlaw before. It will not worry me if the Scots call me so again."

"No, I am King of England and this is England. The people need protection. I will come with you."

I looked at his knight and nodded. He would have to watch the King. "Cedric, how many are in the camps?"

"The largest is at Jedburgh and there are more than a hundred and fifty men there. The others have between sixty and a hundred. The one which is two miles from here has two knights and ninety men. While we waited for dark to make our escape we counted them."

"Then we ride tomorrow. We sweep down the Tweed and we take as many of them as we can. Then, Constable, you and your men will need to watch the border a little more closely through the next months. Once the harvest is in and the animals culled then there will be little for them to raid. Even if we do not succeed in killing or capturing all of them we will hurt them. I will hold a council of war as soon as we have broken our fast. Tell the leaders of the conroi to meet me in the Great Hall."

There were just a handful of us left. Sir Edward, Sir Alfred, Sir William and Sir Fótr joined the King and his solitary knight. Sir Richard looked nervous for even Alfred had more experience of battles than he had. Sir Edward was the most experienced warrior. Only I had fought in more battles. He looked over to the King and his knight, "My lords this will not be a battle. The men we fight will have arms and some may be mailed but they have come to the borderlands as robbers."

The King said, "Even the knights?"

"Especially the knights. Unlike the Earl, the Scottish knights will keep the best treasure for themselves." He looked at me and then turned to the King, "Your Majesty, I mean no offence by this but you and Sir Richard should stay close to the squires. It will not be a battle but that does not mean there will be no risk. There will be arrows and thrown spears. Their boys will hurl stones and they can kill just as easily as a sword. There is no shame attached to hiding behind a shield. Sir Richard, you have a great responsibility."

The King reflected for a moment, "There are many who would think your words insolent Sir Edward but I see you bear the scars of many battles. In addition, you are the leading knight in the Earl's conroi. I will heed your advice." There was an edge to his words. He had not liked the lecture. It had been necessary but Edward was bluff and not noble-born. He would not dress his words.

Alfred saw Edward flush at the tone. "My brother, William, wanted to be at the fore. It took Skipton to show him the dangers of battle. I remember when I was your age, your majesty, and I saw my father's knights winning battle after battle. They made it look easy and it is not. I think you will find tomorrow instructive."

"One battle wins all?"

I shook my head, "There may be three battles tomorrow. We head south sweeping up the Scots and dispersing them. This is a chevauchée. This is a raid into Scottish land. If we

119

can hurt them then the constable will have a safe and quiet winter. The north will be safe from raids and we will be able to turn our eyes south." I looked pointedly at Sir Richard, "You will need to speak to James of Corfe. Some of his men will guard the King along with you but we will need the rest. I would have him at the council of war."

The King frowned, "He is a commoner. He is not a knight!"

I smiled, "You may not have noticed, my liege but I have more men at arms than knights. I think your James of Corfe will do well enough."

What remained of the night was spent in preparation. William had little to do for me. My horse was prepared and my mail and sword were burnished and ready. He spent time speaking with Alfred. The two were close and that pleased me. I had had neither brother nor sister. I knew that my Aunt Ruth had been close to my father. I had grown up alone. My mother and father had been taken from me all too quickly. It was good that my boys were brothers in arms. I prayed in the chapel. I was risking much. I had the King of England with me. He would witness the most brutal of combats for the Scots hated the English and they would fight tooth and nail. His knight, Sir Richard, would not have experienced what was to happen for this was no tourney. The Scots would attempt to hamstring horses and slip daggers beneath mail. When you struck you struck to kill. A wounded Scotsman was worse than a wounded wolf.

I slept little for I was worried and when I rose I woke William. I did not mean to. After he had dressed me and donned his leather jerkin we went to break our fast. There was fresh bread along with the local cheese. It was harvest time and there were ripe plums and greengages. Fresh eggs completed our meal and I headed for the Great Hall. My knights were the first to arrive. That I had expected. The captains, James of Corfe, David of Wales and Henry Youngblood followed. They had been ready already but they would not dream of arriving before Sir Edward and my knights. The knights of Durham arrived next and then the rest filtered guiltily in. I was about to begin when the King and Sir Richard wandered in. Everyone stared at him. For the first time in his life, the King was truly embarrassed. I saw it in his face.

"Do not wait for me, Earl. I will be, as you so rightly told me last night, a bystander."

I nodded, "Thank you, King Henry. My plan is simple. We divide into three battles. The knights of Durham will form one battle and will be led by Sir Geoffrey FitzUrse." My future son in law had impressed me thus far. As he would soon be a knight of the valley it was important to me to see how he could lead men. I had to have a commander and I knew none of the others. I saw him nod. He seemed to grow a little for he knew he had been honoured. "Sir Richard will lead the knights and men at arms of Norham and Bamburgh. I will lead the men of the valley and a contingent of the King's men. We cross the river here for we are all mounted. Sir Richard will ride to the north of me and my men. This is their land and they know it better than any. Sir Geoffrey will stay close to the river. We sweep through their camp. The King's men will secure the camp and deal with prisoners, mail and any treasure. The rest of us will not stop but ride south in an orderly fashion. We halt a mile from Kelso and repeat the attack. Ignore the town, for now. If we have not suffered heavy losses then Sir Richard will secure the town and Sir Geoffrey and myself will continue to Jedburgh. We hold what we have until dawn the next day and then bring back whatever booty we have to Norham." I saw nods of approval. "The King will ride in disguise. He can have neither banner nor device. It is one thing for a killer of priests and the bane of the Scots to raid but not the King of England." I realised that I was giving a command but I caught Henry's eye and he nodded. "Let us ride!"

I would not hide from the Scots and William would carry my banner. He would be in the third rank. The King and his escort would be amongst the other standards and the squires. Sir Richard led the way to the river. He knew it better than any. We had had dry weather and the river was not deep. As we mounted the other bank I saw Sir Richard wave. He would ensure that he and his knights did all that they could. I knew he felt guilty about his lack of vigilance. We rode a mile north and then halted. I turned to make certain that the King was in position. He was. This would be a test for Sir Geoffrey for he would have to judge the right moment to head upstream.

We were all ready. My scouts were good men and they had given us an accurate estimate of distance. If Sir Geoffrey was early or late then he would have to deal with the consequences. I raised my spear. I knew that it would soon shatter but it was an easier weapon to use against men on foot whilst on horseback. I rode next to Alfred and Sir Edward. Fótr and William of Hartburn made up the other knights. Ridley and Henry Youngblood completed the front rank. My men at arms followed and then James of Corfe and the King's men. My archers would be used once the enemy fled. They were better against serried ranks. The Scots would be in a loose formation. Cedric and Will had told us exactly where the first Scottish camp lay. The thundering of our hooves alerted them. Ordinary warriors might flee but the lords had horses and they would not. They would be prepared. The woods through which we galloped did not suit horses and we were not in a completely solid line. That did not matter. I hoped to reach them first so that they would think I was the main threat. When Sir James and Sir Geoffrey suddenly piled in from the flanks then I hoped our victory would be complete.

When I heard the shouts from ahead and the neighs of horses then I knew that we were close to the camp. I pulled up my shield. The Scots had little mail but some of the deadliest weapons known to man. Their war hammers could smash a horse's skull to a pulp. I saw the brighter colours of surcoats. There were knights ahead. Men were forming a hurried shield wall. I pulled back my arm. I saw a Scot wearing just breeks. He had no helmet but he had a two-handed axe and he began to swing it in a figure of eight. I had no intention of losing my horse to such a weapon. My horse was well trained and the terrain meant we were not travelling as fast as we normally did. I headed directly for him and that presented him with a dilemma. He needed me to be on one side or the other. His swing meant he would strike my horse from the side. When I was twenty paces from him he adjusted his feet and moved to my left, away from my spear. I pulled Bella's head to the right and then to the left. He wore no helmet and I saw confusion. His axe head dropped a little lower. Spurring Bella I pulled back my arm and, leaning forward, rammed my spear over my horse's head and into his chest. His axe weakly struck my shield. He was a big man and I let his weight drag his body from my spear. I raised it just as a knight rode at me with his own spear.

He wore an open face helmet with a nose protector. His horse was fresher than Bella but not as well trained. As he spurred his mount towards me I saw that the knight was struggling to control the beast. I could have ridden Bella with just my knees. He rode directly for me and I saw him pull back his arm. We rode shield to shield. We would both have to use our spears over our horse's heads. I had done this before. As we closed I stood in my stirrups and drove my spear downwards. My action made him thrust upwards. There was less for him to hit and, in the event, he hit my shield. I twisted as I rammed my spear downwards. He deflected my spear but only as far as his thigh. Blood spurted and my spear was torn from my hand. He rolled over and off his horse. William would have been watching. He would secure the prisoner.

Drawing my sword, I looked for my next opponent. The Scots were fleeing. I spurred my horse. Bella was a good horse and she could jump. The dead and wounded lay behind me but the detritus of the camp lay before me. She jumped over piles of unused spears. I saw a youth, little older than the King. He looked around in a panic when he saw me. Turning he continued to run. I used the flat of my sword to smack into the back of his head. He fell in a heap. He would wake with a headache as his memory of his first battle. I reined in when I reached the edge of the woods.

I turned in my saddle, "David of Wales, the ones who flee are yours!"

My archers, keen to have useful employment, galloped beyond me into their natural terrain. My archers could loose from the back of a horse. The Scots would only be twenty or thirty paces from them. They would not have to draw fully back. My knights and men at arms had subdued the Scots. The shocked survivors had not been expecting such an attack. They had thought we squatted within our walls.

"James of Corfe, secure the camp. I leave you in command."

"Aye lord."

I saw the King and Sir Richard edge from the safety of the woods. William galloped over to inspect Bella. He handed me a fresh spear. As my men checked their own beasts and their girths the King reined in. "That was speedily done, Earl."

"It helped that they kept a poor watch. I do not think that they were ready to attack. There look to be places left for more camp fires. You had best instruct James of Corfe to keep a watch for reinforcements."

Alfred said, "I will tell him, Earl. I think that it may have been a knight they expected for they left space by the tent of the knight you slew." He turned to ride to James of Corfe.

"Your son is confident for one so young."

Sir Edward rode up, "Good training, my liege. Ridley the Giant made him practise daily and young Alfred learned to defeat him. When you can beat a man twice your size then all else is possible." There was genuine pride in his voice. I knew that he hoped his own sons would turn out as well as Alfred.

The conroi led by Sir Richard and Sir Geoffrey began to edge through the woods where they had captured many of those fleeing our attack. I saw that the camp was secured and when Alfred rode back I said, "A column of fours. We head to Kelso."

As we headed down the river road my son said, "You know that we will not reach Jedburgh until dark, if at all."

I nodded, "I know but we have to try. The alternative would be to halt at Kelso. The first camp was the immediate danger. The next two have monasteries and towns close by.

We threaten them and they will realise the danger of even contemplating a raid in the future."

"Your father is right, Alfred. I heard stories from my father of the Warlord. He did just this. The Scots feared him. He was the one who captured the Scottish King and gave twenty years of peace to the borders." Sir Edward was my link back to the time of the Warlord.

Ridley the Giant rode just behind Edward and he added, "Cedric Warbow told me that the people of Bamburgh now have double the numbers of villagers that they had twenty years since. The Warlord might be long dead but his shadow still lies upon this land."

I had much to live up to.

My archers rejoined me when we were five miles from Kelso. "We have ensured that any who survived the attack are fled back to their homes. The camp at Kelso is between the Abbey and the river. I saw the banners of four knights there. There is little cover for the last mile or so. The ground slopes down to the camp and the river from Ednam Hill. You will be charging across open fields where they graze their cattle."

"Cross the river, David, and have your men south of Kelso. When the Scots flee you can stop them."

"Aye lord, but there are people up and about on the roads. This will not be like the attack on the camp. They will spot you as they close. This time they will be ready."

"Thank you, David. Then it will be a battle from which the King will learn." He rode off and I turned in my saddle, "Henry, send two riders. Tell Sir Richard and Sir Geoffrey that we halt a mile from Kelso. We will need to change our plans."

"Aye lord."

Alfred said, "A charge?"

"Aye, we have the knights and our men at arms are well mounted. The Scots, save for their handful of knights will be afoot. It has been many years since they faced a charge of heavy horse. It will test their resolve. We will be charging downhill. I will let Sir Richard's men bear the brunt of this

125

charge for he and his horses can rest while we head for
Jedburgh."

We stopped in the lee of the hill called Ednam. It rose like
a green pimple. We knew that the town lay beyond. We had
been lucky and not been seen by any who used the road. I
wondered if David of Wales had shifted them. "Sir Richard
you and your knights will lead the charge into their camp. Sir
Geoffrey and I will support you. Ride hard and do not worry
about those who flee. David of Wales waits for them. Your
majesty, if you and the squires ride to the top of the hill you
will have the best view of the battle."

"This will be a battle?"

"They have knights and there is an Abbey and town
nearby. The ones in the camp had no one to see their valour.
These will want to show their courage. The squires will stay
with you."

With open ground before us we could form longer lines
and ride boot to boot. Sir Richard had knights in his front
rank and his men at arms behind. My conroi formed the third
and that of Sir Geoffrey would be the reserve. We followed
Sir Richard's men at arms. As we neared the top and began
to descend I saw the camp. The town and Abbey lay on a
piece of higher ground. If this had been a month later then
the ground where they camped would be a bog. We were just
cantering when I heard the horns from the camp. A drum
sounded and I saw the Scots mounting horses and grabbing
spears. The slope enabled us to gather speed without hurting
our horses too much. We still had some miles to go to reach
Kelso.

The handful of Scottish horsemen placed themselves on
the left flank of the line of spearmen. They were protecting
the town. The spearmen were largely without mail. Most had
the small round shield called a targe. They were well made
for they had layers of wood laid at right angles and were
covered in leather and studded with metal. Their swords
were short ones. They presented Sir Richard and his men
with a hedgehog of spears. This would be a test of nerve as
much as a test of military skill.

I glanced down my line. We had kept together and our spears were vertical. It made riding easier. I saw the spears of Sir Richard's men as they swayed to the horizontal. Now that we were on flatter ground I could see little of the Scots but I heard the clatter, the crack and the shouts as Sir Richard's men struck their line. A Scottish horn sounded and the Scottish knights charged into our right flank. I hoped that Sir Geoffrey had heeded my instructions. We supported Sir Richard and he protected us. As Bella leapt over the body of one of Sir Richard's men at arms I lowered my spear. Sir Richard had broken through the wall of spears. His own spears and lances lay shattered. Not all of the Scots had perished and one faced me with his targe and short sword. I punched over the small targe and into his left shoulder. Twisting as I withdrew it my spearhead came clear.

Behind me and to my right I heard the clash of knights as my daughter's future husband struck the Scottish knights. Above the cries and the sound of steel on steel I heard a Scottish voice, "We yield!" We had defeated them.

We had no time to waste. We had to get to Jedburgh. Sir Richard had wounded men but there were priests in the abbey who could heal. I waved my sword and the King and the squires galloped down from the hill. Sir Geoffrey joined me as we headed down the road. It was the middle of the afternoon and we had ten miles or more to cover. "That went well, my lord."

"Aye it did and you have justified my faith in you. That was well done."

He smiled, "I could not allow my future wife's father to be in danger."

We halted two miles south of Kelso. David of Wales awaited us there with the Scots they had ambushed. There were thirty. Half were dead and half were prisoners. "Have some of your men escort them back to Kelso."

Just then the King reined in, "That was a magnificent charge!" I saw the joy of battle in his eye. He had thought it easy.

"Your majesty, it was against men without mail. Had we not succeeded then we would never have held our heads up again. We have some miles to go. If you wish then you can stay here at Kelso."

"No, Earl, I have been a spectator. If my warriors can fight and ride then I can ride and watch."

As we rode down the road Alfred said, "The horses are spent. We cannot charge them again."

"You are right and besides that would alert the Scots. We will try something different." I waved David of Wales forward. "It will be at night when we attack. Take your men to the bridge over the Jed. Hold it and stop any fleeing. We will make a night attack on foot."

Sir Edward said, "And the horses?"

I turned, "King Henry and the squires can be horse holders. I am guessing that will be a new experience for you, majesty?"

He laughed, "All of this is new and do not worry. I am aware that I have much to learn and if part of that means holding horses then so be it." The son was nothing like his father and that was a good thing.

We crossed the Tweed and headed south. The Scots would know we were coming but they would expect us to come from north of the Tweed. By taking the southern route there would be more who would be sympathetic to England. David and his archers would clear a path for us. In plain cloaks and without surcoats they could be seen as outlaws or brigands. As the afternoon faded to dusk I became more hopeful of success.

It was dusk when we crossed the Jed by the Mill. Mordaf and his brother greeted us. "David of Wales asked us to keep the miller and his family safe." He grinned. "We only extracted two sacks of flour as payment!" My men were resourceful. "The Captain suggested you leave your mounts here, lord. It is but a mile to the Abbey and they are camped hard by there."

"Dismount." The horses were lathered and exhausted. We had ridden them too far. They would enjoy water and oats which had yet to be milled. We left our cloaks by our horses as well as our spears. We would not need them. I took off my helmet. A coif would suffice. The King dismounted.

128

"Your Majesty I will send someone back for you. Your men can fetch our horses."

"Good luck, my lord!"

"A warrior always needs that and the Good Lord to be watching over him."

Once we had forded the river I divided my men. "Sir Geoffrey take your conroi and sweep up from the river. Remain silent until the alarm is given and then shout as though you lead an army. We will attack from the Abbey side. God willing, we will meet in the middle!" He nodded and we parted. Alfred and Edward flanked me. Fótr and Sir William tucked in behind and they were flanked by Ridley and Henry. It was a formation with which we were familiar. I remembered, from previous visits, that the Abbey was on a higher piece of ground and the valley sides rose steeply. The tents and the camp would have to be closer together. This town was larger than Kelso and there would be more civilians. They were on the flatter ground south of the Jed. We moved silently. We were on grass which was grazed by sheep and cattle. They had been gathered ready for the cull. They moved obligingly out of way and their noise masked ours.

Ahead I could see the campfires. Men were moving before them and there appeared to be a great deal of movement. We had either been seen or a survivor had reached them. I drew my sword, after pulling up my coif over my arming cap and began to run. The others soon picked up the pace. We were running over grass and we were coming from the east and the dark. We were not seen. Sir Geoffrey and his men were. I heard a scream and then a shout of, "Cleveland!"

The diversion helped us as men ran towards the river. There was a tent of knights who had been tardy to rise when the alarm was given. Perhaps they had taken the time to don mail. We ploughed into them. We had no choice but to fight for they stepped into our path. I punched my shield into the face of the nearest knight as I raised my sword. At the same time, a knight swung his sword at my side. Alfred's shield flicked out and stopped it. The weight of the men behind us knocked three of the four knights to the ground. I held my sword at the throat of the man I had knocked over, "Yield or die!"

He had little choice and he shouted, "Yield! I yield!" The others all followed suit.

"Back in your tent and do not move." Knights always had the option of yielding. Ordinary warriors did not and consequently, they normally fought to the death or fled. One band, I took them to be shield brothers, decided on the former and ran at us. I was pleased I had not worn my helmet for these moved quickly. They lacked mail but made up for it with a ferocious attack. I saw as one deflected my sword with his targe that he had a dagger in his left hand. I had used the technique. The wickedly pointed tip came for my middle. I too had fast hands. The edge of my shield just managed to stop it hitting me but my move exposed my shoulder. He hit me hard. If I had not had metal disks on my shoulders then the mail might have been damaged. The Scotsman was grinning as though he enjoyed the battle. I decided to use my own guile. I feigned a lunge and when he brought his sword and shield together I spun on my right leg to bring my sword into his unprotected side. My sword scraped off his ribs but, even though he was mortally wounded, he still tried to kill me. I knocked him away with the edge of my shield. Edward and Alfred had killed their foes and Fótr had led four of my men at arms to attack another shield band.

When I saw men fleeing towards me then I knew that Sir Geoffrey had won. They saw us and turned to head for the bridge. As we disposed of the last of those who refused to surrender I heard the cries of the Scots as they ran into David of Wales and his archers. We had defeated these raiders and prevented a terrible ordeal for ordinary folk living south of the border.

"Fótr, there are some horses over there. Take one and fetch the King and our horses. He will want to be here for this victory."

"Aye lord."

Sir Edward, Alfred, collect the mail and weapons."

"Aye lord."

"Sir William organize the prisoners."

"Aye lord."

I sheathed my sword and laid down my shield. I slipped the coif from my head. Sir Geoffrey was still close by. "I thought, lord, that when the alarm was given then we were done for."

Shaking my head, I said, "These are brave fellows but our mail and organisation will always win in the end." He sheathed his sword. "You know that you can stay in the Palatinate with Rebekah. I know that Elton is a small manor and you might have hoped for more."

"It is rich, lord for it is close to Rebekah's home and she will be happier being close to her mother and sister. Besides I have spoken with Sir Fótr and he seems to think that we can grow wheat."

"I have heard that it can be done. I am used to barley and oat bread!"

Just then my knights and men at arms began to herd the captives together and to pile up the weapons and mail. Behind me, an imperious voice said, "Was this well done, Earl? You have broken the peace!"

I turned and saw a dumpy little man who looked incredibly well fed. It was the Prior. He had two churchmen with him and a grey beard who looked to be the chief burgher. "I have broken the peace? Explain to me, Prior, why there are three armed camps close to the border? My men crept close to the camps and heard them plotting. This would have been a raid on English land. I stopped it! Do not speak to me of peace!"

"No matter what the intentions it was you who crossed the river and drew first blood."

"You argue like a lawyer and I have little time for them either." I heard hooves on the grass. I knew it would be Fótr.

The Prior was determined to have the last word, "I shall make representations! The King shall hear of this and the King's Council. If the boy will not act then I am sure that the Bishop of Winchester will!"

King Henry threw back his hood, "I am King Henry, tell me, Prior. Tell the boy!" The Prior was stunned into silence.

"The Earl acted with my full permission. He has ensured that these animals will not kidnap our women nor steal our cattle. And I am here to tell you that if we even suspect that there is a raid in the offing then we will act. I am a boy but, Prior, you should fear the man I will become!"

I smiled for I saw the King growing.

Chapter 10
The lull before the storm

We spent a week at Norham. We ransomed the knights and their men. The ordinary warriors were surprised. They had expected a warrior's death. Our leniency surprised them. We took reparations from the Scots and two hostages. Sir Richard would guard them at Norham. We set the time they would be held as a year. That done we headed back to Stockton. We had all made coin from the action. That had not been our intention but with winter coming it was useful. The Palatinate knights and those from Bamburgh returned to their respective castles. Sir Geoffrey penned a letter for Rebekah.

The end of autumn and the start of winter hit us as we crossed the Tyne. It was raining and windy but the rain had the edge of sleet to it and that would presage winter. I smiled as I saw the King try to envelop himself in his cloak. This was the north and it was a harsh and unforgiving environment. It was, as Sir Edward might have said, a little fresh. Alfred nudged his horse next to mine as Sir Edward and Sir Fótr headed towards their manors. "I know that I upset you once and I would not do so again. When do you think we should wed?"

I smiled, "Women like summer weddings. They like flowers and the sunlight. You, I think, wish to make her your bride as soon as you can. I do not mind. I will be heading back to London soon with the King but you do not need me to be at the wedding."

He shook his head, "You are the reason we found each other. Had you not intervened then she would still be a prisoner of an evil man. I will speak with Matilda but is a Christmas wedding a bad thing?"

"There is no such thing as a bad wedding. Unless, of course, you are a king and are forced to marry. Speak with Matilda and then your mother. I do not think that the King will be in any hurry to leave for the south." I turned in my saddle. The King, his solitary knight and his captain had become close on the journey south. I watched their animated talk. He was free from the restrictions of the Council and he was enjoying discovering just who he was. I hoped for a long sojourn in my home. I missed my wife and my daughters. I was about to lose one of them.

One good thing about arriving from the north was that we had to ride through Stockton. It was always a pleasure. Even without the King, it would have been a warm welcome. With him, it felt as hot as the Holy Land. They applauded and they cheered. They called my name, Alfred's and the King's. The whores from the alehouses called out lewd comments to the men at arms and archers who passed by. With Scottish coins in their purses, they would enjoy their homecoming. My own homecoming was slightly warmer than my last one. Riders had returned to warn them of our arrival for we had wounded. We were expected. As we entered the inner bailey grooms rushed to take our horses. Already a fog was forming on the Tees and a fire accompanied by mulled wine beckoned.

Margaret kissed me and whispered, "It is good that you are home and that you had no losses."

"I was lucky."

"That is because you are a good man and God smiles on you." She stopped, "And the wedding?"

"Alfred will speak with you but I think he leans to one sooner rather than later."

"And I agree. Poor Matilda was treated so badly in Skipton that it will take skill to make her happy again. And the King?"

"I have yet to speak to him." I stopped. "Have there been missives from the south?"

She nodded. "Three from London and one from Pembroke."

"The ones from London can wait. They are from the Council. I will read the one from Pembroke." I shook my head, "I must be turning into a witch for I know what it will say."

"The Earl Marshal?"

"Aye." I tore the seal.

Pembroke
Earl Cleveland,

I have the sad duty to report that my father, William Marshal, Earl Marshal of England and Earl of Pembroke died last night.

I would thank you for the service you did him and the responsibility you took from his shoulders. He was able to enjoy a month with his family. Such a time was rare. He served England and was abused for it. You and the King were in his thoughts to the end. I hope that King Henry realises the sacrifices my father made for his country. When time allows I would speak with you.

I fear that the Welsh will take advantage of my father's death. We have lost two border castles already. The Welsh gather like carrion on our borders. I pray to God for a strong King.

William Marshal,
Earl of Pembroke

It was a sad letter and a disturbing one. The new Earl appeared to blame the Royal family for their father's death. The Earl Marshal's words came back to me. He and his son had fallen out. This did not bode well. When I reached the Great Hall, I was almost assaulted by Isabelle and Rebekah. They hugged me and grabbed my arm. Rebekah whispered in my ear, "My future husband is alive?"

135

I took, from my belt, the letter Geoffrey had given to me. "Here, I know the welcome was for Geoffrey and not me. Go and read."

She looked hurt, "Geoffrey will be my husband and will hold a large part of my heart but you are my father. You have all of my heart for without you I am nothing," She kissed me and fled.

Isabelle said, "You have yet to find me a husband and so I shall cling to your arm until you do!"

I laughed, "You are not yet sixteen!"

"Yet Isabelle, King Henry's mother, was wed at twelve! That is one of the perils of educating your daughters. They know more than they should." She leaned up and kissed me on the cheek. "I am teasing, father. Rebekah and Alfred can have a wedding this year. Then when I have my husband chosen it will be the biggest wedding of the year!" Isabelle was the cleverest of my children. I pitied her husband. She was more like Aunt Ruth than any.

I hurried to my room for I felt sweaty and dirty. I would have, if the King allowed, Christmas at home. Who knew when I would have another. I would make the most of it. My wife followed me and helped me to undress. A servant had already brought in hot water and soap. My wife was proud of the fact that we could afford such luxuries. As she dried me she said, "The Earl's death makes you the most powerful noble in the land."

"There are others who have great power."

"Yet you command the respect of the great and the good. It is no secret that the Earl Marshal thought you his successor. If you chose you could rule this land through King Henry."

I held her at arm's length. "Do you really believe that?" She said nothing. "If you do then you do not know me. I seek to serve England and its king. If someone else could or would do it then I would be happy. I would hunt and watch my grandchildren grow!"

She smiled and kissed me, "I know. I was just testing you. You have spent so much time away that I know not who you are sometimes. It is good to know you are still the same as the young knight who rescued me."

I disliked the games women played!

I was the first down to the Great Hall and my Aunt joined me. She smiled, "When I was younger I would spend hours preparing a face to meet and greet other faces. Now I just smile. This is my face. You can like it or not. I care not a jot. You had a good campaign?"

My aunt was not like other women. The early death of her husband and the lack of children had imbued her with an interest in all things military. I did not condescend and I told her exactly what we had done.

"And the King listened?" I nodded. "He is not like his father then!"

"He listened and he is young. He will grow. He showed signs of that rarity amongst kings; common sense!"

"The servants said William Marshal is dead."

"Aye."

"He was a great man but your great grandfather was greater, as are you! England will come to thank you for what you do for Henry." My aunt believed that her family was the best in the land. When she passed over to the other side we would never see her like again. "So we have two weddings. The girls would like them separate I am sure but economics and needs of the manor would say that they should happen at the same time."

"That is not for me to decide! I am just the father!"

She laughed, "Fear not you have good children! I have brought them up well! Enjoy this night and enjoy the weddings. You have earned some pleasure! I will watch the King for signs of weakness!"

The homecoming feast was joyous. Even though Sir Geoffrey was still in Durham, Rebekah knew he was alive and she was able to ask her brother about the campaign. I think the King revelled in the good humour which pervaded my hall. He was used to a dining experience that was dependent upon where you sat and who you knew. Here there was no pecking order. Sir Richard had grown into his role and the two were quite close. The fact that my captains,

137

steward and priest attended the feast seemed to bemuse the King. For myself I just enjoyed the sight of all of my family gathered together. There were no harsh words and all got on with each other. Remembering the Princes' revolt, I knew that it could so easily have gone in a different direction.

Tam the Hawker had been hunting and the deer we ate had been hung perfectly. The wine, from my manor in Anjou, was from a good harvest. The bread was a favourite of mine. It was a mixture of barley and oats. The soup was a fish soup that would have put those of Paris to shame. I found myself drinking too much and eating more than I should. I did not care. I was aware that I spoke less than any other. That was because I enjoyed hearing their words. The King relaxed and became slightly tipsy. I smiled as I saw Sir Richard trying to manage him. He failed. When the King fell backwards from his chair a situation that could have been disastrous was deemed hilarious and all laughed until they cried, including the King. Sir Richard caught my eye and shrugged. King Henry had, for the first time in his life, a family. It was mine but I did not mind sharing.

Despite the drinking, I was up early and after I ate a little bread and cheese to settle my stomach, I strode through Stockton's streets. I wished to enjoy the company of my people. The burghers had all been up since dawn. I was greeted warmly. They used my title but did not do in a way that made me uncomfortable. Those who had provided for us asked if that which they had given was suitable. Those whose husbands, fathers, sons and brothers served with me kissed my hand and thanked me for their safe return. A walk around my streets made my feet find the bedrock that was England.

Harry the Fletcher had his workshop at the northeast end of my town. It was close to the river gate which lay there. He and his sons were busy fitting fletches to the arrows when I reached the gate. "Morning, my lord."

"Morning Harry, boys. How goes the world?"

"We are happy that you continue to fight the enemies of England. David of Wales came last night to order more arrows."

138

"He did not have to use as many as usual."

Harry nodded, "They are not the knight killers he asked for. It was the barbed ones." I nodded for I was already thinking of the next time they would draw a bow in anger. "David said that the King stays in Stockton."

"He will be our guest."

"It is an honour for our town and we hear there will be weddings too."

I smiled. The news was probably in Stockton's streets while the words still echoed in my hall. "It will be a rarity. There will be two winter weddings."

"So long as they are happy, lord, then it matters not. I married Agnata when I was but fifteen. It was right and my three sons and two daughters are proof of that. I wish Sir Alfred and Lady Rebekah well. They always spoke courteously to us."

As I headed back to the castle I thought on his words. Margaret and I had been determined that our children should be brought up to be polite to all. That policy could now be seen to have worked. While in many manors the lord and his family were regarded as a necessary evil here in Stockton the people felt part of the manor. When my children ran Seamer and Elton they would, I hoped, carry on that legacy. The weddings would also bring prosperity to the town. I knew from Aunt Ruth that in the time of the Warlord if ladies wished fine clothes they had to travel to York to buy them. Since we had put the cut in the river, we had more trade and now we had seamstresses who made fine clothes for our merchants were able to buy good cloth. Ladies now sent to Stockton to have their clothes made. Egbert would have a new tunic made for me for the wedding. Margaret, our daughters and my Aunt would summon Mary Finestitch to the hall and I would pay in gold for their finery. That would trickle back to Stockton and all would benefit. We had plenty of coin. The ride to Scotland had brought gold and silver as well as good horses. The Scots would rue their rash decision to raid for cattle. They would have to do what they always did when a raid on England failed, they would fight amongst themselves.

As I entered my castle then I knew that I could no longer put off reading the letters from the council. I had wanted to read the one from William Marshal. I did not want to read these. I sat in my office. There had been a chill in the air and so Egbert had heated and honeyed my ale. I sipped some before I slit open the first letter. It was just a simple one to tell me that the Carta Foresta, Charter of the Forest, had been drafted and that it just required the King's seal. There was a request for him to return and sign it. I was pleased that the charter had been drafted for that would make the majority of the land happy. There would be some lords who resented sharing their forests with the poorer folk but as the King owned more forests than any few ordinary people would suffer. The Bishop of Winchester wondered when we would return. The second letter was a little more urgent in tone. This time it was from Hubert de Burgh. The date was a week later than that from des Roches. He asked when would the King be returned to his council. The third was positively rude. It stated that the Charter of the Forest had been issued with the King's seal applied by Hubert and the letter demanded that the King be returned to London where he could rule. I smiled. What the Council meant was that they would have more legitimacy to their rule if the King was there.

I summoned my clerk. Leofric had been born with a hunch. His father had been John Wayfarer. As Leofric's mother had died in childbirth my wife and Aunt Ruth had brought up the boy. His infirmity meant he could not be a warrior as his father had been. It had been my aunt who had taught him his letters and, more importantly, his writing. He had a beautiful hand. His deformity did not impede his skill and he actually benefitted from sitting and writing. He was happy and had married Ada, one of Aunt Ruth's maids. I hoped that John Wayfarer was in heaven and happy that we had cared for his boy.

"Yes, my lord?" He had a wax tablet. He would use that to make notes and then draft the letters. If he made a mistake he was quite happy to rewrite them but I rarely found an error that needed a new letter.

"We have letters to send."

He nodded. "Parchment or vellum lord?"

Vellum was calfskin and was an expensive item. Parchment was a little cruder and could come from any animal. "Vellum for the letter to the King's Council and William Marshal. Parchment for the others."

"Aye lord."

I did not dictate. My aunt had taught Leofric the right phrases to use. I knew that he would happily ask my aunt for verification if he was unsure. I told him what to write to the Council. I explained what the King had done and that he would be spending Christmas in the north. I promised that we would return south when the weather improved. The second letter was for William Marshal. I sent my condolences for his loss and promised that I would help him if I could. After his father's words at Windsor, I was more guarded than I might have been. The other letters would be the same. They were invitations for my knights to the weddings. We had set the date; the day after Christmas, St Stephen's day. The Sheriff of York would be the one who would have the furthest to travel. If the roads were bad then I knew he might struggle to reach us. There were lords from Durham I would invite. I invited the Bishop of Durham but I knew that it would be unlikely that he would travel. Richard Marsh was a dedicated Prince Bishop. He kept the Palatinate safe and the frivolity of a pair of weddings would be a distraction.

I knew that I was giving Leofric a great deal of work. "The important letter is the one to the Council. If that could be ready by the morrow then the others can wait until the end of the week."

"I will have them all done by the end of tomorrow, lord. The invitations will not take long."

After he had gone I left my office and went to the warrior hall. I would need two riders to take the letters. The Sheriff would be able to send the one to the Council by sea. It was a safer way than by road. Henry Youngblood knew which two to send. He was a fair man and a visit to York was something of a perk. He did not play favourites. "I will send

James and John. It is some time since they enjoyed the ale in The Saddle Inn."

"Good."

"There is one more thing lord. Ralph of Appleby has four men who wish to be men at arms. They arrived while we were in Scotland. They had served Sir Henry of Gargrave. It seems they were the last of the old knight's retainers. They were forced to leave the land when Lord Hugh of Craven began his reign of terror." He hesitated. "They had been living as outlaws in the Forest of Bowland. They brought little with them."

"Does the Lady Matilda know them?"

"Aye lord. Ralph told me that she wept when she saw their pitiable condition. Ralph is a kind man and he kept them in the warrior hall while we campaigned." I looked at him. He knew the question in my eyes. Had their experience made them resentful? Were they still fit enough to be men at arms? "They are good men lord. One was the sergeant at arms. John of Bolton had served old Sir Henry all of his life. His wife died when Lord Hugh came. He has nothing save Lady Matilda. I think they came here to look after her as much as anything."

I nodded, "And when my son becomes Lord of Seamer then he will need men at arms. I will go with you and see them."

We went to the warrior hall. The rest of my men were busy for the campaign in Scotland had necessitated repairs to war gear and the coin they had accrued needed to be spent. They were the only four in the hall. They rose when I entered. "I am the Earl of Cleveland. Henry tells me that you wish to serve me. I would hear it from your lips."

I knew that the one who spoke was John of Bolton for he had grey hairs in his beard, "Aye lord we would serve you and your son for we hear that he is to marry Lady Matilda." I nodded. "We swore an oath to Sir Henry. We did not break the oath but thanks to the treachery of another we were unable to fulfil it. We would like the opportunity to do so."

"Then we will fit you out as my men at arms. Henry will find you the surcoats and war gear for I believe you lost yours." They nodded. "I will speak with my son but I am certain that he would wish his future wife's protectors with him at Seamer."

Before I could leave John of Bolton said, "There is one thing you ought to know, lord, there were men who served Sir Hugh who escaped. There were twelve of them. They made a camp in the forest close to us. A month back a young knight and his squire came and the whole band headed south. We thought you should know for we heard them talking and they wish you ill."

"The knight, did you see a device?"

"No, lord, just his spurs. He was young and he spoke little."

As I headed back to the hall my head was buzzing. It felt like I had a wasp's nest in my head. I had so much information in my brain and it was as though there was a battle going on. Fighting a campaign was child's play compared with managing a manor! Alfred, William and the King were laughing when I entered the Great Hall. The three of them seemed to get on well. They looked up as I entered. Alfred said, "The King was just telling us of his council. They sound like pompous men!"

"Aye but until the King here attains his majority then they wield the power in England. The death of William Marshal handed that to them." The humour left the King's face. "They have sent letters demanding that you return to London, your majesty."

I saw him chew his lip and then look at Alfred, "I am King and I will attend my friend's wedding. Then we shall return to London!"

"Well done my lord!" Alfred clapped the King around the shoulders.

"Perhaps you should send a letter to your Council eh, King Henry? I am sending riders with my letters on the morrow. My clerk, Leofric, will write them for you if you wish." He brightened and nodded. "William take the King to Leofric."

"Aye father. Come my lord. Leofric is like a hermit. He inhabits the northeast tower. He says he likes the sunrise!"

143

When he had gone I spoke to Alfred about the men at arms. "Of course. I will be needing men at arms and archers." He looked at me hopefully.

I smiled, "The manor alone is not enough? Now you want my men too!" I said it playfully.

"Not your best men, of course."

"Make a list of the ones you would like but Seamer is not as rich as Stockton."

"I have a chest of coin. Following my father's banner has brought me riches. I will make Seamer richer."

I admired his confidence but knew that his manor was not on the river and he would not have the trade he needed. I would not see him go short. If Stockton prospered then so would my son for he and William were my legacy for the future.

While the women prepared for the wedding which would be in just over a month's time I rode with the King and Alfred to survey the valley and for the King to meet the lords who lived there. Not all were warriors. When I had been exiled men had been given manors and farms by the King. Not all had been to war but they were, at least, loyal now to me. I knew that when I took my warriors knights away there were lords who could call up the fyrd and protect the land from unforeseen danger. I smiled when King Henry met such lords. He thought that they should all wield a sword and fight. I was impressed with Alfred. He spoke to the King with ease and it was the same manner he used with those who worked the land. His impending marriage had changed him. He was no longer the headstrong young knight who had happily clambered through a cave. He thought of the future and a life beyond Stockton.

As December approached the weather began to bite. Tam the Hawker came to me, "Lord it will be a hard winter. We should hunt the animals and cull the weaker ones. It will help the rest to survive."

"Do we have food to put out for them?"

"Not as much as we normally do. It is the deer who will suffer. The wild boars survive come what may."

"You think it will be a wolf winter?"

"Aye, lord! They will come down from the high divide."

"Then we will hunt. Where do you think best?"

"The woods north of Hartburn. The farmers have cleared Hartburn woods for the deer and the pigs were eating their crops. The herds all headed to Elton."

I nodded, "And until Sir Geoffrey is there will be no hunting. I will tell my lords and we will ride seven days from now."

"It would not do to delay, lord." He knew his animals and he knew my lands.

The King and William were excited. I was worried. Tam had explained that there were a number of older animals that needed culling and two of them were old stags. One had a peculiarly shaped black horn. The men called it the black stag. Tam had told me that he had been trying to kill it for some years. It hurt stronger stags and thereby weakened the herds. This was our chance but a rogue stag was not to be contemplated lightly. I saw Alan the horse master. We needed horses that could hunt. These were smaller and more nimble beasts. They would be intelligent. That was fine for an experienced horseman like myself or Alfred but the King and William had only hunted before in highly controlled conditions.

I took Sir Richard and my son, Alfred, to one side the day before we hunted. "Sir William and I are experienced hunters. Tam and Alan will be with us and they are good with a spear. I intend to take David of Wales and Cedric Warbow. You two must ensure that William and the King come to no harm." I made sure that I looked in their eyes. "We are culling animals. There is no glory in this."

Alfred smiled, "We will do as you say, father, but the King and William need to face danger here with a simple animal and then they can face danger on the battlefield."

My son had no children of his own. When he did then his attitude would change.

The women barely noticed our preparations. All was about the clothes and the flowers. Despite the fact that it would be winter they were determined to have flowers. Plants were dug up and placed in pots before being brought

145

into the castle. Evergreens would be used to give colour to
the chapel. I did not understand why they fussed so. The
important part would be the vows. Sir Geoffrey was vacating
his Durham manor and bringing down his people to Elton a
week before the wedding. He would not give up the manor.
Another would farm it and give half of the profits to Sir
Geoffrey. He would still owe service to the Bishop and to
me.

We took bows as well as spears. The King and Sir Richard
just had spears. They had not been taught to use a bow. I
think both thought the weapon beneath them. Captain Dick's
legacy meant that we all recognised the virtue of the bow. Of
course, none of us would be able to send an arrow as far as
those who used one every day and had been trained from an
early age to use one but we could still use them for hunting.

We rode first to Hartburn and then headed west towards
Elton. The manor house at Elton had long fallen into
disrepair. Tares and weeds sprouted in what had been the
herb garden. My daughter and her husband would have much
work to do but Rebekah knew the problems and my wife had
told me that our daughter was looking forward to making the
house what she wanted. The woods were at Coatham
although there was a line of trees from Hartburn which
allowed the deer to wander between them.

Tam took us to a path that would bring their smell to us
although he knew where they would gather. There was a
beck that meandered through the wood and there were still
green leaves and berries there. The folk of Hartburn had
stripped Hartburn's bushes already. Our people did not need
the Charter of the Forests to forage. We had servants and
spare horses. We left them in an open area close to the game
trail. David of Wales and Cedric followed Alfred and me.
The King, William and Sir Richard followed behind the rest
of us. We headed down the trail until Tam dropped to his
knees and began to examine the ground. He held some dung
to his nose and sniffed it. He unslung his bow. Alfred and I
did the same. Our squires held our spears. The arrows we
used were barbed. If we were lucky then the animals would
be dropped quickly but it was more likely that it might take a

146

couple of arrows, especially for the wiry black horned stag. I nocked an arrow and held the bow and arrow in two hands. I concentrated on putting my feet where Tam had placed his for we had left the path and were now heading down a slope. It was leaf-covered and slippery.

The herd had left a clear trail and even I could see it. Tam's skill was in knowing exactly where they would be found. We seemed to travel a long way until Tam held up his hand and we repeated the signal down the line. He pointed and I saw, in the distance the herd. I say herd but there looked to be two: a larger one and a smaller one. The ground had flattened out and the two herds were munching the bushes over a three hundred paces stretch. Tam made a circling signal. As Alfred and I stepped closer to him I waved for the rest to come forward. This would be a tricky time. William and the King would be eager to see the animals and one hurried and hasty move could prove disastrous. Fortunately, they managed to reach us without incident.

When Tam was satisfied he set off down the slope. We would not be hunting the young or the mighty stag with the huge antlers. The healthy females would be left alone too. The old and those with an injury were our prey. Tam headed towards the smaller herd. I recognised the black antlered stag. With him dead, the healthy females would join the other herd. I could smell the deer now. Every so often one of the males would lift its head and sniff. They would not smell us. The breeze was in the wrong direction. Our movements down the slope were painfully slow. There were trees and their trunks between us and the animals. Tam was trying to get us as close as we could to them. As we descended I saw that one of the females favoured a hind leg. She would need to be culled. There was an older one too which moved more slowly than the rest and there was another who was thinner than any of the others. They would be the ones we would hunt. Once they and the black antlered stag were dead we would follow the herd and pick off the slower ones. It would make the rest of the herd stronger. If Tam was right and this was a wolf winter then they would need to be as strong as possible.

We were fifty paces from them when Tam stopped. He turned to look at me and nod. I pulled back my arrow. We had seven arrows ready to fly into our targets. The three we would choose and the black antlered deer were close enough. Even as we pulled back ready to release fate intervened. As the arrows flew the stag moved behind a doe. When our arrows slammed into the three targets the two arrows aimed at the stag missed. The herd fled. They raced upstream. The other herd were also spooked. They could not smell us and they followed the other herd. This was an unfortunate turn of events. Two of the deer we had hit ran with the others. They would fall but not straight away. It became a disaster when the black antlered deer ran directly at us. Poor Tam tried the almost impossible he sent an arrow at the stag's head. It was moving so quickly and it was hurried. The arrow cracked off the antler and Tam hurled himself from the path of the deadly beast. Alfred and I each sent an arrow towards it and both hit it but neither was mortal. The animal came for me. I was aware that the King and William were behind me. I threw my bow to the ground and began to draw my sword. I was too close to the stag and its bloodied shoulder threw me to the ground before my sword was clear.

I lay on the ground and saw the stag turn to run at the King. He was transfixed. David of Wales and Cedric Warbow sent arrows into the animal but it still came on. William ran to his side and braced a spear on the ground. Sir Richard did the same. It was inevitable that the stag would hit them. Then Alfred ran from the side and swinging his sword two handed hacked through the hind leg of the stag. It was a maddened beast that flailed its strange antlers from side to side but a deer cannot run on three legs. David of Wales and Cedric Warbow sent two more arrows into the animal and it began to fall. William and Sir Richard plunged their spears into the neck of the stag and it fell at the King's feet. The King's spear was still in his shaking hands.

Tam raised me to my feet. "I am sorry, lord."

"It was an accident and could not be helped. We are lucky that my son had such quick reactions. Thank you, Alfred!"

He was cleaning his sword and he waved a hand, "I could not allow my little brother and the King of England to die. We did not cull as many as we should have."

David of Wales was already gutting the animals. From his voice, I knew that he felt guilty about not bringing down the stag. "With your permission, lord, I will bring my archers out with Tam. We will cull the herds for you. This is better than practice at the butts."

Sir William of Hartburn nodded, "He is right, lord. I was sure that the King would die!"

I looked at the King and a shaken Sir Richard, "Are you alright, your majesty?"

"I thought I would die. I could not move my feet."

I pointed at my son, William. He had his sword drawn. "My son knew that he had to defend himself. If you are in danger then draw your weapon. William, why did you not run?"

"The King had to be defended. Did you run at Arsuf, father, or did you not guard your father's body?"

"Sir Alfred you have saved the life of England's King. I swear that if you ever have need of my help you shall have it!" The King grasped Alfred's right hand in his two.

Alfred shrugged, "My liege it was an honour to save you and I have a tale to tell men which might rival that of Arsuf! The knight and the black antlered stag!" My son was modest. Many would have sought advantage from the King but not my son. I was even more proud of him.

The rest of the King's stay was peaceful although he spent every day with William, Sir Richard and Sir Alfred. They practised. He needed to become a swordsman. The King knew his deficiencies. This was the winter when men hunkered down and contemplated spring but the King had not yet reached his spring and knew that the encounter with the stag had been a warning that he was not yet ready to face men who would try to kill him. The practice allowed me to complete the duties as lord of the manor which I had neglected. I would have to return to London with the King and the valley would be without a lord of the manor. The days seemed to fly by for we had two weddings. When Sir Geoffrey arrived, we went with every man at arms and archer to clear the land at Elton. It was winter but the snow and ice had yet to make the ground unworkable. In the week before the wedding we did the hard part. We dug out the foundations and embedded the mighty beams which would hold up the walls of the hall. The mortar mix would take a week to set properly. After the wedding Sir Geoffrey would be able to build the rest of the hall no matter what the weather. All that we had done was to make the outline of the four walls. What went on within would be my daughter's choice.

My archers were successful and we had plenty of meat for the feast. They had even managed to hunt a young boar. I preferred the taste. For the first time I could remember the Christmas celebration was almost an afterthought for the weddings the next day were the time when we would really feast. My wife shed a tear at the wedding. Nanna and the two girls, Anya and Brigid, wept tears of joy. I was just happy for the young people. They had their lives and their futures ahead of them. I envied them that.

Both couples would live in my hall for a month although the two knights had their men working on their manors during that time. The King was growing restless by the time it was the end of January and we were preparing to leave for London when a rider rode in from York. He handed me two letters and gave one to the King.

"My lord the Welsh have attacked Pembroke. William Marshal is besieged and sends to you for help."

I tore open the letters as did the King. I was ordered, by the Council, to take the King to London and then to march to the aid of the Earl of Pembroke. The King held his letter. "They wish me to go to London while you fight the Welsh."

"We will leave on the morrow!"

"No, Earl for it will take days to summon your knights and it is your knights and men at arms we will need."

"We, my liege?"

"Pembroke is part of my realm. The Earl Marshal made it his home. I will send a letter to the Council and I will tell them that I accompany my Earl General to Wales. I will not fight but I will watch and I know that I will learn!"

And so we gathered men and wagons, tents and supplies for the ride to Wales. The King would be fighting his first real war.

Chapter 11
The Welsh Plot

I would not leave my land denuded of warriors. I would take Sir Edward and Sir Peter. I asked the Bishop and the Sheriff of York to watch over my land. I had, in addition, Sir Fótr, Sir Alfred, Sir William and Sir Geoffrey. I had the best men at arms and archers in the land. I sent letters to London and York and then we set off for Chester. The King, although young, had shown that he had a quick mind. We could save almost three weeks by riding south and west. More importantly, we could pick up good warriors along the way. The Earl of Chester and the men of Chester knew how to fight the Welsh. Gilbert de Clare was Earl of Glamorgan and he too was a powerful lord. This war would not be won by the fyrd or even a muster of border lords. We would have to use a small army made up of the best of warriors. These would be men who knew how to fight the Welsh. Chester and Glamorgan knew how to do that. William Marshal could defend and he would do until we arrived. The King was correct. Speed was of the essence.

It was winter and I took more servants and spare horses than I would normally have done. The incident with the stag had shown me how fragile was the King's life. He needed more guards but we just had the ones led by James of Corfe. As we headed for Carlisle I spoke with Sir Richard and James. "There will be men who excel on the battlefield. I cannot watch everywhere. Find those you think could serve the King. He has but one knight and a handful of men. It is not enough."

James asked, "Lord, should the council not choose them?"

"Who would you trust to guard the King? A Council appointed by lords and bishops or men you have seen fighting on a battlefield?" He nodded. "All that I ask is that you consult with me or Henry Youngblood or Ridley the Giant."

"Why lord?"

"For we have been doing this for twenty years. I have been betrayed before now and all of my men know the signs. I look a man in the eye when I speak with him."

One thing which worried me, on the way south, was the lack of information from Chester. The Earl had lands which were close to the Welsh. He should have known what was going on. Was this some game being played by the King of Gwynedd?

When we reached Chester, the King had learned how to campaign. We had slept out in tents once or twice on the way south and the wind and the rain had swept in from the west. He had learned how to use a latrine and sleep on the hard ground. He understood the benefits of extra blankets and a cloak wrapped around it all. These were little things which we took for granted but for the King they were new. They helped to make him a better man. Worse days would come.

Ranulf de Blondeville, the Earl of Chester, had been the stepfather of Prince Arthur. That alone meant he held me in high esteem even though I was younger than he. He had another side to him, however, he had wished to be Regent of England. Had the first regent been any other than William Marshal then he might have opposed it but the Earl had been the greatest knight since my great grandfather. I knew that he still harboured ambitions. However, he made us welcome and we sat before a roaring fire in his castle of Chester.

"I thank you again, Earl, for your intervention in Skipton. I confess that I would never have appointed that knight to the manor."

"It is done now, lord."

"Aye, we have a more urgent threat in the south." He smiled at King Henry. "Your first campaign, your majesty.

The Welsh are treacherous but I am sure that we can end this conflict peacefully." He smiled, "My nephew John has married the daughter of Llewellyn. We now have an alliance and I am certain that we can persuade him to put pressure on his allies."

The King asked, "Then why, Earl, have you not done so before? You might have saved English lives and I could have been saved a long ride across England."

"I am sorry, my liege, but it was one of your council of Regents, Hubert de Burgh who acted and sent you an unnecessary missive. I would have dealt with it myself." I now remembered that there was ill-feeling between the two men. That explained much. "Besides I have much on my mind. I swore an oath when Prince Arthur was murdered that I would go on Crusade. I leave in a month. That is time enough to make a peace. I have sent emissaries to King Llewellyn. He will meet us at Powys."

Henry looked at me for he was uncertain of the geography and he trusted me, "It is in the Kingdom of Powys closer to the centre of Wales."

The King nodded, "So you are saying, Earl, that we do not need to fight the Welsh?"

"I pray not. The King ordered his men to return some of the land they took in the first campaign. He will see sense. However, we take the fyrd with us. Their numbers will attest to our determination."

The King nodded but I was not convinced. The fyrd were more often than not a liability rather than an asset. At the feast thrown in Henry's honour, I spoke with Gonville de Blondeville. He liked me and I trusted his judgement. "What is happening here in the borders?"

"Earl, this has been going on since before you took Skipton. It has only come to light now because William Marshal appealed to the Council."

"You are saying the Earl knew of this?"

"I am saying that he has had much on his mind. He has no son and he sees the crusades as a way to atone for whatever ill he has done and father a child. When he can see Calvary then he believes that he will be able to have a son of his

154

own." He nodded to Alfred, "You have two sons. Can you imagine life without them?"

I confess that I could not. They were my future. I was proud of both of them as I was of my daughters but sons could inherit castles and titles. Daughters could not. When the Earl died who would be Earl of Chester? I began to see the motives of the Earl. He was not disloyal but he did not have the interests of the King at heart. Had he been appointed Regent then he may have been a better advocate for England. I would need to speak with King Henry privately. This was a world he did not know. We tarried too long in Chester. The fyrd and the knights took almost two weeks to muster. Time was passing. Eventually, all was ready and we left.

The Earl of Chester, whether deliberately or accidentally, prevented me from being alone with the King. He rode with him as we headed for Powys. The army we took appeared large but that was an illusion for the Earl and his knights would be leaving for Southampton once we had met the Welsh King. He had ships waiting to take him to Crusade. The fyrd who trudged behind us would return to their farms and King Henry would be left with my handful of knights. I did not like the situation. Had I made a mistake? Should we have gone to London first?

Sir Edward and my son, Alfred, rode next to me as we headed through the drizzle filled day. The wet seemed to permeate all the layers of clothes which we wore. Our hoods covered our heads and our horses plodded at the pace of the poor farmers behind us. "Look, my lord, it matters not that most of the knights will be leaving us. If we have to fight the Welsh then you know that knights are not the answer." Edward was low born. The son of a hawker he had been a man at arms with me in Sweden. He had never fought in a tourney. He knew not the rules of war and of chivalry. He just knew how to fight. "David of Wales and our archers are more than a match for the Welsh archers. If they hide in their rocky crags then David of Wales and his men will winkle them out."

155

"Edward is right, father. My fears are somewhat different. I have left my bride of fewer than three months at home and we come to fight for land which is not even England."

I nodded. I understood my son's position. What he did not understand was the wider world. "William Marshal is not just Earl of Pembroke. He rules Ireland for the King. What if the Irish rebel while the Earl is in Wales? There may be plots here that we do not understand. The King is young. Perhaps we can have the Marcher Lords join to force Llewellyn to be less belligerent."

Even as the words came out of my mouth I knew that it was unlikely. The lands of Pembroke, Gower and Glamorgan were English islands surrounded by resentful Welsh. Many Marcher lords would seek arrangements with Welsh Princes and would happily see their peers destroyed. Welsh politics were like a snake pit. I began to agree with my son. The Tees Valley and its people were worth fighting for and not Wales.

The problems of taking the fyrd from their homes in late winter soon became apparent. I saw the King taking note. Not only did they slow us to a crawl, the further from Cheshire we travelled the greater were the desertions. It did not help that many of the lords would be following the Earl to the Holy Land. We reached Powys Castle after a slow ten-day ride from Chester. Our horses and surcoats were bespattered and besmeared with mud. I wonder, now, if that had been King Llewellyn's plan all along. He and his lords had gleaming mail and clean surcoats and, when we reached the castle, we looked like a ragged band of brigands. King Henry, however, showed his nobility.

"King Llewellyn, it is good that we meet thus. This is neither your land nor mine. Where is the Prince of Powys these days?" Henry was a clever King. He knew that King Gwenwynwyn ab Owain Cyfeiliog had been the last King of Powys and William Marshal, the Earl Marshal, had taken his son, then but a child, Gruffydd ap Gwenwynwyn to London where he could be protected.

I saw an angry tic in the old Welsh King's eye but he smiled, "Gwenwynwyn ab Owain Cyfeiliog is dead and I watch over his son's kingdom for him. I am as a father to the other Welsh princes and I am here to prevent bloodshed. Come. Let us retire into the castle for I am sure that you would appreciate a bath and warmth. Our land can be a little harsh."

King Henry had shown the Welsh that he might be young but he would not be pushed around. I saw now that Ranulf, Earl of Chester, had bought his own security by tying his family to that of the Welsh King. We would get no help from him. In fact, I began to wonder at the delay which suited the Welsh and not the Marcher lords. Had we been kept away so that the Welsh could gain more ground?

Only the senior lords were admitted to the castle. My knights and those brought by the Earl had to camp. I knew that Edward and Alfred would use their time wisely. They would discover which of the knights who would accompany us were to be trusted. Egbert and William would share my chamber and that was no bad thing. I did not trust the Welsh King. If there was murder in this castle he could wash his hands of it and say it was the result of another's treachery. Sir Robert, his squire and their servants were given a large chamber which was attached to that of the King. He would be safe. I was confident that King Henry would be able to navigate the tricky waters of negotiation. I would be close but we had spoken at length in Stockton. It had only been the last half month or so when we had been apart.

After we had stripped off our mail and washed we donned clean clothes. "William go to the King's chamber. Ostensibly you go to ask if the quarters are satisfactory but, in reality, I wish you to find out if he is happy with the way the Earl is conducting these negotiations."

"Aye lord." William, Alfred and the King were close. More importantly, the King trusted my sons. The Earl of Chester would have spies watching the young King as would the Welsh. A lowly squire would not be seen as a threat.

Egbert had envisaged that there might come a time when we were not fighting and would need to be presentable. He had two spare tunics. One was brand new. I had worn it just once, for the weddings. "Which of these, lord?"

"The newer one. The Welsh King thinks to embarrass us. When William returns I will have him clean my scabbard and sword."

Egbert nodded. "If you let me have your spurs, lord, then I will polish those too." My men from high to low were loyal and, more importantly, knew how to think.

William was away some time. He was grinning when he returned, "This is like a nest of rats and mice, father. As soon as I left I was followed. I know not where they thought I was going but I took the two of them on a merry chase. It gave me the chance to explore the castle. When I reached the kitchens, I rounded on them and asked where were the King's quarters. They were confused and had to lead me all the way back here for the King is but two doors away. I suspect they think me stupid. Let us keep it that way."

"Good lad and what did the King say?"

"He is disappointed with the Earl. Like you he does not trust that he will do that which he said."

I nodded, "Prince Louis did England no favours by offering the crown of England to the Earl. He did not accept but it planted a seed there. I think the Crusade is to take him from England. He believes there will be rebellion and he can profit from it. Go on."

"King Henry is adamant that he will not give away any land. The Welsh King thinks he is a boy but he is determined to show the world that he has grown under your tutelage." I nodded. "He asks that you sit close by him when he meets the King."

"And the Earl?"

"King Henry is no fool lord. He will say that as the Earl is on his way to the Holy Land his adviser should be the Earl who will be at his side should war come."

That was clever. If the Earl was playing a treacherous game then that would be reported to the Welsh King and any threat made by Henry would have substance. In addition, even the Welsh feared the Earl of Cleveland. "You have done well. Clean my sword and scabbard. Egbert has your tunic from the wedding. We will look presentable this night. I will send for Edward and Alfred."

I did not wish to risk dirtying my tunic and so when I reached the gatehouse to the keep I asked one of the sentries to fetch my two lords. At first, they feigned ignorance of my words but I knew that they spoke English. I had a number of Welshmen in my ranks and I could speak a little Welsh. I repeated my words in Welsh but with a harsher tone. They nodded and one scurried off.

While I waited it gave me the chance to look at the castle. It was Welsh built but they had stolen ideas from the Norman castles of England. The keep was a large one and the gatehouse was two large rounded towers. The castle was built upon a hill and the camp for our men, not the fyrd, was in the huge outer ward. It could be taken but it would be costly.

Alfred and Edward arrived and I headed back into the castle. I took them to my chamber. Egbert bowed and, taking the spurs, said, "I will take these into the corridor lord. I can clean them there."

He was clever. If the Welsh thought to overhear our conversation then his presence and the cleaning of the rowels on the spurs would mask any conversation being overheard.

I told them what the King had said. Alfred nodded, "He is wise not to trust the Earl. His knights speak of nothing save the Crusade. The Earl cares nothing for Pembroke. His lands will be safe. I fear he plays a game to gain a throne. He now has an ally in the Welsh King. We know that Louis of France supports him and there are many Frenchmen in the Holy Land. If we fail in the marches then the King's position will be weakened."

"And what of the knights who do not accompany the Earl?"

"There are some knights from Gilbert de Clare, Earl of Gloucester and Jocelyn de Braose leads the knights of Gower." I waited.

Sir Edward said, "I trust not the men of de Clare. He fought with Prince Louis. It is only because his lands are threatened that he is with us."

"And de Braose?"

159

"Although his family sided with Prince Louis I like Sir Jocelyn. He is young, like me, but he has fought against Deheubarth. He does not like the Welsh for his land is surrounded by enemies. He can give us valuable information."

Sir Edward said, "You think we will have to fight?"

"I am sure of it. The Welsh King has shown his hand. He thinks that he has power over the Earl of Chester. He can have his allies make war and take more land. He is called the Great by the princes who once were kings. He sees his Kingdom as the whole land of Wales and not just a rocky stronghold in the north-west of the land. He plays a good game of chess. He sacrifices pieces and thinks ahead. He would crown himself lord of a land that does not yet exist. He will give King Henry assurances and hope that the King goes timidly back to London."

"But we will not?"

I shook my head, "I am afraid not. You will be kept away from your bride a little while longer."

Edward put his arm around my son, "She has a new home to build. Women like to build nests and if you are anything like your father then your son already grows within her!"

Edward could be a little too plain-spoken at times and I saw my son blush.

I changed the subject and asked my two knights to have our men at arms and archers speak with those in other conroi and battles. They were good judges of character. When they left Egbert returned. "You eat with the other servants, Egbert?"

"Yes lord. The King's two servants, Paul and Matthew also eat with us. We will eat with the servants of the lord of this castle."

William asked, "Who is that?"

"I suspect that it is King Llewellyn himself. Keep your ears open, Egbert. Sometimes servants can be indiscreet. Let us hope these Welsh ones are."

Although the feast was a celebration and there was no official business I saw the game being played. The Earl and the King were trying to mould the King. They thought him young and impressionable. They tried to ply him with drink and they attempted to have him make indiscreet comments about the Council. I knew that they were wasting their time. We managed to annoy them as soon as we arrived for the young King insisted that I sit at his right hand. He sat next to the Welsh King. It left the Earl of Chester to my right. He had to speak with Sir Robert. I had come to trust Sir Robert and knew that he could be relied upon to say little and learn much. As the evening wore on he became more frustrated and I saw Llewellyn become more irritated. Finally, Llewellyn asked outright what King Henry intended.

King Henry gave the most innocent smile imaginable and said, "Surely, King Llewellyn, that is for our formal discussions on the morrow. Here we are in our cups and this is a social occasion is it not? Tomorrow I will let you know my demands and we will all have clear heads and minds."

That proved to be the end of the attempts by the Welsh to delve into the King's mind. A couple of Welsh harpists and singers entertained us. The singers were tuneful enough and they played their harps and rotes well but as I did not understand the language they were largely wasted on me. Instead, I studied the warriors in the hall. One day I would need to fight them. I looked at their faces and their devices. Ostensibly from Gwynedd, I was under no illusions. There would be warriors from Powys and Deheubarth here. They would be spying out our forces. King Llewellyn was playing a clever game. He sought a throne which did not exist. It was the throne of Wales. Even before the Romans came it had been a confused tangle of tribes who fought each other more than they fought the Romans. The first King Henry had maintained that anarchy and it had allowed him and his knights to conquer much of the south. England now had the best land in Wales. Powys was the only jewel left and as its future king was a guest of King Henry then we would have that soon enough.

When the King chose to retire I accompanied him. Going up the stairs he said quietly, "I think this Welsh King thinks he has me defeated already."

"That he does but you did well this night. I will sit by you tomorrow but I think I know what will happen. They will use the threat of a united Wales to make you concede land. Do not do so."

"That will mean war."

"Even if we agree it will mean war. They will see it as a weakness. Do not fear the Welsh. Even without the Earl of Chester, we can win. We use the men of Glamorgan, the Gower and Pembroke. They may fight amongst themselves but they will unite behind you. When they are defeated and Pembroke is safe I will take you back to the Council and I will endure their wrath."

He laughed. We had reached his room, "You do not seem unduly concerned."

"In truth, I am not. Your father's wrath hurt me and my people for he had teeth. The three who rule England now do so for a few years until you have your majority. They have a limited time."

"You would do without them?"

"They serve a purpose. Both the Bishop and the Chancellor appear to have skills of organization. Let them tot up their columns and tally marks. You are the one who will lead."

"I will write to Hubert de Burgh and tell him where we are. I will ask for men to join us at Gloucester."

"An excellent suggestion. Even if his lordship does not join us then any troops he sends will be welcome." I turned to William, "In the morning, help the servants empty the chamber and we will meet you at the camp. The less time we spend here the better. Who knows what mischief the Welsh are getting up to while we are delayed."

I rose early and prepared myself for the day of negotiation.

To ensure that all was done well the King of Gwynedd had brought the Bishop of St. Asaph. At the feast he had spent the whole time consuming as much food as he could. As he blessed us all before the meeting began I could see the ill effects of the meal. King Henry waited for the King of Gwynedd to make his proposals before he said anything. I

162

could tell that young Henry was nervous but I doubted that the others would. I had seen his fearful face and that had been when we faced the deer.

"King Henry you have come to my land prepared for war but I am here to tell you that there is no need. I swear that I will instruct Prince Maelgwn ap Rhys to cease taking land from the Earl of Pembroke. Peace will be returned to Pembroke." He sat down, leaned back and smiled as though he had done all that was required of him.

King Henry waited and then stood, "And what of the lands and castles they have taken? When will they be returned? What of the reparations for the damage done?"

The Earl of Chester showed his true colours, "King Henry, King Llewellyn has offered us peace. Will you now break it?"

"We came here because I was told, by you, Earl Ranulf, that we could negotiate a peace with those Welsh princes who have taken from our countrymen. I thank King Llewellyn but what he offers does not go far enough." He turned to me and began to rise, "Come Earl, let us raise the men of Shropshire and Hereford. We will show this Prince Maelgwn ap Rhys that he cannot raid England without paying a price."

King Llewellyn became angry, "He has not taken English land! It is Welsh land he has reclaimed."

King Henry turned and said, quietly, "It was Welsh land and then my great grandfather killed the king who lived there and took it. My grandfather enlarged it and my father also did so. Be careful King Llewellyn. I may be young in years but I have a wealth of experience at my side. If you do not fight alongside me then I might have to consider you an enemy." He stared at the Earl of Chester. "Your daughter has not married one of my family and there are no ties." The silence lay like a heavy black cloud. Would it yield thunder? The King waited what seemed too long and then he said, "I will leave now and travel south to Glamorgan. If I see any knights of Gwynedd in the marches then I will deem it to be a declaration of war. I do not make war on Gwynedd ... yet!"

163

King Llewellyn had regained his composure. I knew not what he was plotting but King Henry had done the right thing. "I am disappointed, King Henry. I feel that you have been badly advised." He shrugged, "However, I have done all that I could to make a peace. You are quite right what happens in the Marches is naught to do with me save that those princes owe me allegiance. If they seek my help then I may have to fulfil my obligations."

I rose too. The King nodded at me. I spoke, "Then King of Gwynedd think hard for if you save your allies then you may lose your kingdom."

"Is that a threat, Earl?"

"No. But you should know the consequences of attacking our country and our King." I turned to the Earl of Chester. He had remained seated. "And perhaps the Holy Land will be the safest place for you, Earl. When you return I will be waiting."

He recoiled. Llewellyn shouted, "You will let him insult you?"

I laughed, "Should he wish to defend his honour then speak now. The day is young and I have yet to exercise."

I knew he would not. He was not a fool. He knew my reputation. He shook his head and waved a dismissive hand. "The killer of churchmen is not worth the trouble."

"Perhaps I will travel to Outremer! I know the country well. Unlike the Earl, I fought to defend a King there."

We headed for our camp. Sir Robert was the one who did not seem to understand what had just gone on. "But the Earl is the one who brought us here!"

"And he brought the fyrd which slowed us up. We came at a walking pace. We were deliberately delayed so that the Prince of Deheubarth can make even more inroads into Pembroke and Gower. We must leave now. If we push on we can be at Gloucester by dark."

The King nodded. "I will send one of my men to London with a message for the Council."

"Majesty send at least four. Treachery abounds." He nodded. "Perhaps all of this is my fault. If you had not stayed for the weddings we would have been in London now."

We reached the camp as he said, "And there the Council would have prevented me leaving again. I believe I am intended to go to the Marches. This will be like a baptism of fire. I know that I cannot fight but I can watch and I can learn. I can show my people that although I am young I am ready to fight for all true Englishmen."

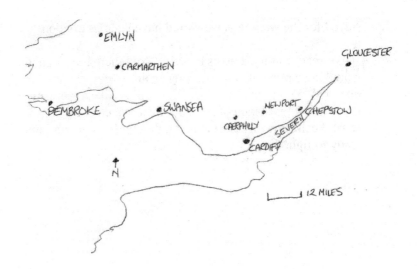

EMLYN

CARMARTHEN

GLOUCESTER

PEMBROKE

SWANSEA

NEWPORT

CHEPSTOW

CAERPHILLY

SEVERN

CARDIFF

N

12 MILES

Chapter 12
The Bloody Marches

It was a miserable march south to the Severn. The roads
were muddy and it took us longer than it should have. But
when we reached Gloucester we had a good welcome for it
had always held for the King from the time of the first Civil
War. Ralph Musard was a good knight. A little bluff but a
doughty warrior and as loyal as any. He sent for all of his
knights as soon as he realised what was our purpose.

"All the knights and barons in Gloucestershire are loyal to
the crown. They always have been and they hate the Welsh.
Folk around here remember that the Welsh always took
advantage of English wars to raid animals and ravage
women. There will be no end of men flocking to your
banner."

"And does the Lord of Glamorgan still hold that land?"
The King had learned to ask the pertinent questions.

"Aye lord. Baron Gilbert has good castles and defends
them well. You will not have to fight your way to reach
him."

"Have you maps for us to study? It has been many years
since I was in this region."

The Sheriff sent for maps and we pored over them. Now
that the Earl of Chester was no longer manipulating us we
were able to have my knights and captains together to look at
the maps. It was then that I met Jocelyn de Braose and I
concurred with my son's opinion. He was a clever man who
knew war and, more importantly, knew the land. He studied
me closely. At first, I felt uncomfortable but my son

explained that he admired me so much and had been desperate to meet me.

He kept silent for a long time and then ventured, "Your Majesty if I might suggest?"

The King looked at me and I nodded, "Go ahead."

"Baron Gilbert has a strong castle at Cardiff. Prince Maelgwn ap Rhys has taken Caerphilly and made it a mighty stronghold to the north of Cardiff. From there he can raid both Glamorgan and Gower. A threat to Caerphilly would relieve the pressure on Gower. My uncle would be able to rally his forces and come to our aid."

"Your uncle?"

"Reginald de Braose."

I was not fond of the Braose family. William de Braose, now dead, was involved in the murder of Prince Arthur. I knew I had failed that troubled boy. However, just as Henry was nothing like his father I had to hope that neither Reginald nor Jocelyn were anything like William de Braose. "We will need to send a messenger to him to let him know of our intentions. We have perilous few men until de Burgh sends reinforcements."

The eager knight said, "I will send a messenger. I have men I can trust." I had seen the men who travelled with him. They looked like warriors who could handle themselves.

In my heart I wondered just how many men would come from London. I had secretly planned on helping William Marshal without the aid of de Burgh. The loss of the men of Cheshire might cause a problem of numbers. On the other hand, the lack of men from London meant that I had complete command. The King had no regents to countermand his orders and the other barons and earls all deferred to me. That was how I wished it to continue.

I turned to the Sheriff. "We leave on the morrow. We are all mounted. The muster can follow on foot. The conspiracy to keep us in the north was for a purpose. I think the King of Gwynedd will be sending men to the aid of Prince Maelgwn ap Rhys."

That night I sat and spoke with the King, Alfred and Edward. The rest of my knights retired but we had a strategy to determine. Edward was the one with the practical experience of a man at arms. He understood how ordinary men would fight. He knew the language of the archers. When the King or Alfred tried to suggest something, they could not do he told them in no uncertain terms. Other than that, he was silent. I tried to allow the King and Alfred to come up with a workable battle plan. I only intervened when I had to. It was important that the King felt he was in command. I needed him confident enough to take on the Council of Regents.

In the end it was a simple plan. Often, they are the best for then there is less to go wrong. We would do what the Welsh expected. We would charge with our heavy cavalry. William would wear the King's surcoat so that the Welsh thought that the King led the battle line. My son was a similar size to the King. When we retreated we would, I hoped, draw the Welsh to charge us and then we would unleash our own secret weapon; our archers. I was sure that the Welsh would not expect an English army to have archers as skilled as ours. The feigned retreat had worked for William at Senlac Hill. I hoped it would work for us.

It took a whole day for us to cross the Severn and reach Newport. We had sent riders to warn Gilbert de Clare of our movements. Edward was still unhappy about the Marcher Lord who had switched sides and fought alongside the French. "You can't trust a turncoat, my lord and to fight for the French!"

"I confess that I am unhappy too but if we rejected every baron who opposed King John then it would be a small army."

King Henry said, "Yet, my lord, my father treated you as bad if not worse than any other lord but you did not raise a weapon against him."

I was silent for a few moments. The King had raised unpleasant memories for me. I still remembered the desecrated grave of my grandmother. "Two things, my liege; firstly, my heritage. My great grandfather saved England and King Henry. My father gave his life for King Richard. The other was William Marshal. I trusted him. He supported your father. I do not deny that I did not like your father. I probably hated him however that was not for his position but his abuse of power. You know that you will need to reaffirm the Great Charter." He looked at me. "The Pope ruled that it had been unlawful for your father to be forced to sign the charter. He was right to do so but the charter has much good within it. There are many barons who still oppose you because your father repudiated the charter. You could reissue it and you would win over many men."

"But I do not like all that it says!"

"Some parts could be changed; they would be small parts but the whole is now public knowledge. It is not only the barons and the nobles who like it. There are others who were given rights too."

"I will think on this. First, we will go to the aid of William Marshal. I will speak with other lords."

Alfred said, quietly, "But remember that the Marcher lords have more freedom than those in England. They owe allegiance to you, your majesty, but they do not pay taxes. They would be happy for the charter to be forgotten. You would know their minds better if you spoke with the nobles of Gloucester and Hereford."

"Good advice and I will heed it." My son might well be the ally and friend the King needed. They could both grow together and England would be a better place because of it.

Cardiff Castle had the look of a frontier stronghold. It had been motte and bailey and made of wood but now it was stone and dominated the land around. Gilbert de Clare was not what I expected. Firstly, he had a shock of bright red hair which explained his nickname, Red Gilbert and, considering he had fought against King John, he surprised me by dropping to his knee before the King. "You do me great honour, King Henry. That you came to our aid touches me beyond words! From this day forth I am your man. Ask anything of me and I will obey."

The King was also taken aback. Later I learned that his conversion went back to the time he was captured and imprisoned by William Marshal, Earl Marshal of England. The old man had changed de Clare so much that the former rebel married the Earl's daughter Isabel. I think even Edward began to change his opinion.

As we walked into the castle he added to our information. "I am pleased that you arrived when you did. Another week and the land between here and Gower would be in the hands of the Welsh. They have been driving a wedge between us. We have fought many skirmishes in the last month. I think they were making a great push to take as much land as they could."

I gave the King a knowing look. I had been right. There had been a deliberate attempt to slow our progress south. "I had planned on attacking them at Caerphilly."

He looked surprised but rubbing his red beard he said, "Aye that might work. A bold strategy."

"Jocelyn de Braose suggested it. He said his uncle could then join us from the west."

"Then I will muster all of my knights." He rubbed his hands. "It will be good to attack! I have had enough of squatting behind our walls. A knight needs a horse between his legs!"

His hall was smaller than that at Gloucester but the baron insisted that as many knights as possible enjoy the comfort of his hall. The Earl's wife, Isabel, was particularly attentive to me. "My father thought better of you than any other man he knew and that includes my brother. I know that he thought long and hard before burdening you with a task which would take your whole life up."

King Henry looked around, "I am a burden?"

Lady Isabel blushed, "I meant no harm, King Henry, it is just that my father gave so much time to your father and England that he had little time for his family."

I smiled, "Peace. There is a Council of Regents who will guide King Henry. I will be here for counsel when the King needs me. I am a warrior and not a politician. Your father, Lady Isabel, was both and I admired him for those skills. I am too plain-spoken to be a politician. I would draw my sword and let that speak rather than my tongue."

I saw that the words had an effect on King Henry. "I can never be the warrior you are, Earl. I have improved and that

171

is thanks to your son and your men but I am more like my father than my uncle."

I nodded, "Richard was a man's man. I believe that resulted in a premature death. Taunting an enemy is never a good idea."

Another change happened and it was as a result of Lady Isabel's words. Henry was young but each day he was evolving. Some changes were clearly visible. He was taller. His beard was fuller. He was broader in the chest. It was the differences inside which were harder to see. I detected them in his manner. It was in his eyes as he looked at his barons and captains. He was now but a couple of years from his majority.

He turned to me, "I should like to be crowned again with proper regalia. My mother's crown does not seem appropriate. Perhaps I should contact the Pope."

"When you return to London speak with the cardinal. The Pope has shown that he has your interests at heart."

Henry was becoming a King. He knew he had to look like a King. He wished to be remembered wearing a crown of England. His father had lost the crown and the jewels in the Wash. This would be a clean start for King Henry.

It took two days to muster the men we needed. Red Gilbert sent his scouts to discover the Welsh. They were rampaging through the north of Glamorgan and Gower. We learned that the Welsh had over three hundred knights. Gilbert de Clare was at first suspicious of that number for the Prince of Deheubarth did not have that many manors in his lands. When his scouts described some of the standards and devices I recognised them as knights who had been at Powys. They were knights of Gwynedd. I told the King and he did not become angry. He merely said, "I warned him but he thought me a youth. I will remember this slight and Wales will suffer."

When our host was ready we marched. We had just two hundred and ten knights. The men at arms I had brought from my valley brought our heavy cavalry up to more than three hundred but the Welsh would know that we had fewer knights. The lack of spurs and shorter hauberks told them

172

that we had mounted men at arms. What they would not know was the quality of those men. De Clare, de Braose and the Sheriff of Gloucestershire did not know their quality. They were surprised when I consulted Henry Youngblood and Ridley the Giant.

It was the King who spoke for them. "Do not disparage these men, gentlemen. I have seen them and whilst not noble-born they will give a good account of themselves and the Earl has a good plan which has my full approval."

William was resplendent in the King's robes. He rode a fine horse while the King was dressed in a plain surcoat and rode a palfrey. He was playing the part of Sir Robert's squire. Garth carried the King's banner and he too wore the King's device. It was a ruse. If it succeeded it might give us an unlikely victory. The scouts had told us that the Welsh had many hundreds of archers and spearmen. Our one advantage was that their only armoured men were their knights. Even my archers had padded gambeson and leather vests studded with metal. They wore a simple round helmet and carried a sword. My archers could fight with bow or sword. Most importantly they would ride to battle. The Welsh scouts would think that they were light horsemen and would not fear them.

We rode up the road which ran by the Taff River. We could not manage a stealthy approach. There were too many of us. The Welsh knew that we were coming. We had intelligence about their defences. They were using the wooden castle at Caerphilly to anchor their line. The ground rose from the valley side and the slope would sap the energy from our horses. The Welsh who had taken over the farms of de Clare's people fled. The ones they had driven from their homes were either dead or waited in Cardiff. The fyrd of Glamorgan marched with us and they were eager for vengeance on the Welsh. Until the Normans had come with King Henry's great grandfather there had been few farms. It had been the first Marcher lords who had cleared the land and made it productive. That was one of the main reasons that the Welsh wanted the land so desperately. De Clare and his people had done the hard work and they wished to benefit.

We only had eleven miles to travel and we reached the Welsh lines at noon. We formed our battle lines as we neared the Welsh. They had quickly embedded stakes. The stakes were to protect their spearmen and archers. Obligingly they had arrayed their knights in three lines before the stakes. We had three battles. I was with the fake King, William, in the one at the centre. De Clare led the men of Glamorgan on the left and Musard, the Sheriff of Gloucestershire, the rest of the knights on the right. The fyrd were arrayed in three ranks behind my mounted archers, the King and his bodyguard. The King and the archers would look like a reserve of horsemen. Sir William of Hartburn's squire, Robert, carried my standard and my son's squire, Henry, the horn. Their signals would be vital to our success. The Bishop of Gloucester had ridden with us and he blessed us and our standards as we gathered for the attack. My son William was prominently at the fore. He had to be seen. It was his build and his surcoat which would deceive the enemy. Only his eyes could be seen. My son was excited at the honour. To him, it was a game. As he turned to face our men he raised his arm and they cheered. It was exactly what a young king would do.

As the Bishop retired I nudged my horse next to him. "Remember Will, you are not to get in danger. If you were to fall then the whole plan would disintegrate. You must play a fearful boy king. Do that and we might win."

"Do not worry, father. I am just excited at the prospect of leading a charge! I will be a knight the next time this opportunity comes my way. Let me enjoy this."

Alfred nodded, "Do not worry, lord, with you and I at his side he is safe, Besides the Welsh will not try to kill him. They would take him prisoner."

Alfred was right but I was a father and that was what we did, worry! I did not want to lose my son so young.

William played his part well. He rode from the line and turned, "Today your King rides to battle for the first time. Follow me and we will have a swift victory." All knew that my son had volunteered for this part and the cheer which resounded was heartfelt. It further helped the deception. He returned to the line and Walter handed him his spear. He spurred his borrowed warhorse. It had a mail hood as most of our horses did. We were fighting Welsh archers! William was a good rider and the horse was an old, experienced one. We began the steady climb up the slope.

The Welsh began jeering and catcalling as we moved in our three blocks of knights. It was Alfred and me who set the pace. We walked. Then we began to trot. Our spears were held vertically. The Welsh horsemen stood firm. They would want our ranks thinned before they committed to the attack. I was disturbed that I knew their archers would be ordered not to hit the King. That meant that Alfred and I would be less likely to be struck. Edward, Peter, Fótr and the other knights would be in greater danger and that concerned me.

When we were one hundred and fifty paces from the Welsh knights I shouted, "Gallop!" We would not spur our horses we would just increase our speed. The spurs would be saved for the last forty paces. Soon the arrow storm would come. As the archers were behind their knights then the arrows would come vertically. We lifted our shields as one. The higher we held them then the more protection we would have. All of my knights and even my men at arms had metal strips across our shoulders. Even an arrow like a knight killer would not penetrate the plate. The danger was to our horses.

The arrows began not long after we began our gallop. I saw a ripple along the Welsh line which told me that their knights were going to counter charge. The shower of arrows descended. They rattled off shields like hailstones. I heard the whinny of horses struck in the rump or shoulder by an arrow. The arrows would not be barbed and knights and men at arms would pluck the arrows from the wounds. I did not look around to see the damage. I had to judge the time for the retreat. I lowered my spear when I was just twenty paces from the leading Welsh knight. I recognised him from Powys. He was a large red bearded knight. His device was a white gryphon on a black background. He had a mask over his eyes but his prominent beard told me who he was. He had a lance. I lowered my shield. The Welsh archers would not risk their own knights. The arrows slowed then stopped. William pulled back on his reins to allow Alfred, Edward, Peter and I to edge forward. We would take the impact of the enemy spears and lances. I pulled back my arm. I had learned, long ago, that it was easier to hit a knight in the leg. The red bearded knight obliged me by coming at my spear side. His lance was longer and he would strike me first. I managed to place my shield horizontally over the cantle of my saddle as he punched at my middle. It was a safer strike than going for the head. He drew his shield to protect his own middle. The lance struck my shield and cantle. The wooden cantle took some of the force from the blow. Even so when the lance shattered the blow hurt. I pulled back and punched. The visor on his helmet impaired his vision. He did not see my spear and it tore into his thigh and stuck in the wood of the saddle. His horse veered to the left and tore the spear from my hand.

I drew my sword. I had no squire with a spare spear. A lance came at my left side. William was still behind me and the knight who thrust his weapon at me saw the chance for glory. He punched and I did the only thing I could. I punched back. There was a crack like thunder as his lance shattered on my shield and I felt my arm shiver. The knight had a helmet with a nasal and he looked in shock for he was certain I would have fallen. Had he used a spear then he might have done more damage but my punch had deflected the broken lance along the side of me. I stood and brought my sword above his shield. As I did so I saw Alfred and Sir Edward carving their way through the Welsh. This was what they both did best. My sword hacked under the metal plate protecting his shoulder. I did not penetrate his mail but the blow was hard enough to unbalance and to hurt him. I was helped by the fact that he was reaching for his sword. He began to tumble from the saddle. His weight began to drag his horse down too.

I turned to look at the Welsh knights. A second battle was heading for us. Now was the time. "Henry sound the horn. Robert, signal retreat!"

All of our men were expecting the command and almost as one they turned. The exceptions were myself, Sir Alfred, Sir Edward, Sir William, Sir Fótr, Sir Geoffrey and Sir Peter. My men at arms would form a protective screen around William. The Welsh would expect that. The seven of us would hold up the Welsh and give our men a head start. Inevitably the two wings would fall back more slowly and that was part of my plan. When we were in position we would turn on our pursuers and bare our teeth! The seven of us formed a wedge. The second Welsh battle had lances. We chopped and hacked at them before they reached us. They punched and stabbed with splintered stumps. Our mail held. A broken lance is like a useless piece of wood. It is not even fit to use as a club. One knight punched at my shield and although my numb arm was of little use the blow did no harm. I swung my sword hard. I aimed to strike him diagonally, above his shield. I must have hurt something for he wheeled away and blocked the next three knights trying to get at me.

Sir Edward shouted, "Enough heroics, lord! The King is safe!"

What we had done would be expected of loyal bodyguards. I wheeled Bella's head around and spurred my horse. I slipped my shield around my back. Alfred was just ahead of me and the other three before him. I saw the joy of battle on Alfred's face. He was using a helmet with a nasal. "Had we stayed, we could have had ransom!"

"There will be coin enough, son. Let us win first." I felt arrows as they struck our shields. I hoped that none would strike Bella. Ahead of me I could see that William had reached our lines and reined in behind Ridley and the other men at arms. Behind him was the King. He was protected by James of Corfe and Sir Robert. What I could not see, although I knew that they were there, were the one hundred and twenty archers. One hundred were from my valley. They would be the equal of any on the field but as David of Wales commanded them then the other twenty would perform better than they ever had before! On the two flanks were dismounted men at arms and the fyrd. They had embedded spears. I risked glancing behind me. Prince Maelgwn ap Rhys might have preferred otherwise but his whole army, from knights to peasants were pouring down the hill to fall upon us. They thought that we had broken. I slowed Bella down as we approached our men. My glance behind had shown me that the nearest Welsh horses were more than fifty paces from me. I wheeled her around to place myself before William. I backed her into a space between Ridley and Henry Youngblood.

Will Red Leg was at the rear of our line and he shouted, "Now David of Wales!"

The Welsh were not expecting arrows. Their shields were held before them. As we knew from our scouts the only mailed men were the knights and David of Wales sent his arrows into the men who were not mailed, the bulk of their army, and not the knights. We would have to endure the knights. I turned the first lance which came at me but I could do nothing about the second which glanced off my helmet and made my ears ring. I saw stars but I did not need to see to know where the Welsh were. I swashed my sword in an arc at head height. There was a resounding ring as it hit one Welsh helmet. The squires of our knights had throwing spears and they hurled them at the Welsh knights. They would not penetrate mail but they stuck in shields and saddles. They punctured the Welsh horses' skin. They were a painful distraction that we did not have to endure.

My head cleared. The attack had slowed to a walk. Some horses had been wounded and others had baulked. This would be a confused mêlée. That suited my men. Edward did not fight as most knights did. He had been told, by Aunt Ruth that he reminded her of the mighty Sir Wulfric of Thornaby. He was relentless in his attack. An enemy did not know whence the blows would come. He would rain so many blows in a short space of time that an enemy could not cope with the storm. Peter was Ridley's son and he was as big as his father. A blow from either man would result in a broken arm. Fótr and Alfred both had quick hands and quick reflexes. Fótr was Swedish and he had something of a Viking berserker about him. He fought furiously. The result was that our wall of five knights held and blunted the Welsh attack. The Sheriff and de Clare began to flow around the sides of the Welsh knights and all the time our archers thinned the ranks of the spears and their archers. Plunging arrows found heads without helmets and shoulders without mail. Had they been able to get to grips with their enemy then the Welsh might have held but there was a wall of horses before them. As the horses were forced back by the force of our attack so the fyrd began to slip away. If they had been fighting to defend their homes then it would have been different but they were fighting for land and the ones who would benefit were their lords.

I spurred Bella who began to move forward. She was bigger than the knight who faced me and that meant that I had the advantage of height. I used it and began to swing my sword at his head. He blocked with his sword and sparks flew as the blades rang together. I switched my blow and he had to fend it off more awkwardly than he would have liked. My sword smashed into his thigh. I swung my shield sideways and the edge tore across the knight's ventail. The leather binding broke and the ventail dropped. I lunged with my sword. The point entered the knight's open mouth and tore out of his cheek. To say he was distracted was an understatement. I did not pull my sword back I swept it sideways and it smashed into his teeth and tore open his other cheek. He could not speak but he flipped his sword in the air and held the hilt to me. He was surrendering. I took his sword and pulled his reins. There was a gap next to me and I handed the reins to Walter. I urged Bella on to occupy the space vacated by the knight.

There was now more room to fight. Knights had fallen and horses died. The archers had thinned out the ranks behind and the Welsh were being forced back. Around me, I heard the Welsh knights as increasing numbers surrendered. What had seemed like an easy victory had become a disaster. When the horn sound for the retreat the Welsh were ready to run and run they did. They turned their horses and rode back to the castle.

"After them! Do not let them reoccupy their castle. Sound the charge!"

Our horn sounded and our men were released. We rushed up the hill. Bella was tired but the Welsh were exhausted. I kept a steady pace and she ate up the ground. Alfred and Fótr rode at my side and the three of us drew inexorably closer to a knot of Welsh knights. Their exhausted horses began to tire and they turned in panic. My surcoat was known and two knights surrendered immediately. William and the other squires were close behind for their horses had had nothing to do yet. Two knights turned to face Fótr, Alfred and myself. Even as I blocked the blow from a sword Alfred's blade had hacked into the side of the Welshman. His mail must have been weakened already for Alfred's blade ripped through the mail and the gambeson. He fell from his horse. He would live but only if a priest found him.

We were close enough to see the open gates of the castle and Prince Maelgwn ap Rhys must not have relished a siege for he and his knights continued north. When we reached the castle, I reined in and rode through the gates. I shouted, "Yield the castle to King Henry or suffer the consequences!"

The standard of Deheubarth was lowered. We had won.

Chapter 13
The Battle of Emlyn

Gilbert de Clare followed me into the castle. "Thank you, Earl. It was a clever plan."

"And if I might suggest that, now that we have retaken it, you make the castle a little stronger. You need stone."

"Stone costs money, Earl."

"Men's lives cost more." I saw the King approaching. "You pay no taxes to the King and yet he came here without any fuss to rescue you."

He nodded. I saw him realising that I had brought my own men and had it not been for my archers then the result might have been different.

"You are right. I will do so."

We were still surveying the land around the castle when the King dismounted. He looked excited. "Are all battles so closely fought?"

I smiled, "Your Majesty once the Welsh fell into our trap we were never in any danger of defeat."

"But they came within a few paces of our camp."

"The camp and your person were guarded by resolute men. James of Corfe is a good warrior. Sir Robert knows his business you need to trust the men around you and have faith."

Lord Gilbert smiled, "The Earl is being disingenuous. He and his oathsworn bought the time for the feigned retreat and they ensured that the enemy would follow."

The King nodded, "And now what?"

"Lord Gilbert and I were discussing how we could make this into a stronger castle."

King Henry was young but he liked his castles. He had lived his whole life in castles and he seemed to have an affinity with them. He looked around the land. "You must build in stone. See how the mound of the castle and the small plateau dips. There is a stream yonder. I would build a castle in stone and divert the water to form a lake around three sides of it. You build one bridge over your moat. That way there is no higher land for war machines and the boggy ground you create will make it hard for you to be assaulted."

I saw the incredulous look on Gilbert's face. I smiled, "The King may be young but he is clever. I think it would work. It would be the strongest castle in this part of Glamorgan."

When Caerphilly was finally finished men praised the First Lord of Glamorgan. We knew that it was King Henry's idea.

By nightfall the men too badly injured to be healed were despatched and the wounded brought into the castle. It was still close enough to winter for there to be wolves. We had many prisoners for ransom and great quantities of booty. Gilbert de Clare had more than enough money for stone!

This was not my land and so my men and I camped by the castle. The King stayed in the hall. He asked for William to accompany him. I saw no reason to deny him. De Clare sent out scouts to follow the fleeing Welsh. Jocelyn de Braose had distinguished himself in the battle. He had fought close to Alfred. Padraig the Wanderer commented on his courage. "Feisty little cockerel that one is."

I was pleased for his grandsire had not been a good man. It was encouraging that the bad blood did not go to another generation. He led his men to head to Gower and rejoin his uncle. Having defeated Prince Maelgwn ap Rhys once he was keen to follow up with that victory. As we sat around the campfire Alfred brought up the matter of our return home, "Is it necessary for us to relieve the Earl of Pembroke? We have broken the Welsh. Prince Maelgwn ap Rhys will head back to his own lands now."

I saw Sir Edward shake his head. He knew better. I sighed, "Have you not been listening, Alfred? This is not about Prince Maelgwn ap Rhys. This is about King Llewellyn. I slew one of the knights we saw at Powys and I am sure there were at least four others on the battlefield. The Prince does what he does for land but they are just crumbs from the King's table. He wants a kingdom. That kingdom will be the land as it was before the first King Henry conquered large swathes of it. We need to relieve William Marshal and inflict such a defeat on the Welsh that they become like the Scots and wary of us."

Sir Edward nodded. Alfred sighed, "It is just that I wish to return to my wife."

"Then return. Take your squire and return to Seamer. No one would blame you. You have acted blamelessly in the campaign thus far and covered yourself in glory. I only said that I could not return home."

Sir Edward looked intently at Alfred. My former squire saw this as a test for my son. Fótr and Peter were just bemused. They had wives but they enjoyed campaigning. They liked the profit it brought. Alfred lay on his back and looked up at the stars, "No, I am your knight and I will not leave my comrades. I will stay!"

Sir Edward's smile filled his face. "And I have seen a couple of likely lads to be in the King's Men. They were with Sir Ralph Thornton." Sir Ralph had died, along with his squire in the Welsh attack. There were just a handful of survivors and they deserved a good lord. Who better than the King?

"Alfred why not go with Sir Edward and take these men to speak with the King, his knight and his captain? I think he will be in the mood to take on more men and you can see how your brother fares while you are there."

When they were gone I sat with Sir Peter, Sir Fótr, Sir Geoffrey and Sir William. Sir Fótr said, "I understand how he feels, lord. I would have been the same if I had had to leave so soon after my wedding."

Sir Geoffrey said nothing. He had had to leave my daughter too. His forbearance did him great credit. I knew

183

that he must be feeling the same inside as Alfred. I put it down to the fact that he was slightly older than my son.

Sir William laughed, "Aye and Sir Alfred does not have squawking children to keep him awake."

Sir Peter famously had three children all of whom did not sleep well. He laughed, "Aye, even Sir Edward's snoring does not compare. Your Aunt Ruth says it is a phase and they will grow out of it. Perhaps this campaign will last long enough for that miracle to take place."

Sir William poured more ale from the jug into our beakers, "What I cannot understand is the Earl of Chester and his actions."

"He is easy to understand. He has had his head turned by the Prince of France who suggested he should be King of England. The Earl is like a honey bee. He is always seeking nectar. He changes sides to suit himself. The ones who are a mystery to me are the ones like Sir Falkes de Breauté."

Sir Peter frowned as he sipped his ale. "I have not heard of him, lord."

Sir William shook his head, "He is a bad one, Petr. He was nothing, not even a gentleman. King John had elevated him and ennobled him. He gave him lands. The man became so rich that even the Earl Marshal borrowed from him and yet as soon as the King died he refused to acknowledge Henry of Winchester as King. He squats in Bedford Castle like some robber baron. There are others like him. Lord Hugh of Skipton was one. I would have thought that having done so well from John's misrule that they would have just enjoyed the life they lead."

"Some men are greedy. The Holy Land taught me humility. I am grateful for what I have and what I have I have earned. No one gave me anything."

William had been my squire back then and he nodded, "Amen to that, lord. We saw the best and worst in men. I confess I did not think we would ever leave that land alive."

We reminisced about our times in the Holy Land and Sweden. Alfred returned with Sir Edward. "It went well, father. All seemed happy with the arrangement. There might only be four more men for the King but they will be valuable

184

additions." He smiled, "And I am sorry that I was not the son I ought to be. You are right. And we have spoken to Gilbert de Clare. If we can retake Swansea for Sir Reginald then it will be child's play to do as we have promised and relieve Earl William."

"I will not have need of you in London, any of you, for I will have my men at arms and archers." I saw the relief on their faces. London was not an experience which they relished. "And how is William?"

Alfred laughed, "Still enjoying the glory of the day. The other squires are envious of him and Garth and the King cannot cease singing his praises."

"Aye well, tomorrow he comes back to the reality of grooming my horse and sharpening my sword."

"Let him enjoy this night, father. He will relive the memory for the rest of his life." Alfred was a good brother.

We had just twenty odd miles to go to reach Swansea. The scouts had returned to tell us that while the fyrd had headed north the King and his knights had headed west. They were heading for Pembroke. We had lost men but not enough to diminish our threat and the Welsh who were between us and Swansea fell away. When Sir Jocelyn appeared from the north we found another reason. Sir Reginald had used our attack to gather his men and relieve the siege of Swansea. Gower was now free from the Welsh. Ominously the besiegers had also fled west. We would have one more battle before we could relieve the Earl of Pembroke.

The Welsh were also determined to harass us. Once again, we had relied on another's men to scout and they had been found lacking. Archers sent showers of barbed arrows as we headed down a valley towards Swansea. One of the knights from Gloucestershire lost his squire. The youth was too slow to react and his shield was just a lifetime away when the arrow struck. We wasted an hour hunting down and slaying the miscreants. For the last twelve miles, I used David of Wales and his archers to screen us. We were not ambushed again.

Sir Reginald was grateful for our arrival. He swore his loyalty repeatedly to King Henry. He was aware of the treachery of his father. The ambush meant that we would not be able to leave as early the next day. I sat with Gilbert de Clare, Sir Reginald and the Sheriff of Gloucestershire to plan our strategy. I would have involved the King but the younger knights of both Gower and Glamorgan claimed his time. They were all eager to show their loyalty. If nothing else our journey from Stockton had given King Henry loyal knights who appreciated the effort he had made. I wanted to be sure that the Marcher lords could defend their land. To do that I had to see how they would attack.

Gilbert de Clare was the one with the ideas and he initiated the discussion. "I know my scouts let us down this day lord and I have punished them. Perhaps the Lord of Gower has men he could trust to lead us and watch our flanks?"

"Aye I have but you should know, Earl, that the land twixt Pembroke and here is much disputed."

"They have castles?"

"The only ones are those built by our ancestors. Pembroke Castle was a de Clare castle once. My ancestors built Carmarthen Castle." He smiled, "The father of the Prince of Deheubarth foolishly destroyed it. It will not hold us up."

The Sheriff of Gloucester still brooded about the loss of the popular squire on the road. "Then if they do not hold castles why do we not meet them on the field! Let us be done with these brigands once and for all. The Earl showed us how to deal with unruly neighbours. He captured King William and the Scots have become lapdogs since then!" It had been a little harder than that but I said nothing.

"Then let us bring them to battle." We all looked at de Clare.

"How?"

"Simple enough, Sheriff. We do not head for Pembroke Castle. We head north for Aberystwyth."

Sir Reginald shook his head, "Even as the crow flies that is more than fifty miles. On the tracks the Welsh call roads it would be nearer a hundred and we would be ambushed all the way."

"We would not have to travel that far. Once we reach Carmarthen we turn north. As we know the men of Deheubarth watch us all the way. Once they knew that we headed for their capital their King would have to withdraw men from the siege."

I confess that I saw merit in the plan but it needed the agreement of all of the lords. Surprisingly Sir Reginald seemed to like the idea. "Aye for then we could fight the Welsh on the land of our choosing."

"But if they do not follow us we cannot march through the mountains of Wales all the way to Aberystwyth. Already the men of the fyrd grow weary of the campaign and we do not have enough of their days left."

I was about to say to the Sheriff that he could send the fyrd back when Gilbert de Clare said, "And we need not. It is a day's march from here to Carmarthen. We head north for one day. If they have not come we turn west towards Cilgarran Castle. The Welsh would still think we headed for Aberystwyth by the coast road. I am convinced that they will attack us but, if not, then we would be cutting off their supplies."

The Sheriff shrugged and said, "We will march to Cilgarran and if the Welsh have not attacked then I will have to take the men of Gloucester and Hereford home."

It was an ultimatum although couched in diplomatic terms. The two Marcher lords agreed. Gilbert and the Sheriff went off to tell the captains of their plans. They would tell all the men that we headed for Aberystwyth. I would tell the King of the real destination. We might have spies in our camp and secrecy was paramount.

The Lord of Gower had some wine brought. "Your nephew has impressed us all."

"Jocelyn is a good man although, in truth, he has no right to the name de Braose." I sipped my wine for I knew that Sir Reginald had a tale to tell. He lowered his voice. "My sister, Adeliza, was a wild young thing. When she was but fourteen she ran off with a knight. He came from the Marches. He was an impressive knight but wild. I never knew his father but he won a few tourneys and impressed the young women.

187

He had an eye for them. I do not know if he was even a knight. He came from nowhere and no one knew him. He was a sword for hire. He said that his name was Sir Henry but we later discovered that was a lie. When my father made it clear that he would disown my sister this knight, Sir Henry abandoned her. She was with child. Jocelyn was that child. My sister was a broken woman. She had been abandoned. I fear she lost her mind. My father had women bring up Jocelyn but he was fond of his mother and spent long hours with her. She fed him stories about his father. He grew up thinking that it was my father who was the villain. When my father died and I inherited the title I adopted Jocelyn so that he could have the name and I had him trained as a knight. His mother died when he was ten. I am pleased that he has turned out well for I have moulded him."

"He does you great credit."

"And he is most interested in you and your exploits. In the last year, he has asked many questions about this knight of the north who keeps the border free from foes. I think that he would emulate you here in the borders. When this is over and the Marches are safe once more I would deem it an honour if you would allow him to ride with you as one of your knights. The experience would do him good. He has ridden into England before now with his squire and his men. In the last year, he has become somewhat obsessed by you and your exploits. I think some time with you could be beneficial. He will not inherit land here and learning from you might be the making of him."

"I have to ride to London first but he would be more than welcome to accompany my son to Stockton. The two seem to get on well."

"Good. He will be pleased."

We left the next day but a curious incident occurred which none of us could explain. Harry son of John had been one of the men at arms I had taken to London. He was popular. Some of my men at arms and archers went to the local alehouse for a drink. While they were there Harry had suddenly become agitated and rushed out into the dark. The others thought he had seen a woman. When he did not return they searched for him. They found him dead. His throat had been cut. We might have put it down to robbery but his purse and weapons were all about his person. No one had seen anything and the more superstitious amongst my men put it down to a ghost. It was a loss that we found hard to bear. Had we lost him in battle then that would have been one thing but to be murdered! My men were uneasy. We buried him by the parish church. He was unmarried and so there would be no one to mourn save his shield brothers. They were angry and upset. As was I. As we headed for Carmarthen a theory came into my head. I would mention it to no one until I was sure but I would be wary from now on. There was a killer loose and it seemed likely that they sought another of my retinue.

The castle at Carmarthen had been attacked and destroyed on numerous occasions by the Welsh. We camped there and King Henry became quite agitated. He took the two Marcher lords to task. "My lords, my grandsires took this land and conquered it. They gave it to your families to protect. You do not even pay taxes to the crown! The least that you can do is ensure that the castles King Henry built are maintained! The Earl Marshal did much work at Pembroke and the fact that it has not fallen shows the merit of such building work. When this is over you have just four years to make the castles strong enough to withstand attacks! I will return and inspect them." I almost smiled at the two lords whose heads hung low. They were being berated by a youth!

Our scouts had reported that Prince Maelgwn ap Rhys was at the siege of Pembroke and had been reinforced. We had thirty knights of Deheubarth in Cardiff Castle awaiting ransom. As he had been reinforced by over a hundred knights then either he had an inexhaustible supply of knights or King Llewellyn was sending him his own knights. I suspected the latter. I had Mordaf and Gruffyd shadow the Welsh. They would let us know if the Welsh swallowed our bait. When we headed north we did so slowly. Gilbert de Clare had arranged for many wagons with tents. It added to the illusion that we intended a long campaign. The presence of the King added to the deception. The Welsh would think it was a young king flexing his muscles. The land through which we travelled had been part of Gower but long lost. The farms showed that. The Welsh did not farm in the same way as we did. Our slow progress allowed them to flee and, no doubt, tell others of our advance. We halted at Emlyn. There was another ruined castle here. The King and I could not understand why the Welsh would take a castle and then destroy it. Had they held it then we would have had a very hard job to retake it.

The castle rose on a rocky bluff above the Teifi river. The army camped below it while the King and I, along with Alfred and William explored the castle. The river looped around three sides of the castle. It reminded me of Durham but on a smaller scale. The motte had been built on top of rock and the castle had a stone gate. The Welsh had removed the gates and burned the wooden hall. We climbed to the fighting platform and surveyed the land.

I pointed to the flat ground before us. "We will fight the Welsh here!"

Alfred frowned, "How can you be sure that the Welsh will come?"

"I am not but even if they do not come and we moved west I would fall back here and use this as the battlefield." I banged the parapet. "Our archers can be here. From this elevated position, they can send their arrows further. We array our knights and men at arms between the two bends of the river. There it is but a hundred paces from bank to bank. The archers would be just a hundred and fifty paces from our front rank."

"You would fight dismounted?"

"Aye, King Henry, in this case, I would. Our knights and men at arms are better than the Welsh. We can put the fyrd south of the river. They would be protected but can use their slings and their bows to harass the Welsh whilst keeping them safe." I saw him frown. "Even if they do not attack because we have such a strong position we will have won for they will have ceased to besiege the Earl of Pembroke. Do not lose sight of that, majesty. It is the reason we are here.

The reconquest of these lands is for the Marcher lords. We are here to bring succour to the Earl."

When we rejoined the other lords at the camp we told them of our plan. Unlike the King Sir Reginald and Sir Gilbert understood it immediately. Jocelyn de Braose slapped his squire on the back. He had been told he could come back to Stockton with Alfred. "See, we shall come back from Cleveland with such skills that I will lead an army to retake Wales!"

His enthusiasm was infectious. He was an engaging young man. I saw his uncle smile at the thought of his sister's son rising like a phoenix to conquer Wales. When Mordaf rode in, just before the watch was set, the others wondered if I was some sort of wizard. "Earl, the Welsh have lifted the siege. They march towards us. They will be here tomorrow."

The King smiled, "Well, Earl, it seems we have the opportunity to see if your plan will succeed."

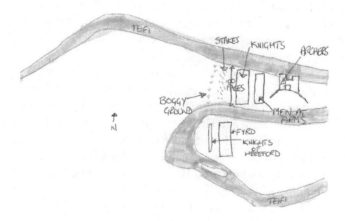

The first thing we did the next morning was to cross the fyrd and the knights of Hereford over the river. They were to give the illusion that our army was spread out further than it was. While it was still dark the archers secreted themselves within the castle. They would remain hidden. None were left in the village and any Welsh scouts would have had trouble seeing them move. Stakes were embedded between the loops in the river. They were there to stop horses. Men could move between them. The men at arms dug a shallow ditch before the stakes. It quickly flooded and then the waters receded. The shallow ditch was refilled. It looked harmless but the water had made it a muddy morass. Men and horses would slip and slide when they tried to cross it. It was a trick and would not win the battle for us. It would just increase our odds of victory.

Then we rested. It would be the Welsh who would be exhausted after a long march from Pembroke. We had many of the knights and men at arms rest within the walls of the castle. Our horses gazed beyond the castle in a loop of the river. When the Welsh came they would see the fyrd in their camp and a couple of hundred men. I wanted them to attack. One positive was there were no civilians close by. There were just warriors. If there was a killer hunting my men they would be easily seen.

Gruffyd rode in during the late afternoon. "They are five miles down the road, lord, and they are coming here." He patted his knife. "I found one of their scouts and he confirmed it. I saw more men heading from the north-west. I think they were coming from Aberteifi. I saw at least ten banners."

"Then that means more knights. You have done well. David of Wales and your brother are in the castle." He hurried to join them. I turned to the other leaders and the King. "Now we wait. The Welsh have taken the bait. Let us see if they will swallow it. Sir Reginald if you would send a rider to Pembroke then we can let the Earl know where we are. I am certain he would like to join us and besides his men marching north can only serve us."

We kept a good watch that night. The people who had fled the town had left supplies and we ate reasonably well. We had taken animals on our slow march north west too. The fyrd would stand so long as they were fed and safe. The river before them could be forded but as there were knights and men at arms before them they were in no danger. If the Welsh used their archers then there was plenty of room to move them out of range. I rarely used the fyrd. I used them now to give the illusion of numbers. Many of them wore the helmets of the men we had killed at Carmarthen. From a distance they might appear to be better armed than they actually were.

Awake before dawn I walked along the stakes with Alfred, William and Edward. Sir Fótr, Sir William and Sir Peter roused the camp and then checked on the archers. I wanted no horns. If the enemy was clever then it would move close to us in the dark and then attack at dawn. It is what I would do for the Welsh now knew about our archers. We stepped beyond the stakes. The ground appeared to have dried but Sir Edward, who was the largest of us, sank to his spurs in the mud. A horse would struggle. He nodded, "I will get the lads to come and use it as a latrine when they rise. Every little helps."

We headed back to the camp and cold food. With luck, we would dine on cooked horsemeat in the evening. The King surprised me by greeting us before the other lords had been roused. He had woken of his own volition. Sir Robert and James of Corfe were with him. Already they worked well together. King Henry said, "I wish James and my men at arms to fight alongside your men today, Earl."

"It will be an honour."

"I am being selfish. I want them to see how your men do. I have watched them and they conduct themselves not like men low born but warriors who know their trade. I believe my men can fight but today will be the test." He took some of the stale bread which William offered him. It had runny cheese and ham upon it. A few months ago, he would have turned his nose up at such fare but now he ate it for he knew it would fill a hole, as Edward was fond of saying. "You think we can win? I heard that Gruffyd saw more knights coming from the north-west. I am still unhappy about fighting on foot."

"If this field suited horses then I would have employed them, my liege. The castle has been left here and we shall use it. If you stand on the gatehouse then you will have the best view."

He shook his head, "I shall sit on my horse in the gateway with Sir Robert holding my standard. The open gate will

193

suffice for I will see the battle and they will see me. I do not want them to think I am afraid of them."

I admired the King's courage. "This will be the first time you have seen knights battling on foot. You will see that sometimes it is an advantage."

Soon we could hear the camp coming awake. Men went to make water. Others joked with their shield brothers. Each had their own rituals they followed. Warriors were superstitious. You could be the best warrior in the world and favoured by God but a slip at the wrong time could result in a wound or worse. Men liked the familiarity of routine and of preparations that had worked in the past. Mine relied on them less than most but I knew that they would still use them. Ridley would touch the wooden cross he had made and then kiss it before tucking it beneath his kyrtle. David of Wales would choose the first five arrows he would use. All his arrows were straight and true but he would use the ones with the best fletch and which felt right in his hand. Before he strung his bow, he would kiss the yew. All of my archers wore helmets. However, they still kept their spare strings beneath them as they had when they had worn a hat. A dry bowstring meant their arrows could fly a greater distance. Even the squires were not immune. William would always feed Bella a treat before each battle. It mattered not that I might not ride. He would often delay his own food so that he could secure a treat: a carrot, an apple, dandelions, anything so long as it was something Bella liked. It was a bizarre ritual for it could only benefit me and not William but it made him comfortable and a comfortable warrior fought better and we would be fighting that day.

I walked back with my sons and knights. We stood by the stakes and peered south and west. We had seen the fires of the Welsh in the distance. Now we could hear them as they woke. Our horses were quiet for they were grazing and still resting. The Welsh horses were noisy. We heard the sound of mail. My fears were laid to rest. There would be no sudden dawn attack. We would have coped but a night battle was always unpredictable. We would now fight as I had envisaged. So long as they attacked then we all knew what to do. They would use horses and arrows to break us down. Inevitably it would come to their knights against ours. If they did not attack then we would wait. I doubted that they would be as well supplied as we were for they had been surrounding Pembroke for some time. They had fled from Carmarthen and Caerphilly. An army that flees cannot carry as much as an army that advanced.

As the sun came up behind us it shone on the helmets, spears and mail of the Welsh. My own helmet had been burnished until it looked like silver. William held it and his own. My coif was around my shoulders and I wore just my arming cap. William, and possibly Alfred, would relish every moment they spent in mail. It made them feel like a warrior. It had been twenty years since I had felt that way.

When the horns sounded in the enemy camp I turned to William, "Sound stand to!"

Our men were awake and in position but the Welsh would expect it. They would be looking for us to mount and advance towards them. They would assume we would fight another battle as we had at Caerphilly. Their Prince would be wary of a trap. I wondered what he would make of our dispositions. The Welsh were moving. I could not see individuals but I saw the metal snake as it crawled from the dark of the west. When the rising sun picked out a helmet it seemed to flash and twinkle. As the light became better I saw banners. Smaller shadows, horsemen on ponies, detached themselves from the column and rode towards us. We had twenty of the fyrd, mainly boys, with us. They were armed with slings. I would not risk them in battle but they had been honoured to be chosen by the Earl of Cleveland. They were in the staked area.

"Alfred go and tell the boys that they are free to annoy the horsemen."

"Aye, lord."

The ten riders galloped close to us. They had no helmets but each had a throwing spear and a small round shield. They would be wary of archers. They stopped just twenty paces from the boggy ground. Had they advanced but a little then they would have discovered the treacherous nature of the footing. As it was they halted and began counting our banners. Just then the eldest of the boys whirled his slingshot and sent a stone to smack into the head of one of the scouts. He fell from his saddle, dead. The other stones were just a heartbeat later. Three men and four horses were struck. One of the men who was struck rose unsteadily to his feet before he was felled by a hailstorm of stones. Two of the horses threw their riders. The survivors fled. More were hit before they were beyond stone range. Our knights and men at arms cheered the boys.

"Now get them behind the knights. The Welsh will be wary and the boys have done their job. The scouts will not have had time to count the banners. They will make up a figure."

As the boys trooped past, with their heads held high, I nodded and said, "Well done! These are warriors I see before me and not boys!" There would only be twenty of them but their stones, sent over our heads at the mounted knights who would charge us could be an irritation which might cause casualties. The cost was a few river stones.

The sun was now up and I saw the Prince and his lords. They were in a huddle half a mile from us. The survivors of the scouting expedition reported to them. After a short debate, the Prince gave his orders and waved his arms. He did not do as I had expected. He formed his men at arms and archers up before his horsemen. The stakes had been a warning. His men on foot would remove the stakes and then he would charge. Each of my knights had three spears at their feet. If the stakes were destroyed then we would plant spears in the ground. The Prince obviously did not trust his peasants. I could see them mobbed behind the knights and squires. Priests came before the host which knelt. This would be a chance to go to war with God's grace. Drums and horns sounded and the Welsh moved towards us. They were singing. The words I could not understand but the sound was musical. Perhaps it helped them to march in time.

The Bishop of Gloucester stepped through the ranks and one of his priests raised the cross. His voice carried above the advancing Welsh, "We fight this day with God on our side against the wild men of Wales. Know that your King watches you and as such you are assured of a place in heaven should you fall." As he headed back to the King I looked at Edward who shrugged. I was not sure of the truthfulness of the priest's words but it did no harm for men to believe that they would go to heaven.

David of Wales would not need a command from me. He and his men would have chosen the correct arrows. Most of those who advanced were without mail. A few had short hauberks but the majority, if they had armour at all, wore leather. It would be barbed arrows and not knight killers that they would use. He would choose his moment perfectly. I had the utmost faith in him. He and Henry Youngblood had been with me since the Holy Land. We had all the same experiences. I trusted my captain of archers.

When the marching Welshmen were almost at the boggy ground I pulled up my coif and fastened my ventail. William handed me my helmet and my world shrank to the two eye holes. I could see that the advancing men were wary of the boys with slings. Their cautious approach stopped them from slipping and sliding in the mud. It just sucked at their feet. They reached the stakes and were just thirty paces from us. They wondered why we did not advance to fight them. Confusion helped us. I heard Henry Youngblood give a command and the twenty slingers who were before him began to hurl their stones blindly. It did not matter that they could not see their target so long as they cleared our knights and they did. Four men fell and others were hit before the Welsh reacted and pulled their shields up. Their leader, a huge man with a thick black beard, no helmet and a two-handed Danish axe, urged them on. He swung his axe at a stake and the blow was so hard that it not only split the stake it plucked it from the ground. Other men hacked and pulled at the stakes. To do so properly they had to lower their shields and that was when David of Wales sent the one hundred and twenty arrows to plunge into the Welshmen. The huge leader took one arrow in his shoulder but he appeared to brush it off. Others fell.

The Welsh were brave. They must have had persuasive priests for they came on. I, like the knights around me, had my spear held in two hands. When the Welsh sent their own arrows at us some knights fell for they were slow to raise their shields. I was lucky. An arrow clanked off my helmet. I had my shield above my head and I saw that David's arrows were now being sent at the archers. It was an unfair duel for the Welsh could not see my archers who were hidden behind the castle's battlements. Soon the Welsh arrows would have to stop for fear of hitting their own men. Already half of the stakes had gone. I had to judge this aright. When the Welsh were just ten paces from us I lowered my shield and, holding my spear in two hands, shouted, "Charge!" Apart from the ten warriors with axes, the rest were largely weaponless. I ran at the giant. He swung his axe in a figure of eight. To a novice it was intimidating. I had seen it before. It did not worry me and I rammed my spear through his middle. I did not intend to but his charge and swinging axe drew the spear into and through him. I dropped the spear and the haft stuck in the ground. The spearhead stood proud of his body which was folded over the spear. I drew my sword and hacked through the neck of the next Welshman. They fled. When I looked along the stakes I could see why. The one hundred knights of ours who had advanced had each speared a man. Along with the ones the Welsh had lost to arrows and stones they had lost more than one hundred and eighty men. They ran.

"Back!" We had lost most of our stakes but when I stood and looked at the ground I saw that they had been replaced by the dead. There were also dead archers further back. My archers had easily won the duel. I picked up one of the two spears which remained and, after laying down my shield, rammed it into the ground at an angle. The head was just four feet from the ground. A horse would impale itself. I picked up my last spear and looked down the line. We had lost knights. Most were wounded and were being helped back to the castle. Replacements stepped up to take their place. We now had a few stakes but they were backed by a line of one hundred spears. We had time to prepare for the

198

next attack as the men on foot hurried back to the horsemen. The last ones limped and crawled. I saw then that the Prince had formed his knights and horses into five lines of fifty men in each line. His first line was made up of knights wielding lances. I saw two smaller groups of spear-wielding light horsemen. They would, I had no doubt, ride in first and try to disrupt us. His fifty knights could not ride toe to toe because of the stakes. Their job would be to punch holes in our lines which could then be exploited by successive charges.

We had enough knights to switch over but we would only be able to do so once. I would have to use men at arms for a third charge. I could rely on my men but I was unsure about the other men at arms.

A horn sounded and the lines of horsemen began to gallop. As I had expected the light horsemen rode in quickly. David and his archers sent their arrows towards them but the two bands meant he had to divide his arrows and fewer men fell than I would have liked. The throwing spears showered down upon us. The boys with slings brought down a couple of horsemen and that added to the eight hit by my archers but three knights were struck and downed. Four others suffered wounds. Then the knights closed with us. When they struck the mud some of them slipped and slithered. The knights fought to control their horses. It was then that David's archers began to cause real damage. Our archers managed to hit four or five of them. Although none fell we had hurt them. The knights began to pick their way through the stakes. This time we did not charge. We waited. The lances outranged us but the blows were not struck at speed. The horses had had to slow down. As I had expected I was the main target. William, behind me, held my standard and it drew them like moths to a flame. A lance lunged towards me. The knight had stood in his stirrups. I could have stepped back but had I done so it would have sent the wrong message to the others. I punched with my shield as the lance came towards me. It splintered and shattered. My arm felt numb. I lunged forward with my spear. Held one handed had I struck his mail I would have done him little harm but, by luck, I struck the throat of his horse. It reared and I pushed even harder. I must have struck something vital for it fell backwards taking the knight with it. The falling horse crashed into the next knight along and Sir Peter was able to ram his spear under the helmet and into the head of the knight. I still retained my spear and I was able to turn and thrust it at the horse and knight facing my son. Alfred's spear had gone between the sword belt and mail. It effectively held the knight there. My spear went into the horse' shoulder and it reared. The spearhead severed the belt and the sword fell. The knight reacted and tried to reach down for the sword. Alfred had quick hands and he thrust the spear into the space between the ventail and the nasal. It broke in the knight's skull. Even as he fell Alfred reached down for his last spear. Once our last spears broke then we would have to use our swords and the Welsh would have the advantage until we could switch ranks.

The wall of staked spears and their losses were too much for most of the knights. They wheeled away. I saw bloodied horses and knights with wounds. One of two were determined to have their moment of glory. It was a mistake. While the second rank of knights galloped towards us the boys with slings and my knights finished off the six knights who stayed to fight. Warhorses were valuable and the six mounts were dragged into our ranks. They were passed back to the castle.

As we prepared for the next attack I saw that there were some men at arms in our front rank. We had the knights of Hereford as a reserve but I was loath to use them as it would expose the fyrd and they were a threat to the Welsh. The second rank of knights had a harder task. Before Sir Edward, Sir Peter and myself lay the bodies of two horses and three knights. It was a barrier. There were neither spears nor stakes there. I could not see the standard of the Prince in the next rank. I had to assume that he was saving his best knights to charge with him. That way he could ensure not only the victory but the glory which accompanied it. What I did see, however, were the shields and devices of four knights from Gwynedd. I had seen them at Powys. This would be a determined attack.

"Close ranks and hold them. Make them bleed for every piece of earth!" I added, for the benefit of my knights. "These are knights from Gwynedd. They will try to kill us!" Every knight was trying to kill or capture other knights. If you had the chance then you ransomed them. These knights from King Llewellyn would want rid of me for my insults. The knights from Deheubarth had not known me. These did. I saw, as they approached that they had besmeared their lances with dung. They would be poisonous. It would probably be human dung and a wound infected with it was usually fatal.

I held my shield before me and rested my spear on the top. The knight with the red and green surcoat was heading for me. He had a full-face helmet and I could not see his face but I remembered his surcoat from Powys. At the feast, he had barely been able to conceal his contempt for me. He would have to either jump or clamber over the dead horses before me. He must have lacked confidence in his horse or his skill for he slowed. As his horse rose above me, its head covered in mail, I saw the lance, tipped and stinking come for my face. I had to not only avoid it striking me I had to avoid the splinters. He struck my shield and I turned the shield so that the lance did not shatter but slid down the side of my shield. As it did so I stepped closer in and rammed my spear into the chest of the horse. I was lucky for it hit its mighty heart. As it burst I was showered with blood. It fell sideways and broke off the head of my spear. I swung the broken shaft at the knight's leg as he fell and then drew my sword.

I broke my own rule. I left the line and climbed onto a horse's carcass. As the knight kicked his right leg free I brought my sword down and it cracked into the side of his left leg. The greave did not cover the side. I heard something crack and he screamed. He tried to push himself up and in doing so exposed his mail covered neck. I lunged and my sword tore through the mail links and into his throat. I ripped the blade out sideways as a lance was thrust down at me. As I deflected it Sir Edward rammed hard with his spear and knocked the knight from his saddle. Even though it meant leaving the safety of my line I ran towards the stricken knight. He was another with a dung covered lance and I thrust my sword up between his legs. There was neither mail nor gambeson there. I twisted as I pulled it out and brought entrails and organs with it.

I felt William tugging me, "Back, father, I beg of you!"

I realised that I was beyond the last of the broken stakes. My knights stood in a defensive half-circle ready to rush to my aid if I failed to heed William's words. I hurried back but we had broken this second attack. Once again, my household knights and I were surrounded by dead knights and their bodies. As I walked back a knight of Deheubarth lay beneath his horse. He had discarded his helmet. "Help me lord and I will yield."

I sheathed my sword, "William, pull him free when I lift the saddle." The horse was a dead weight but by using a broken spear I was able to lever it sufficiently for William to pull his leg free.

"I thank you, lord."

"William, take him to the castle!"

We had held them again but I saw that the knights who had fought in the front rank were weary. It was time to change. "Second rank change places with the front rank." The move brought the Sheriff and Sir Reginald to the front as well as some of my men at arms. Jocelyn de Braose took the place of Alfred. I saw them clasp arms and speak as they did so. I took off my helmet as we awaited the next attack. William had delivered his captive and he handed me an ale skin. I drank deeply. He said, "Father your sword is notched."

"There is no time to sharpen it. I will have to use it as it is."

Alfred took off his helmet as he joined us in the second rank. "We held them. This, I think, will be the crucial charge."

I nodded. The Prince had kept his best men until now. He thought we were ready to defeat for we had been weakened. If he chose not to attack then we would have won and if they did then all we had to do was hold them. That would be easier said than done for our best men had fended off their two charges. Would a line held by the likes of the Sheriff, an old warrior like Sir Reginald and the young de Braose be enough?

"William, take Henry and the other squires. Fetch as many throwing spears and darts as you can."

As our squires ran off Sir Edward said, "I am not sure there are many darts, lord."

"No matter how few there are we can use them. Our spears are shattered. We need to attack them every way we can. David and his archers can only do so much. The Welsh are not sending their men without mail. They wait to see us broken and then they will send those to us. We break this attack and we win."

Sir Peter said, "That sounds desperate lord."

"These are desperate times. King Llewellyn has sent his men to aid the Prince. Those extra men have made the difference."

The squires returned with eighty or so throwing spears and thirty darts. I had them distributed to the men who were now in the second rank. Our third rank was made up of men at arms who either did not have mail or, like Ralph of Appleby, had mail but had suffered a wound. They were there for moral support. I glanced across the river. I was tempted to order the men of Hereford and the fyrd to join us but I held my nerve. I looked at the ground behind us. It was flat to the castle. If we had to then we could fall back and fight before the walls. Then the fyrd could use their weapons. The switch had already moved us back four paces. Sir Reginald and the Sheriff had wanted a patch of ground unencumbered with bodies, blood and guts.

A Welsh horn sounded and the lines began to move. I donned my helmet and picked up my throwing spear. The Prince was using all of his horsemen in two lines. Their approach was more cautious. He had seen the knights slip at the muddy section. The stakes were now completely gone but there was a wall of dead over which they would have to clamber. These were the best knights Deheubarth had and they jumped the horses and men. Some of the bodies became mangled by hooves but this was war and the Prince was gambling all. They did not hit our line at speed. It was little more than a canter but they were facing men who were not as good as we had been. None fled but there was a distinct lack of confidence amongst some of the knights of Gloucester. This was not their land.

Lances were raised and thrust. There was a clatter of splintering wood and I saw that the Sheriff was wounded. Jocelyn de Braose showed great courage by stepping across the Sheriff so that he could be lifted to his feet. Ridley the Giant and Henry Youngblood braced them with their shields. I pulled back my arm as the Prince's standard bearer pulled back on his reins to make his horse rear his hooves at Sir Reginald. I hurled my spear. The standard bearer had had to stand to make his horse rear. The banner fluttered behind him and my spear hit him under his right arm. His left arm pulled his horse around and the standard of Deheubarth fled the field. The Welsh continued to press and I saw that we were losing too many men. The neck of land between the rivers narrowed behind us. We would have a narrower frontage to fight.

I took off my helmet and shouted, "On my command take five steps backwards! Now!" The five steps proved to be ten for the Welsh pressed and pushed. Our flanks became more secure and, donning my helmet I pressed my shield into the back of Sir Reginald. Then I heard the sound of stones and arrows on metal. The Sheriff of Hereford had brought the fyrd to the river bank. They were pouring arrows and stones into the right sides of the Welsh. There the enemy had no shield to protect them. The flanks of the horses were exposed. I was close enough to see the stone which struck the Prince on the side of the head. It stunned him. It was the final blow. A horn sounded and the Welsh fled backwards. They left twenty dead knights and countless riderless horses. We had won the battle now we had to win the peace.

Chapter 14
King's Council

The King rode forward when it was clear that the Welsh had ceased to fight. I ordered the fyrd and the men of Hereford to cross the river and bolster our numbers. We took the wounded to be healed. The Sheriff had to be carried. Six more knights had yielded and they joined the ones we held at the castle. The Welsh would rue the day they destroyed and then abandoned the castle at Emlyn. The steady rain of arrows had sapped their will to fight. "Fetch our horses forward."

Sir Reginald said, "You would continue to fight?"

"I do not wish to but I will make the threat. Our horses are fresh. If we mount then the men on foot will be hunted down and slaughtered."

The horses were fetched and the men of Hereford and the fyrd began to swell our numbers. It had an effect. There was a debate at the Welsh camp. The Prince's standard-bearer and the Bishop approached our lines. I saw that the standard-bearer had his right arm in a sling. I stood with the King, de Clare and de Braose to speak with them. The standard-bearer looked to me although his words were for the King. "My lord, we would clear our dead from the field and then we would speak of peace."

I nodded, "Aye for we have many knights to ransom and there is the question of reparations." I turned to the King. "Where would you speak, King Henry?"

He smiled and pointed to the castle. "Tell your Prince that I will meet with him inside our castle. I would do so before it is dark. We have an appetite and there is much Welsh horseflesh upon which to feast." I hid my smile. The King had learned much. He was telling the Welsh that we had won and we would determine the terms.

The Bishop looked at the standard-bearer and said, "Yes, Your Majesty, it will be as you determine."

After they had gone I said, "Ridley, have our men collect the treasure and have some of the horse carcasses butchered. Light fires on which to cook them. William, fetch Mordaf and Gruffyd." We walked back to the castle. I saw the healers working on the wounded. Some would lose limbs, others would lose their lives but we had lost fewer men than we might, thanks to the intervention of the fyrd.

My two archers greeted me with happy expressions, "Yes, my lord?"

"Ride around the rear of the Welsh camp and get as close as you can. I would know what they are saying."

They nodded. Mordaf said, "It will be dark when we return, lord."

"No matter. These talks will resume on the morrow. Unless I miss my guess, the Prince is not the one who is in command here."

Gilbert de Clare asked, "Then who?"

"The King of Gwynedd or one he trusts."

I handed my sword and helmet to William. He would put an edge to my blade. The King's servants, aided by Egbert and the others, had found some chairs and a table in the wrecked castle. They had placed them in the inner ward. I saw that James of Corfe had ringed them with his men. Wearing the King's livery, they made a statement. The King of England had won the battle. The King, Sir Reginald, Sir Gilbert and myself sat on one side of the table. We had the only chairs. On the Welsh side was a log. It was lower than the chairs on which we sat and they would have to look up at the King. Egbert and the servants knew how these things worked. They brought us beakers of ale to quench our thirst. William brought a bucket of river water and he helped me to clean most of the blood from my mail. Blood was easier to clean when it was fresh. We did not have time to fetch a fresh surcoat but the bloody one I wore would be a reminder of how many Welshmen I had killed.

The Welsh Prince, the Bishop and the four lords he brought with him rode through our men who were stripping the dead of their weapons, mail and valuables. They dismounted and walked to the table. We offered them no ale. I saw the tic of anger in the Prince's eye as they sat. The King said nothing but pointedly drank some ale and then smiled.

The Prince was looking at me. Eventually, he said, "You have a well-deserved reputation, Earl. You fought well."

"You lead brave men too, Prince."

Silence fell. Finally, the Bishop said, "There are men whose souls need me, my lords. Let us speak of peace and then I can return to minister to their needs."

The King nodded, "You are quite right Bishop. Prince Maelgwn ap Rhys, we came here to right the wrongs of your attack on our Marcher lords, their lands and their people. God has been on our side and we have prevailed. You will return all captives taken in your raids. You will take your men from any castles and manors you have occupied." He paused and the King nodded. "In addition, I will have you swear that you will not attack Gower, Pembroke or Glamorgan again. Those lands are not part of Deheubarth."

"Your majesty, they were!"

The King smiled, "And now they are not and we have the right and the might to defend them." It was as clear a statement as one could make and the King nodded. "As for reparations… I need to speak to my lords for it is they who have suffered."

"Reparations?"

"Punishment! King Henry, my great-grandsire, took ten thousand head of cattle when he defeated Gwynedd. We will debate this night what we require." Already the smell of cooking horseflesh was drifting towards us. "Victory has given me an appetite." He smiled, "You will need to speak with your lords and the Bishop has souls to save."

They trudged unhappily off. I smiled at the King. "You are learning, my lord."

"And your scouts may discover more which might aid us. Besides I was not certain what reparations we wanted."

Sir Jocelyn had been listening, along with my son, "As much as we can get. It will stop the Welsh from taking from us. It worked with the Scots."

"It did."

While the food was being prepared I went to see my men at arms. None of my archers had suffered a wound but some of my men at arms had. I saw that their wounds were not serious. Poor Harry son of John had been the only man we had lost. His death and the cause still niggled in my head. "When the talks are done I will take my men at arms to London. The wounded and the archers can return with my knights to Stockton."

Ralph of Appleby said, "The wound will not impair me, lord."

"I know, Ralph, but I only need an escort. There will be no fighting." I hoped that was true. The Welsh had prevented me from helping to secure the rebel castles for the King. Bedford and others still held out but I knew that the Council needed the King in London. I would travel home after London before the serious work of securing England for King Henry could begin.

Not long before dark, the sentries on the walls reported a handful of banners coming from the south. They did not worry me but I had men at arms and archers mount to investigate. When they rode in it was the retinue of the Earl of Pembroke. He brought with him his son Richard and twenty knights. When the King approached the Earl dropped to one knee, "My liege, I hoped that you would come to my aid but I knew that we are on the edge of your world. I thank you."

"Rise Earl, it is the Earl of Cleveland you should thank for he is the architect of our victory!"

William and I had fought together and he grinned as he clasped my arm, "Thomas, you are ever the rock my father said you would be. He spoke of you to the end. He said you were King Henry's hope and I can see it is true." He surveyed the wounded who were being tended. "We came as soon as we could. The rest of my men will be here by morning. Has the battle been fought?"

"Aye and we won thanks to the Earl's plan. We made demands and tomorrow their Prince will return so that we can tell them what reparations we demand."

While their horses were attended to we told the Earl of our demands. He nodded, "You are right about our castles, lord. We allowed them to fall into disrepair. It was a mistake. I swear to you that it will not happen again." He sniffed the air. "Are we too late for food?"

Gilbert de Clare laughed, "The Earl's archers slew many horses. There is more than enough."

We were still eating and the sun had long set when Mordaf and Gruffyd rode quietly in. I gathered our captains and lords together so that they could hear their report. "You have hurt them badly, lord. They can muster barely a hundred knights. The fyrd are already heading north and west. We saw a covey of men at arms sneaking off with stolen sumpters laden with booty. The men of Deheubarth are defeated."

I heard a note of caution in Mordaf's voice, "But?"

He grinned, "Aye lord, there is a but. The King of Gwynedd is there with twenty of his knights. We managed to get close enough to the campfire of the King and the Prince to hear some of their words. The King was unhappy that the Prince lost some of the King's best knights. There is discord in their camp."

King Henry said, "Discord; that is a good thing, surely."

Mordaf nodded, "Aye King Henry but King Llewellyn wants the war prosecuting further. He said he has men coming from Powys to reinforce him. He was angry that the siege of Pembroke was lifted."

I nodded, "So it was as we thought. The King of Gwynedd is behind this." I turned to William Marshal. "Could you have someone reach your men? I think that the sight of an army arriving from the south-west might just discourage any further talk of war."

"Aye lord."

"They would need to time their arrival perfectly. When the Prince and Llewellyn are at the peace table would be best."

"Let me go, father!"

The Earl of Pembroke looked at his son. "Aye. Take my knights with you. Their banners will add to our enemies' dismay!"

After they had gone we devised a strategy for the talks which would benefit us and discomfit the Welsh.

We rose at dawn and I had the men stand to. Mordaf's words had been a warning and I would heed it. We saw the Prince, Bishop and knights as they rode towards us. The Earl of Pembroke was disguised with a cloak but he stood close to the negotiating table between Jocelyn de Braose and my sons. The Prince looked like he had slept but a little. I spoke before they could. I wanted them off guard. "Bishop, it seems a little disingenuous of you to speak of peace when there is another in your camp whose voice holds more sway than Prince Maelgwn ap Rhys."

"My lord, I know not what you mean!"

"You are a man of God and I do not expect lies from you. King Llewellyn of Gwynedd is in your camp! You sir," I jabbed a finger at a knight, "fetch him hither or this meeting is over and there will be war!"

The Prince's shoulders sagged and he nodded, "Do as this wizard demands! It seems he can see through the cloak of night and hear conversations which should be private."

We said nothing while we waited but William, my squire, slipped away to tell the sentry on the highest tower to send the signal. The men of Pembroke would begin their march. We had to wait for some time before the King appeared. He was accompanied by his son, Dafydd ap Llewelyn. This was his second son for his eldest, Gruffyd, had been held hostage by King John and Dafydd ap Llewelyn would be the next King of Gwynedd. He was barely a youth but his presence showed the importance of our battle.

He sat. None of us bowed. He glared at me. King Henry smiled, "Now we can talk not only reparations but peace between the Welsh and the English!"

"Peace! I come here to tell you that I will bring more men and we will drive you from our land."

King Henry nodded, "And you expect that the men who are marching from Gwynedd will defeat us?"

The King looked shocked at our knowledge. He glared at the Prince, "I said nothing, my lord. They have spies in our camp."

The King waved a dismissive hand, "It matters not you have too few men here to do any harm to us."

I had been watching William on the gatehouse. He waved, "King Llewelyn, I pray you to come with me for I have something to show you which might just change your mind and your policy." He hesitated. "Come I swear that you will come to no harm and it might help you make a wise decision." He rose, somewhat reluctantly, and we went to the gate. I pointed. The Earl's son had done well. It looked like an enormous army was approaching. "If you wish war then we will fight this day and I promise you that we will win. None of my knights used their horses yesterday and this is a fresh army. You and the Prince lead a battered shadow of the army you brought. Our fyrd stands firm while yours flees." I pointed to the north. The last of the fyrd of Deheubarth had seen the banners and were fleeing. "Do not speak of war. Speak of peace and you and your son might live."

"You threaten me?"

I laughed, "Of course I do for I saw the knights you sent to me with poisoned lances. This is personal and you have made it so. Do you really want to make an enemy of me? Would you not rather I go back north and become the bane of the Scots once more?"

He nodded and a wry smile creased his face, "You are a hard man. I would I had one like you in my ranks."

He was a beaten man and the negotiations flew by. We received five hundred head of cattle. The borders were guaranteed. Ransoms for the knights were promised and the three counties were each given a chest of gold. As the talks ended the King of Gwynedd pointed at me. "You are responsible for all of this and yet you have nothing from it. Why?"

211

"Because I promised the Earl Marshal that I would protect King Henry from any enemies; all enemies. I keep my word. You are either the friend of my King or you are my enemy. The choice is yours."

We left three days later when the ransoms were paid. Alfred led my knights, archers and half of my men at arms north. They took the ransom and the treasure we had taken from the field. Jocelyn de Braose and his men accompanied Alfred. I now saw why he sought to serve with me. He had more opportunities for advancement than in the Marches. I left with the Sheriff, the King and his men. The Marcher lords would strengthen their castles and we would ride to London.

Once we had left the Sheriff in Gloucester I was able to continue my work with the King. I explained why I had done what I had done and my strategies. He was like one of the sponges they take from the Mediterranean Sea bed; he soaked it all in. As we rode along the old Roman Road which had protected the province in times past I saw him looking at castles and defensive positions. The battle had allowed him to have a good view of the land and the way the castle controlled it.

"I hope that the work has begun on the Tower."

I was not convinced that the Council would have seen that as urgent. Of the three of them, only de Burgh was what one might call a military man. They struck me as men who liked to count piles of coins. "I know we have been away for many months but it takes time to assemble the materials and then to build."

He pointed to the road, "My tutors told me that the Romans built this road at a rate of almost half a mile a day."

I had heard such figures but I was not sure of the veracity of them. They struck me as priests finding more reasons to applaud Rome. "Perhaps on a good day when the land was flat. They had almost six thousand men to do the building. You will have far fewer."

He thought about it for a while. "We used men who should have been punished. There must be many others who commit crimes."

Padraig the Wanderer was riding just ahead of us and he could not help quipping, "In London, they probably commit them by the minute!"

"Padraig!"

"Sorry lord."

King Henry smiled and said, "But he is right. Instead of lopping off limbs, blinding or putting in the stocks, it would be of more use if they were to serve me and build my castle."

I did not want to get into that area and so I smiled, "Then, lord, suggest that to the Council. I think the idea has merit."

"And you will not be there."

"No, King Henry. I am needed in my valley. When you need me for war and martial advice then send for me and I will be at your side forthwith."

"The Earl Marshal said for you to be my mentor."

"For war, lord, I am a warrior and not a politician."

"Yet you came up with the Charter of the Forest and your manor is the best run that we have visited. I think you do yourself an injustice, lord." I nodded. The King rode in silence for a while. "You are probably right. I have had good lessons in, what is it, more than a year since you took me under your wing? I will put those lessons to good use but know that if I send for you then it is urgent. I would have you come with all of your men to my aid. Then we may be ready for the next lessons."

As we neared London my men rode closer to us. The death of my men at arms seemed to have something to do with London. They were wary. There had been rumours of a woman when Harry had been killed. I wondered if Morag, One Eye Waller's doxy, had been the one to end Harry's life. It was the only plausible answer to a puzzle that had kept me awake since Swansea.

Riders must have told the Council that we were near for when we spied the city walls just a mile or so ahead Hubert de Burgh and a column of men rode up. They were dressed in the King's livery. De Burgh ignored me. "Your majesty! It is good to have you back and safe from the wild Welshmen!"

The King did not slow up and Hubert de Burgh was forced to turn and speed up to keep up with us. He looked

213

vaguely ridiculous and I think it was an intentional act from the King. "I was never in any danger and we have done that which has not been done since the time of my grandfather. We have cowed the Welsh. We have cattle and coin and, most importantly, we have a secure border. In my view that is worth the short time, I was away from London. Has the Charter of the Forests been drafted?"

"Aye lord and awaits your seal."

"The Tower, the work goes on?" His words were like the arrows of David of Wales' men. They were relentless.

"It does but do not expect to see much progress."

"I will be the judge. I have seen much since I have been away. My eyes have been opened. Do not expect me to be a compliant boy. You will not find one. You will find a king in the making. I know that I am not a king yet but I am more of one as a result of the last, what is it, more than a year away from the confines of Windsor! This bird has learned to fly and he enjoys the freedom!" It was as clear a statement as was possible.

De Burgh threw murderous glances my way. He had been moulding the young King to increase his own power. I had not done that. I had tried to make Henry the best king that he could be. "Well lord, I am pleased that you are back. As you can see I have hired more men to follow you."

"Then Sir Robert and James of Corfe can help me to inspect them. I have seen my warriors fighting and know that the Earl of Cleveland made good choices. I now know what to look for. If they do not meet my standards then I do not want them." He turned to William. "I think William of Stockton that I will miss you more than any other and that includes your father. Chancellor, I would have young men my own age at court. They should be the sons of nobles. William here is a good example of the sort of man I would like. You and the rest of the Council are too old. I want young men who will become warriors so that when I go into battle I will be surrounded by men that I can trust and rely upon."

He had returned to London like a whirlwind. I had not intended it but the Welsh War had been the perfect way to see how to lead men and how to deal with tricky and treacherous enemies.

Hubert de Burgh turned to me and said morosely, "And will you be staying in London too, my lord?"

"You will be pleased to know that I return to Stockton. I have told the King that if he needs me he just needs to send to me but I would appreciate a little more notice than I received for Pembroke!"

"Lord, you heard as soon as I found out."

I had spoken with William Marshal and now knew the timeline of events that led to my summons. "No, my lord, you did not. You should have had an idea of the danger before it erupted. When you received the news, you spoke with the rest of the Council and then drafted a letter."

"Of course!"

"Then those three days could have been saved and we might have reached Wales sooner."

The King smacked the cantle of his saddle, "Well said, Earl! That will be our watchword. Let us not do tomorrow that which we should have done yesterday!"

I felt proud that I had begun to do that which the Earl Marshal had asked me in that antechamber in Windsor. Henry was not the finished article but he was taking shape.

We stayed in the Tower, much to the annoyance of the Council who were more comfortable at Windsor. The Constable of the Tower had men working hard on the walls, ditch and new towers. The new tower was taking shape and the walls looked to be much improved. I helped the King to cull a third of the men chosen by de Burgh and waited while we interviewed and accepted replacements. I gave advice on the walls and the new defences. On our last day, while William and the King rode through the streets of London to receive the acclaim of the populace for the victory in Wales I sat with the three members of the Council. It was des Roches and de Burgh who questioned me most closely.

They wanted to know exactly what the King had done and what he had agreed. Des Roches said, "You seem to have made an enemy of Llewellyn the Great."

I laughed, "It is he who gave himself that title. He is an enemy. He tried to take land."

"But we get no taxes from that land."

"The King has ideas in that area. He is no fool, my lord. He is quick to learn. You would be making a grave mistake if you were to underestimate him." I sighed. "One more thing, he listened to his barons. All agree that the Great Charter should be reissued and King Henry should sign it."

For the first time, Pandulf took an interest, "The Pope ruled that it was unlawful to make the king sign the document."

"But the King will not be forced to sign it. He will be happy to do so. There are some parts that need to be rewritten but he will sign it. Think how powerful that would be. The lords like Sir Falkes de Breauté will be marginalized. The King and his Council will have more legitimacy."

Pandulf nodded, "I think we have been guilty of underestimating you, Earl. You are more than a warrior who kills for England."

Hubert nodded, "Earl, you have done much to turn a boy into a man. Let us have him now. We can make him a King. England trusts the three of us to do that. Will you not do so also?" I said nothing. "Go to your family. I know that the Earl Marshal regretted the time he spent away from his on the service of the King. If things become desperate we will send for you."

I knew they were trying to be rid of me and my influence and I had told the King I would leave. I made them sweat and looked to ponder the question. Then I nodded and I saw the relief on all of their faces. I was a threat, not to England nor the King but their position. They were right. Part of me was relieved that the King would no longer be my direct responsibility but another part of me was sad for I had enjoyed the experience. We spent a couple of productive hours where I gave them my own ideas. I was satisfied but I could see that there would be a power struggle between de Burgh and des Roches.

We left the next morning. I was touched at the parting. The King gave gifts to both William and myself. They were rings. He had had three made and they all had a dragon on them. They were to commemorate the Welsh War. He gave each of the men at arms a dagger with a dragon upon it. Finally, he embraced both William and myself. I had never heard of any King who did that. I too was touched.

As we headed north William told me about some of the conversations they had had. "He was determined to reward us and he liked the idea of the symbolism of the dragon. It represents Wales and yet it is a mystical beast. He was going to have one made for Alfred but he did not like Sir Jocelyn."

"Sir Jocelyn? I thought he was a fine knight!"

"He may be but the King was a little jealous that my brother gave more time to Sir Jocelyn than to him. Also, Sir Jocelyn seemed to ignore the King."

I had not thought about that but on reflection, I realised it was true. I had been so concerned with the war that I had not noticed that. My youngest son, like the King, had also grown!

Chapter 15
A time of peace

The journey home did not pass quickly enough for me. As we passed through the towns on the Great North Road I sensed that there was more who were happy with the King than there had been but there were still parts of the land where barons, who had grown used to rebellion, still thought that they could oppose the rule of the King. My work was not done but, for a time, I could enjoy some time with my family and my people. The castles we stayed in reflected that. The lord of Knebworth, the Lady of Lincoln both confirmed that there was a little less unrest because of the King's actions. They had seen that he was a king who could go to war and to win.

I enjoyed the company of William. My men at arms and Egbert were as familiar to me as my mail but William was something new. He had been a boy when Alfred had been knighted and he had almost insinuated himself to become my squire. It was a measure of his skill that I barely noticed the change from Alfred to him. His time with the King had brought out a side of him I had not expected. He matured before my eyes. He could talk to my men at arms and servants with the same ease as he conversed with a king and they all held him in the same esteem. I had two sons in whom I could be proud and I would ensure that unlike me when I was little more than William's age, they would have a future. They would have land which was guaranteed and could not be taken away on the whim of a king. It was in the interests of my family that King Henry become a successful king. I found myself looking forward to watching them grow. They would be able to take over from me. William would make a good knight and now that Alfred might soon be a father he would have his own dynasty to lead.

Henry Youngblood came to me at Lincoln. We stayed in the castle. We were both welcomed there and familiar with it. While most of the men enjoyed the pleasures of the town, after we had eaten, Henry asked to speak with me privately. I was more than happy to do so but I wondered why. The constable, Nichola de la Haie, gave us a small antechamber for our discussion. She was a fine woman. She was the only female constable and yet she was far more resolute than the feckless Earl of Chester.

"Lord it is not a meaty matter. I have served you since the Holy Land. I have been proud to do so. I confess I grow weary of travelling the country and after the wound to Ralph of Appleby and Harry son of John I fear for my mortality. You need younger warriors to follow your banner. I would continue to serve you, lord, but I would if you would have me, be castellan of Stockton."

I was relieved. His words had sounded as though he was leaving me, "I feared you would leave my service!"

"Never lord. it is just that I have a family now. I have grandchildren. They are but a year and fourteen months old but I have barely seen them. I know that one day the Good Lord will take me. I would spend as much time with them, before my time on earth is done, as I could. I want them to remember their grandfather. I missed my own children growing up. I can make up for that with my grandchildren." He paused, "I hope you are not angry."

I clapped him about the shoulder. The constable had left a jug of wine and two goblets. "Of course, not and your words echo the thoughts which have been in my head too. Come let us drink together as two old comrades. You are right to do as you do. Who knows I may already have grandchildren and will feel the same as you do."

He took the proffered goblet and shook his head, "You, lord, have little choice in what you do. You cannot resign your title. I could not be a lord for the responsibilities would weigh too heavy. I admire you more than you can know." He raised his goblet. "Here is to the last twenty years."

"Aye, much blood has flowed but we are still together."

The wine tasted good. "Ridley the Giant could do as I do but I fear that, like me, soon he may wish to stay at home."

"Who knows, King Henry may be a king who does not need us."

"With the Earl Marshal dead, lord, he will need you and your men more than ever. It is good that David of Wales is married to his bow. He seems happy to leave his family at home. He will continue to be your captain of archers." I wondered about that. Would David of Wales relinquish his title and position too? I would not blame him but I would miss him as I would miss Henry Youngblood.

The journey north saw me in a reflective mood. I thought my life would stay the same once King John was dead. I was wrong. I had to look at what I did and make a life that would suit all. My wife was patient and forbearing but she saw little of me. I had come to know my son on campaign but what of Isabelle and Rebekah? Did I know them? How would they and their children remember me? By the time we reached the ferry, at Thornaby, I had decided to make the most of each moment with my family and my land. I would be called away again but, until then, I would be Thomas, lord of the manor of Stockton.

It was late afternoon when we arrived but my son and the rest of my men had arrived many days earlier and a watch had been kept for me. Consequently, I was greeted by a wharf full of people from my wife down to Tam the Hawker. They seemed pleased to see me and I was touched. When I saw Matilda, I saw that she was with child. I would have a grandchild. My heart filled with joy. For some reason, I felt close to tears and I knew not why. I was a warrior and warriors did not weep.

I was greeted as a conquering hero and yet I had done little. The two battles we had fought had never been in doubt. My wife hugged me and kissed me. She whispered in my ear, "You are to be a grandfather!"

220

I laughed, "Even an old warrior knows that Matilda has not just been overeating. When is the child due?"

"The child should be born soon."

"And Rebekah?"

My wife shook her head, "God has not blessed them with a child yet. She and Sir Geoffrey are at Elton. They have finished their hall and live there now." She smiled. "They will be trying for a child. Tonight, we eat simply but I will send for Sir Edward and Sir Fótr as well as Sir Geoffrey to attend a celebration tomorrow night. We should have a feast to toast your safe return. Our son and his wife have only waited for your swift arrival. They will head to Seamer the day after the feast. Matilda is anxious to make her new hall into a home." She turned to William. "Come, my son, for you have grown and your brother and Sir Jocelyn have been telling me that you are now close friends with a King! Let me hug you before you become too important!"

Isabelle rushed to me and threw herself into my arms, "My father, the hero!" Her arms squeezed me tightly. She said, in my ear, "Alfred has told me of some of the things that you did. It is not necessary to be the hero of Arsuf every day of your life! Let others take the risks too."

As she drew away I said, "A man cannot change the way he is."

She nodded, "I will have the wine ready when you reach the castle." She laughed. Her laugh was like tinkling water. "You still have many people to greet!"

Alfred and his wife approached, "Congratulations!" I clasped his arm

Alfred looked happy. "Victories, treasure and a child! I am truly blessed. You left the King safe?"

"As safe as any man surrounded by bookkeepers. We have made a start, my son and now it is up to the Council to teach him politics and diplomacy. I am happy that he knows how to fight a battle. Sir Robert is a good knight." I looked around. "Where is Sir Jocelyn?"

"He and his squire, along with his men, rode out to Seamer. We were unsure when you would return and he and his squire said that they would ensure that the work was moving on apace." He laughed, "If I did not know better then I would say that he had a woman somewhere. He kept sneaking off in Wales and came back smelling as though he had been with a woman." He shrugged, "Bachelor knights eh? They plough where they will!"

"He is a good knight. I had hoped he might become one of the King's men."

We began to walk back to the castle. "He wishes to learn about you and how you rule this valley. He spoke of nothing but you on the journey home. He asked about the most minute detail of your routine. Edward tired of it and told him to shut up!" Alfred laughed. Edward never changes."

I shook my head, "There is nothing remarkable about me."

"That is what Sir Edward said. He became cross when Sir Jocelyn began to ask about your favourite rides. I confess I did not understand the reason. You seem to be an obsession for him. Still, that is why he has come here to learn how to be more like you. I suppose that he has to study every detail of you."

Matilda giggled, "And Isabelle will not be unhappy that he stays close by. I think she likes him."

"Ah, and Sir Jocelyn? Does he return the feelings?"

Alfred shrugged, "He only seems to have an interest in you and becoming the best knight that he can be. And, as I say, there may be a woman he has secreted." We entered my inner bailey. "He knows that he will never inherit the Gower. He made enough coin in the campaign to have money but he wishes to be a lord of a manor. I think he hopes that you will give him one."

"He would be better served following the King. I will speak with him when he returns."

It was a cosy meal that we enjoyed. Only Rebekah was absent. It was good to have my family around me. My wife and Isabelle gave me all the news from the manor. They knew who had died, which mothers had given birth; who had become parents. They told me of new families coming to the town and the manor. It was a litany of trivia and yet a relief after looking at lists of dead warriors. I had not lost any men save Harry son of John but other lords had. De Clare and de Braose had lost loyal knights and warriors. I knew myself what it was like to lose oathsworn. There was a pang of guilt for you knew that you had led them into battle.

My wife, Matilda and Isabelle retired before my sons and I. Matilda was tired. Isabelle had no Jocelyn to admire and my wife, well, I think she went to prepare our bed.

Alfred spoke and I knew why he had kept this news for the three of us alone. "When we came through Skipton we spoke with the lord there. He told us some disturbing news." I looked at him. "It seems we did not manage to account for all of Sir Hugh's men. Some must have escaped for there was mischief after we had left for Wales. He sent to Sir Ralph for help and they discovered the remains of the camp they had used. They are fled."

I nodded, "We knew that from the four men we hired."

William said, "Surely, they are just brigands. They can cause no more trouble."

I remembered the letter. I told my sons about it. "Sir Hugh had a son. It seems clear to me that that reprobate of a baron wished to leave something to his son. Who knows what message he sent to him. If there was a son then they may have found him. If they joined him then they would seek vengeance or perhaps the manor."

Alfred shook his head, "The son can have no claim on the land and the men would be hanged as bandits."

My son had missed the point, "Alfred, that is not the danger. We are the reason that this unknown son lost a father. I killed him and we hanged his squire. Vengeance may be on his mind."

"Then we will be vigilant. My little brother is little no longer. He is almost a man grown. He can watch your back and your men at arms can smell a villain!"

I nodded but I could feel the hairs on the back of my neck prickling.

I rose early. My wife had made my welcome complete when I had returned to my chamber. I woke feeling like a new man. The sense of menace I had felt the night before was gone thanks to my wife's tender embraces. After I had spoken with Geoffrey I left to ride to the home of Ridley the Giant. He had a farm which lay to the north of my town. It was close to the Oxbridge and stood on a piece of high land. He had a fine view of Hartburn woods. My people all rose earlier than those in my castle and I was greeted by all that I passed. It made me feel part of the manor again. Once I crossed the bridge the land rose to the hall on the hill.

Marguerite, his wife, loved the farm. She was Swedish and their life on a farm in that cold northern land had been hard. Here in England, it was easier and she loved the variety of crops they could raise. Ridley was away so much that it was she who was the farmer and Ridley's success in war meant that they never had to rely on the success of what they grew. His two daughters and their husbands lived on the farm with them. The two men had been warriors but preferred the life of a farmer. It suited Ridley for he was no farmer. Even as I rode up I saw him stripped to the waist and hewing logs. He was still preparing for war. The axe he swung was a weapon even though his actions were peaceful.

"Good morning lord. You are up and about early!"

"As are you." I dismounted and Alf, one of his sons in law, took my horse to water her. "I thought to speak with you privately."

He swung the axe to embed it in the log. "This sounds ominous, lord."

"Not really. Henry Youngblood spoke to me. He tires of war and wishes to see his grandchildren grow. He will be the castellan for me. I thought to ask you to lead my men at arms." I added, hurriedly, "If you wish to spend more time with your family then I would understand."

He grinned with relief. "I would be honoured. I thought I had done something wrong."

I shook my head. "There is one thing, however, Hugh of Craven had men who escaped. I fear they may wish to make mischief in my land. Keep a good watch for strangers eh? Your farm has a good aspect."

"Aye lord. I still worry about Harry son of John."

I stroked my beard and told him my suspicions.

"You may be right. Morag was a sneaky bitch. We will watch for a woman too." He poured a pail of water over his sweating body. "Then we are home for a while?"

"We are. I hope to see my first grandchild born before we go to war once more."

"Then as the new leader of your men at arms, I will assign two warriors to watch you."

"That will not be necessary, Ridley."

He looked at me seriously, "Lord all of us owe all that we have to you. Robert of Newton and Sam Strongarm are young. They have no families. They can watch over you and both can help Master William practise the art of being a knight."

For some reason, as I rode back to Stockton I felt happier. I had too much to live for and the thought of a knife in the night ending that was too much. My wife was keen to make this a celebration to remember. Anya and Brigid, the two young girls rescued from Sir Hugh's clutches, had not left my castle. Aunt Ruth was still helping with their recovery but they were much happier these days. Nanna looked after Matilda but Aunt Ruth and my wife used the girls, who had become young women, as almost ladies in waiting. They helped to organise everything and it was they who greeted me when I returned to my hall. "Your lady wife said that you should send riders to invite your knights and their families for the feast."

"Yes, lord, she was insistent that you should do so as soon as you returned."

I smiled for I could hear the tone my wife would have used. She would have been annoyed that I had ridden abroad before sending riders. "Tell her I will do so." They were about to turn away when a thought came to me. "Are you able to speak of your time with Sir Hugh yet? If not then I will understand."

The one called Anya nodded, "We have cried away the pain of those times. Lady Ruth told us how to deal with those memories. We can speak but not, I pray, of the horror we endured."

"I would not know that. I cannot conceive how a man can do what he did. Did Sir Hugh have a son?"

"He had no wife, lord. No woman would be able to abide living with him. There was no son."

"And there was none who visited him, perhaps in the last year before I came?"

"No sir… oh I forget myself." Anya looked at Brigid. "Those hooded men who came. Who were they?"

Brigid said, "I know not." She looked at me. "It was more than six months before you rescued us lord and not long after the Lady Matilda was brought to Skipton. Three hooded men arrived late one night. One was a servant for he slept in the stable and they were gone by dawn."

"You did not hear their names nor see their faces?"

"No lord but the reason I remember them was because Sir Hugh did not send for us that night. We had a night where we were not…"

I held up my hand, "I would not ask more save this. Were they old or young?"

They looked blankly at me and then Anya said, "One wore mail and had spurs."

"Aye, and they both had swords but their hoods covered their faces."

"Thank you." As I headed to the warrior hall I reflected that I knew more now than I had done. I would ask Sir Ralph if there had been a knight amongst the men he had hunted.

I sent riders to invite my lords and then went to the Great Hall. There were duties and responsibilities I had neglected whilst being on campaign. There were trials to arrange. I would need to hold a courts baron. I would need to inspect the archers when they met at St. John's well for their Sunday practice. My priest, Father Harold, would have notice of births, deaths and marriages which I would need. Many lords simply allowed their steward to perform these acts. I was not one of those. It brought me close to the people.

Geoffrey, Father Harold and myself spent what remained of the morning going through all that I needed to know and, more importantly, to do. My wife ended the meeting by shooing away the priest and my steward, "Come, it is time for food and I need time with my husband too!"

They backed away and I was left with my wife. I sighed for I knew that she would not have asked the two men to leave unless she had something important to tell me. "Yes, wife, what is it? If it is Isabelle and her infatuation with Sir Jocelyn then I know."

She waved a hand, "That is nothing. He is handsome and young. He is not the man for our daughter. He is pleasant enough but she will get over him. This is more important. The keep is no longer large enough for us. We now have Anya and Brigid living here. Soon we will have grandchildren and I would have them stay with us. Babies and young children require a great deal of space."

I was relieved. This was a problem with which I could deal. "We could build an annex in the bailey but that would make that area crowded."

"No, there is enough there already."

"Then we build upwards." We had a square keep. There were four small towers. They were really turrets. My keep had just two floors and a cellar. The proximity of the river meant that when there was flooding then the cellar filled with water and one year the Great Hall had been flooded. "We build two floors and move the Great Hall upstairs. This can be divided up into chambers. I will take this opportunity to increase the size of one tower. I have a mind to have a solar as my father did." I looked at my wife. She looked disappointed. "What is wrong my love?"

"I expected an argument. I thought you would complain about the expense."

"The expense is nothing but I must write to the King to ask permission. The extra floors are not a problem but if I am to build a tower then that might be deemed an aggressive act. I do not want to give other barons the opportunity to use me as an example. Does my idea meet with your approval? I know that there might be flooding in a bad winter but you do not want young children to have a great number of stairs to negotiate."

"It is an acceptable risk. I feared it might impair your ability to defend the castle."

"We have good gatehouses. As we will be buying stone and having a mason employed then I will have a barbican built at the south gate. It will be a more imposing entrance. I also thought to have a church built for the town to use. The one inside the castle is too small. Little more than our chapel it is barely large enough for the garrison. I thought to have one built on the high ground overlooking the common and St. John's well. I will speak with Father Harold. It would mean another priest."

She came to me and kissed me, "You are a constant surprise. Here was I expecting an argument and you have already come up with more ideas than I. When did you think of these improvements?"

"When I travel I do not just fight. I have eyes and I look. I have stayed in many castles and halls. Most are worse but some are better and I have looked at those. After we have eaten I will seek out Walter the Mason. I dare say he will be grateful for the work."

"And the coin?"

"I brought back a chest and we have more in the strong room. I have enough." It was true that I had plenty of gold for I had worked hard as a sword for hire to make profit. I used money to hire men but that was my only expense. My farms were profitable and the taxes from my town brought me a good income.

I found my mason with his labourers. Cedric the Chandler was reaping the benefit of increased trade along the river. After a long voyage, north ships often needed to buy new tackle and sails. Being based by the river he needed sturdy foundations. He was having a stone quay and workshop built upstream from the castle and the wharf. It was close enough for me to walk there.

"Walter."

They all stopped. The men all gave a bow. "Yes, lord?"

"I will not keep your mason long, Cedric. I have work for him."

Cedric would pay good coin but I was the Earl! Walter wiped his hands on his apron and pick up his wax tablet. I was not sure that he could read but he understood his own marks. "Yes lord. I have nearly finished the work for Cedric. It will be time for the carpenters and joiners next. What do you require, my lord?"

I led him back to the castle. I heard Cedric bark at the men to continue working. Time was money to Cedric. I pointed out what we wanted. He listened as I went through all the work. He could see the site for the church, the barbican and the extension. He scribbled his marks on his wax tablet. To me they made as much sense as the marks I had seen the Egyptians use on their temples but he seemed to understand them. He sucked a deep breath and scratched his ear, "It will be expensive lord."

I laughed, "I am not a fool, Walter. I know that it will cost gold. You are a good mason and, if you wish to continue to work in my town then you will not rob me. Whatever it costs I will pay."

He shook his head, "I would not dream of robbing you, lord. It is just that it is such a big job that I will have to employ other masons and their labourers."

"Good for I want the work to begin as soon as possible."

"I will send word to the other masons and I can begin work four days from now. I can start on the foundations for the church and the barbican. The keep will need to wait for the stone to arrive."

"Good. Come to my hall on the morrow before you begin work for Cedric and I will have silver for your expenses. Could you do a drawing so that I may see what it is like?"

"Of course, lord and you can change it to whatever design you like. This will be good for my sons. They are both apprentices and I want them to see how to build a church. One day we may build an abbey or a cathedral."

"I doubt that there will be one in Stockton."

"The way your town grows, lord, who knows."

By the time I began to prepare for the feast I was weary. I could fight a battle all day and still not feel fatigued but my mind felt as though it had been invaded by bees. Egbert had a bath ready for me. "Are you a mind reader, Egbert?"

"No lord, Lady Margaret said you would need one." He picked up a jar, "She gave me some rose and rosemary oil too, lord."

I laughed, "Then I must have impressed her." As he undressed me I said, "Thank for all that you did on the campaign. You had three of us to watch over."

"I enjoyed it, lord. I have no family of my own and Master William and Sir Alfred are like sons to me. It does not seem that long ago since they were racing around the hall playing with wooden swords and now they converse with kings and fight England's enemies. You must be proud."

"I am, Egbert, I am. Now that I am to be a grandfather I can watch a young family grow once more."

He laughed, "Without the sleepless nights lord!"

Egbert cut my unruly hair and trimmed my beard while I bathed. He used a strigil to scrape the dirt from my skin and then, after I had been dried, he oiled my hair and body. I felt like a new man. As he did so we talked. "Tell me Egbert what do you make of Sir Jocelyn?" He was silent. "Come Egbert, he is a guest in my hall and I do not ask for gossip. I value your opinion."

"I confess that I do not like him." He sighed, "Servants are invisible lord. Men, you and your sons apart, do not see them. It means that they can see all. They can see the smile which disappears when someone turns. They can see the clenched fists. Sir Jocelyn feigns friendship but I fear that he seeks a position."

I was surprised. The servant agreed with the king! "Feigns friendship?"

"Aye lord, I am sorry to say so but it was you, Sir Alfred and Master William who were given the false smiles. I think he is here for a manor and I like neither his servant nor his men. The servants all got on and helped each other when we served in Wales. The King's were as friendly as any. Sir Jocelyn's kept apart. He seemed more like one of those cutthroats Sir Jocelyn calls men."

The words '*cutthroats*' were alarming, "Thank you for your honesty. Keep a good watch on him for me eh? I can see that I have been blind and preoccupied."

While I had been away my wife had had the seamstresses make a new tunic for me. The material was light. It would not be robust enough for a campaign but would be comfortable at a feast. I donned it.

When I reached the hall, Rebekah ran to greet me. She hugged me, "Thank you for keeping my husband safe."

"It was the other way around. Your brothers, husband and my other knights all guarded my back. My task is easy knowing that I have such men behind me." I saw that my knights had all arrived with their wives and their families. The silence which had greeted my arrival was now replaced by a buzz of conversation. I took the wine from the servant and then saw that Robert of Newton and Sam Strongarm were waiting patiently in the corridor. I turned, "Ridley has spoken with you?"

"Aye lord and we are happy to be your bodyguards. Geoffrey has found us a chamber in the west tower. It is more comfortable than the warrior hall. We will watch your room at night."

"You have no need, Sam."

"It will not be a problem, lord. We can divide the night into watches. We have no other duties unless we are on campaign. It is good. We will, with your permission, go to our room and rest. You should be safe enough at the feast."

I laughed, "I should be safe enough in my bed."

Robert lowered his voice, "Lord, Captain Ridley does not do this on a whim. When we were at Emlyn Mordaf heard Welsh voices threatening your life because of the humiliation their King endured. The Welsh are nasty lord! They would slit a man's throat over a dirty look. We will watch!"

I had known of the threats but dismissed them. I had been threatened often and so far, none had even come close to ending my life. There were Scots who had sworn to kill me. I had no doubt that Sir Hugh's men and his son wished me a grisly end. I did not fear them. I would take my chances. I

231

returned to the Great Hall. It was a celebratory mood. I saw that Sir Jocelyn had returned and my daughter was trying to attract his attention. She had yet to learn the subtle art of wooing. I confess that I was a stranger to it. Her mother and I had, had been thrown into a romantic situation. After Egbert's words I would view Sir Jocelyn a little closer and with a more critical eye. I wondered if his rejection of my daughter Isabelle was also colouring my judgement. Sir Jocelyn saw me and strode over. There was hurt in Isabelle's eyes as he ignored her.

"Earl, you have a fine castle and a fine land. I hear that you intend to improve the castle?"

"Aye with grandchildren on the way it will not be big enough. Already we have outgrown the home I built when first I erected the keep." I remembered that King John had forbidden me to build a keep and I had to be circumspect and crafty when designing it. I had built a hall but I built one which could be easily converted to a keep. When I had captured King William of Scotland then King John had given me permission to build a keep. I just converted the hall. I added crenulations and turrets. By the time I had fitted a fighting platform then it was a defensible keep.

"I had hoped that my squire and I could stay here with you. I have much to learn. There look to be many manors which need a lord."

Now I saw the truth in Egbert's words. He wished to stay in my hall and for me to give him a manor. I did not like to be used and, as I saw my daughter's face I said, "I fear it would be too overcrowded for when the work begins we will have even less room. Stay with my son or my daughter. Sir Geoffrey is but a couple of miles up the road. There is much you could learn from him."

There was a little anger as well as disappointment in his eyes. But his mouth formed a smile, "No matter. I will rise each day and come here to Stockton. If I can take your lessons back to my uncle then we can make the Marches as safe as the northern border."

"I never take such things for granted. The Scots could rise at any time. There are lords who live close by here who can flaunt the rule of law and I have to deal with them too. The moment you relax your vigilance is when you lose."

Sir Fótr had moved closer and heard the last part, "Aye, Sir Jocelyn. Last year we had a knight at Skipton who behaved most abominably towards Sir Alfred's wife, Matilda. Then she was not his wife. It was only Sir Thomas' prompt action which saved the girls held there."

Sir Jocelyn still seem preoccupied with his accommodation for he ignored Fótr's words. He looked to be thinking about something else for his face darkened.

"What I will promise, Sir Jocelyn, is to take you on a tour of the castles. You have begun to make good castles but as Emlyn, Carmarthen and Caerphilly fell easily then I think you have much work to do."

The smile returned and I saw that Egbert had been right about the mask, "Thank you, lord."

The entrance of Sir Geoffrey and Rebekah ended our conversation. I had liked Sir Jocelyn but he seemed obsessive. It was as though he wanted to be the shadow of either my son or me. Now that I knew his real motive I regretted my decision to bring him north.

My wife was delighted with the party for it was joyous. The only cloud was my daughter Isabelle's disappointment in the lack of attention Sir Jocelyn paid her. As Margaret said, when we cuddled, "It would not have hurt him to smile at her." I wondered if he was shy and did not want to encourage her. He could, on the other hand, have been one of those men who liked other men. Most joined a religious order. Then I realised that he might have a woman already in mind. Perhaps he was already married and that would explain the woman Alfred suspected was close by. There were women who followed armies. It would explain much.

The next day I took my men out to Elton. Sir Geoffrey had built a hall and there was room for Sir Jocelyn, his squire and his servant but there was no warrior hall, no bakery, no stables, in fact, none of the buildings which a lord of the manor needed. We used my archers and men at arms as labourers and, by the end of the day had a stable erected. It doubled as a warrior hall for one night. Sir Jocelyn had helped us to build. Like the rest of us, he was stripped to the waist. As we sluiced off the sweat he said, "Is this not a waste of time for warriors and archers?"

"On the contrary, it helps them to work together. They share a common goal. Their bodies will be all the better for this different type of exercise and besides, it was for fellow warriors and my daughter."

He donned his surcoat, "Now I begin to see how you have built such loyalty." He pointed to Sam and Robert, "Those two follow your every move. Such loyalty!"

"Ridley has decided that they will be my bodyguards. There have been threats against my life. It is probably the Welsh or the Scots. I do not fear such threats but I would hate for someone I loved to be hurt as a consequence of an attack on me."

Even as we were busy building new rooms for the grandchildren Rebekah brought us the good news that she was with child. My world was becoming more complete each day. The news spurred on my men to work even harder.

It took a week to complete the buildings. In that time Walter and his men had begun the foundations for my barbican and church. Father Harold worked closely with the mason. It would be a marriage of the builder and the priest. Time seemed to fly as we all pitched in with the work. During this time, we heard that Hubert de Burgh and the King had managed to defeat some of the lords who had still to accept Henry as King. It seemed I might not be needed and that pleased me. The King had told me that he intended to use our lessons well and he had made a good beginning.

It came as a real shock to me when my son and his wife arrived at my castle. Matilda was in a litter. My son looked nervous. "The midwife says that the baby will be born soon."

My wife said to Matilda, "The baby is in the right position?"

"Aye!"

"Come we will get you to bed and fetch the women! Anya, Brigid!" They scurried off.

234

He shrugged, "They speak a language I do not understand. I thought to have my child born here in Stockton. You have a doctor and healers. I just have a priest."

"You need not apologise. We are delighted. Your mother and Aunt Ruth as well as Nanna, Anya and Brigid will all be on hand to help the bairn into this world."

As soon as my wife and the other women disappeared with Matilda then all thoughts of the building work evaporated. The men were forgotten. All was about Matilda. The only one who seemed put out was Jocelyn. I suspected it was because none of us had any time to continue with his education. He left, with his squire, to ride through my woods and explore my land. We had more important matters to deal with. I took my son to view my building work. He was not particularly interested but it kept his mind from his wife. When her cries rang through my castle he reacted like a rabbit hunted by an owl. He froze and stared at me.

"Son, this is women's work. You would not blanch on a battlefield but you are now in an unknown land. Nanna and my wife know what they do. Trust them." He nodded. I took him around the foundations explaining to him where the various buildings would be and what they would look like. I was just filling the silence and keeping the fears from terrorising his mind. The labour went on all through a long afternoon and into the night. I noticed that even my men at arms were becoming nervous. They could cope with men screaming in battle as they were eviscerated but young woman's pitiful cries were too much. It was with great relief that the screams stopped and Aunt Ruth came out to speak with us. "You have a son, Alfred, and he is healthy. Do you have a name?"

"We have two. He shall be Henry Samuel. Henry is a lucky name for the best kings our family have served have been called Henry and Samuel." He looked at me, "He is named for the grandfather I never knew."

I did not get to hold Henry Samuel until the next day. I had forgotten how fragile they were and I feared to hold him too tight. Aunt Ruth and my wife were delighted. Rebekah and Isabelle looked at their first nephew. All were touched.

He was healthy and had all of his parts. The birth seemed to inspire my town and my castle. Despite the lengthening nights and the end of autumn, there was hope and excitement in the air. Instead of dwelling upon the doom and the gloom of impending winter, we all looked forward to Christmas. The work on the gate and the church showed progress and, a week before Christmas I received permission to improve my castle. In truth, we had begun to do so already. The treadmill crane was already in place.

Christmas was the best that I could remember. A helpless child seemed appropriate. All grew closer together. Isabelle's sadness at the lack of interest demonstrated by Jocelyn de Braose was offset by the joy of a baby. Jocelyn and his men chose to visit Gower over Christmas. I think he resented the lack of attention. We barely noticed that he was gone.

We had not had a wolf winter the previous year but, beginning on St Stephen's Day, we had a deep freeze followed by a snowstorm which lasted three days. No one could leave the castle. The river froze. We had a month of such weather before a slight thaw came and I was able to ride my land and give succour to the people who lived in isolated farms. We were lucky that we had had a good harvest and no one died save a couple of old men who lived alone. It was sad but the price was less than we might have expected. By the time Jocelyn de Braose returned, in a much happier frame of mind, the snow had turned to slush and the worst was over. Rebekah was growing larger each day and, despite the conditions, our men worked to finish all of the buildings at her manor. When Matilda was with child again we could not believe our good fortune. I would have three grandchildren!

All the joy dissipated at the beginning of April. I had hoped to be there for the birth of Rebekah's child but a summons came from the Council. We were needed further south. All peaceful means to end the stand-off at Bedford Castle had failed. We would go to war once more. We had to say goodbye and both Geoffrey and Alfred were distraught. The King called and we went.

Chapter 16
The Siege of Bedford

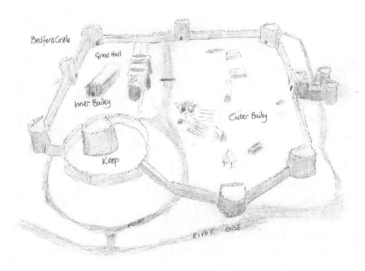

Bedford Castle was a mighty castle. Sir Falkes de Breauté had been given the castle by King John but instead of supporting his son, King Henry, the knight had decided to defy all. He had attempted to capture the Tower of London but King Henry's new defences had proved too strong and my protégé had shown himself to be a leader. Hubert de Burgh had demanded that Sir Falkes de Breauté give up his castle and he had refused. The castle was now defended by his brother, William, with more than a hundred knights of a similar frame of mind. This would not be a rapid victory like Caerphilly and Carmarthen. A siege was bloody!

As we headed south Alfred and Geoffrey were silent. Their silence was more than compensated for by the eagerness of Jocelyn de Braose. He threw question after question at me as we headed south. "But surely with the might of the King and England behind us the castle will fall quickly, Earl!"

"The castle which stands against the King is one of the strongest castles in England. The River Ouse is a barrier and it has been diverted to make a moat. No matter which direction we attack we have to cross the river. There is one huge outer bailey and a small inner one. If we breached the outer wall then archers and crossbows on the high walls of the inner bailey and the keep would decimate any men we sent. The keep is round and they are the hardest to mine. This will be a castle which is only taken by men climbing ladders and doing battle. It will not be easy, Sir Jocelyn."

Surprisingly he did not seem deterred by my warning. "William told me of the attack on Skipton where you used subterfuge and trickery. Could you not do that again?"

"Skipton was built on rocks and we were fortunate that there was a tunnel. I will not be sending my sons up ladders at Bedford. I will be leading my men for we have done this before."

"Then you will be in the greatest danger."

"Where else should a leader be?"

"Then I will be behind you for I would emulate you in all that you do."

I saw the camp spread out before the town. It seemed to envelop the houses. The keep of the castle rose high above the town. There was nowhere to place an engine that would be higher than the keep. It was well designed. When we reached the castle, I saw that the King was there with Sir Robert, his men and Hubert de Burgh. They were not the surprise. It was the number of men I saw around the walls. There were more than two thousand men and more were trooping in from the west even as we arrived. I heard the sounds of hammers and sawing long before I saw the camp. This was not just warriors. King Henry had employed guildsmen! There was no sound of battle. We dismounted as the King approached.

In the time I had been away the King had grown both in confidence and in size. He would never be a giant but he now looked like a man. I saw that he led and Sir Hubert followed. Stephen Langton, the forceful Archbishop of Canterbury hurried behind. The King clasped my arm, "Earl! You have come!"

"As I promised!"

He nodded, "And with your sons and knights then we can prosecute this siege and bring it to a swift conclusion." He turned to James of Corfe, "James, take the Earl and his men to their campsite. I will speak with you later, Earl. I have much to tell you."

He bustled off with the Chancellor and Archbishop in tow. James of Corfe smiled, "Much of the change you see is down to you, lord. He learned to command while watching you in Wales. Come this way, lord. He watched you all the time while we campaigned in the Marches and he saw how you dealt with the Marcher lords. He uses the same method with the Council. I think they are taken aback by the change you have wrought. We have fought battles too. They were not on the scale of the ones in Wales but the King has defeated those who tried to take his tower and he has captured some smaller castles which have held against him."

I saw that men were building a couple of trebuchets, two mangonels and a cat, a battering ram. I saw men from all over England. This was not just the fyrd. I saw that skilled workers were building the war machines. There were stacks of crossbow bolts. I knew that would annoy my archers but the King must have realised he could not find enough archers. The crossbows could keep up a steady rate of bolts but they would not be as effective as archers. It would be my archers who would be the ones to clear the walls.

We reached a spot some four hundred paces from the north wall. "Here, my lord, the King kept this space close to his own. He would have you nearby. I had best return." He lowered his voice, "There have been threats of assassins. We

239

keep men close by the King at all times. Either Sir Robert or myself sleeps across his tent entrance each night."

I turned to Egbert and Ridley. "Put our tents here. Have the men find the wood for their hovels quickly for it looks like the carpenters intend taking every tree and branch they can find. I would have my knights in their tents around mine."

Alfred asked, "You fear assassins too?"

"The Welsh have not forgotten me and there are still the men of Sir Hugh who are at large. The confusion of a siege would be a perfect place for a knife in your back or Sir Fótr's."

"Why us?"

"You were the ones who gained us entrance to the castle. I did not say it was right but in the twisted minds of those who followed Sir Hugh, it would make sense. Sir Edward, Sir William, Sir Geoffrey and Sir Peter can watch over you."

My son said, "I need no nursemaids! Let an assassin come and he will rue the day."

"Son, you have one child and are going to have another soon. I know that I will take all the precautions I can for I want to see my grandchildren grow. That is why I have Sam and Robert sleeping in my tent. If your father takes such measures then I feel you should too."

Jocelyn de Braose said, "My squire and I will act as chamberlains!" He laughed, "It will save us being on the edge of this assembly of knights!"

Alfred laughed too, "Very well but I should warn you that Henry my squire makes more wind than a field full of cows!"

Alan the Horse Master had come with us and he found a field which was close to our camp. The horses would have grazing and water and yet would be safe from the noise of battle. By the time night fell we were organised. The men had fires going and food was cooking. We would settle into a routine now. James of Corfe came for me, "Lord, the King would have you join him for food."

"Should I bring my knights?"

240

He shook his head, "You and he will be dining alone, lord. He wishes conference with you."

I nodded, "Edward take charge." As I left Sam rose and followed. I was now accustomed to having a permanent shadow. My two bodyguards were as unobtrusive as possible. We did not have far to go. The King's tent was less than fifty paces from my own. I saw that his guards had hovels and tents around the King's. Sir Robert was outside the tent which sported his standard. He was setting up two chairs. Two servants brought out a small folding table and laid food upon it.

"We have more comfort here than in Wales, lord. The King has busied himself to ensure that we eat better. We have timber from Northamptonshire; ropes from London, Cambridge and Southampton; hides from Northampton and tallow from London. Sheriffs have provided labourers. We might only have a thousand men to fight but there are fifteen hundred others labouring to bring this siege to a successful conclusion."

The King emerged, "You see Sir Thomas I watched not only what you did well in Wales but where it might be improved. We did not have to take any castles but I saw what was needed. Now sit. Have your man stand with James, out of earshot but close enough to intercept an assassin's blade. Sir Robert has already tasted the food and as he has not fallen foul of poison I think that we can eat."

Was this the same diffident boy who had had to wear his mother's crown at his hurried coronation? What a change had been wrought. I knew that I was only partly responsible but I felt proud of what I had achieved. It was nothing like the achievement of the Warlord but it would do. While we ate the King told me all. Falkes Breauté was not in the castle. He had left that under the command of his brother, William de Breauté. The two brothers were confident that a summons to Pope Honorius would result in a judgement forbidding King Henry from taking the castle. The result of that plea, although the defenders did not know it yet was that William had been excommunicated. The bad news was that the castle was garrisoned by knights and men at arms. It was well supplied and the moat was a major obstacle.

After we had eaten Henry brought out a wax tablet and sketched out his plan for the attack. It was well thought out. He would have a trebuchet and two mangonels hurling stones at the keep while a trebuchet and mangonel on each of the north and south sides would try to break through the walls of the outer bailey.

"You have thought this out well, your majesty."

He nodded, "When they tried to take the Tower I saw the problems they would have. This is the strongest castle in England. It is why they hold on to it for they believe it cannot fall. When it does then a message will be sent around my land that I rule and not my barons. I will reissue the Great Charter but only when Bedford has fallen."

"Good but you should know that we will lose more men than those who defend it."

"Then I will speak with them before we attack and give them the opportunity to surrender."

"And if they do not?"

His face was cold as he said, "Then all of them will be put to death!" It was obvious to me that the attack on London had more than just annoyed him. Sir Robert had told me that Falkes de Breauté had been involved in that attempt to usurp the King's authority. Although the slippery weasel had fled to another castle the King would make an example of him and those who followed him. It was necessary but I did not relish the prospect of a long and protracted siege.

"Where will you want my men?"

"The north wall, the one closest to the town. I can trust your men to behave themselves." We could see the walls. "There where the wall dividing the inner and our bailey runs. You may be close enough to the gate to have to endure missiles but it will divide their forces and we know that they do not have numbers of men. They have quality but not quantity. We will not try to breach the inner walls until the outer ones are secure. Their supplies are in the outer ward."

"You have thought this through well, King Henry!"

"I was already here when I sent my messenger for you. I have ridden around every inch of the walls. The river is our enemy and I can think of no way to defeat it."

I nodded, "You are probably right. This could take weeks, lord."

"I know but I want to win and we will stay as long as we have to."

We drank more of the wine. I noticed that we had fine goblets and the ham which we were nibbling was of the best quality. We were close enough to London for the King not to have to stint. "And the Council?"

A mischievous look came over his face, "I think I have their measure. Pandulf is not particularly interested in secular matters. So long as I agree to most of the religious requests then I have his support. Des Roches and de Burgh do not like each other. There are three of them so I can always win two to my side and marginalise the other. I have learned to do that without you, Earl."

"Such strategies are outside of my experience lord but I am pleased that you have more control and power. Use them wisely, sire."

"Do you chastise me, sir?"

I shook my head. "I have two sons and I would give them the same advice. It is meant well." I took the bull by the horns. "Your father had power but do you think he used it wisely?"

He drank and then shook his head, "But perhaps he was ill-served by lords who just sought land and power."

"Is that not the reason we are here? Falkes and his brother seek great power. Who knows, they may desire the throne."

"As does the Earl of Chester." He waved a hand, "Do not try to deny it. I know that he has gone to the Holy Land so that he cannot be associated with the unrest in my land but I know he is the cause and one day he will have to return. I have a long memory."

By the time I left the King to return to my camp then I think I understood him. Sam followed me back. "The King's guards are worried, lord, about an attempt to kill him. He has annoyed many powerful men and they do not relish him as a man grown with great power."

"Then we will have to watch for these enemies."

The next few days were spent establishing our siege lines. We dug ditches and made pavise and willow boards to protect us as we advanced. There were not many trees left but we found a couple which we made into a bridge for the moat. We would not need it for some time but it gave the men something to do. The mangonel and trebuchet were built in situ. They had a maximum range of three hundred paces but they were built just two hundred and fifty paces from the walls. We used pavise to protect the carpenters who built them. When the siege lines were built we still had to wait for the engines to be finished. To prevent our men becoming bored I had David of Wales and his archers see if they would hit any of the defenders. As most of the garrison was made up of mailed knights and men at arms it was unlikely that we would do much damage. However, it would weaken the resolve of the defenders and once the mighty machines began hurling eighty-pound stones at the walls that resolve would be severely tested.

The first killers were found before we had even started the assault. Our vigilance was rewarded by Robert, who was watching my tent while Sam slept across the doorway. He saw a shadow moving towards the tent. We had a daily password for my knights and Robert gave the first part. "Father."

When the reply came back "Mother" instead of 'Harold' then Robert drew his sword. The killer made the mistake of trying to fight Robert. He failed and paid for his failure with his life. Robert could not afford to take chances. When we searched the body, we found Welsh coins in his purse. That was not conclusive evidence but all Welshmen we did not know came under intense scrutiny from then on. Sir Jocelyn volunteered to help Robert and Sam but I declined. The knight was keen enough but he would be needed soon to assault the walls of Bedford Castle.

After two weeks and no further attempts on our lives, the trebuchets and mangonels were ready. The King gave

William de Breauté the opportunity to surrender. We crossed the river and spoke to the baron across the water. William de Breauté stood on the fighting platform of his keep.

"I give you one chance William de Breauté to surrender. We have your castle surrounded and tomorrow we begin to break down your walls. Surrender and you will live. Fight and you die. All of you will die."

"We have sent an appeal to the Pope, Henry of Winchester. He will judge in our favour."

"I am your King and you will address me as such!"

"You serve a council of regents. My brother and I do not recognise their authority. We cannot be guilty of treason for you are not yet King and, if we have our way, then you never shall be."

I could see the King becoming angrier and yet he kept his voice calm. "Then release your females. None of us can guarantee their safety in the heat of the battle."

I said, quietly, "He is playing for time, lord."

"I know and I have had enough of this play acting. William de Breauté will you surrender or will you die?"

"Our women will stay here for this castle will not fall! We will defend my brother's castle. Do your worst, boy, for this castle will not be taken!"

The last insult was a mistake. Any vestige of mercy was driven from King Henry's heart by the barb. He turned and led Hubert de Burgh, the Archbishop and myself back to the camp. William de Breauté had insulted the King and the Council. I wondered why the Archbishop and I had managed to avoid his ire. Hubert de Burgh said, as we headed back to our lines, "I have ordered extra men, King Henry, to watch our tents."

The King pointed at me. "It is the Earl of Cleveland who is in danger not I. There will come a time when men will seek my death but not until I attain my majority. I have a brother and he would simply replace me."

He was remarkably sanguine about the prospect of being murdered.

My camp was now as tightly guarded as it was possible. All of the knights, men at arms and archers who had

245

travelled from Cleveland were now of one mind. Woe betide any who crossed into our camp. Two men at arms from Oxford had been severely beaten when they made the mistake of passing too close to our lines. The word was spread and none would approach us after dark. We trusted each other. We knew each other. We had stood in shield walls and fought alongside each other. Here I was safe. It would be different once we ascended the ladders and began to fight with men who knew that failure meant death!

Carpenters and joiners had built the trebuchets and mangonels but it would be my men who loaded the machines and sent their stones towards the walls. The trebuchet worked by a counterweight. Padraig the Wanderer had an eye for such things and he would command the larger machine. His first missile would be for range. Once he had that he could adjust both the weight and the trajectory. The mangonel or traction trebuchet was slightly different. It required a team of men to pull it. While the counterweight trebuchet could send heavier stones and could keep sending missiles longer the mangonel was faster to reload but men tired. Until we actually assaulted the walls I would have my men at arms working in teams. Will Red Leg commanded the mangonel.

While some of the other war machines began releasing stones quickly my men were more measured. The machines were well built but others had built them. They checked each rope and joint before they loaded them. They chose the most rounded stones they could. That would be a true test of the machine. We saw one of the other teams sending stones over the walls and into the castle. There they would do no harm. When they adjusted their stones hit the moat. The stones were valuable and four were wasted by the other teams before they even struck the wall.

My men examined every part of the machines and stones. When they were satisfied Will Red Leg looked at Padraig and nodded. Padraig released the stone and it flew true. It struck the top of the parapet. It would take a lucky strike to hit a man. When a war machine cracked all those on the wall looked to the sky and a defender could easily move out of the way. The first stone nudged a stone from the top of the wall. Smaller splinters flew and then the stone careered into the castle. The hit was too high. Padraig adjusted his machine while Will Red Leg let fly with his first stone. He had the advantage of human power. He could remove or add men to give more accuracy. His stone hit six feet to the right of Padraig's but slightly lower.

He shouted to one of his crew, "James, we will not need you for the next strike. Reload!"

From now on they would send stones alternately. That way they would know the effect of their own strikes. The next one from the trebuchet was almost perfect. It hit halfway up the wall. To an onlooker, it would have appeared disappointing. There was neither crack in the wall nor movement. There was just a small cloud of dust. Padraig nodded in satisfaction. His stones would continue to pound away at the same point. The walls could be six or eight feet thick. He was aiming to damage the outer stones which would, in turn, disturb the small infill stones and, finally, the stones on the inner wall. Will Red Leg hit a little lower than Padraig but he too managed a cloud of dust. The two of them kept pounding away all morning. After ten hits Will added James to his team again and the stones hit where they had on the first strike. When we stopped for food the machines would be checked, ropes tightened and the team on the mangonel rotated.

King Henry and Sir Robert came in the early afternoon to view our hits. I pointed, "There is the smallest of cracks which rises up the wall. They will be shoring it up inside already."

"And that is good progress?"

I nodded, "Aye, sire. Tonight, we will hear hammering as they put beams in place. They have a finite amount of timber and when that is gone then they will be able to shore up no longer. It could take a week but we will have a breach and then we will have the outer bailey."

"You do not sound excited about the prospect, Earl."

"I am not for that means that they will have more men to guard a shorter perimeter. This siege must succeed but inevitably we will lose more men than those within."

Each day saw the crack widen. On the third day, the mangonel broke down and had to be repaired. However, we used the repair to use the men to load the trebuchet and our rate of stones remained the same. On the fifth day, one mighty stone from the trebuchet made a direct hit on the crack. The wall seemed to shiver and then the parapet tumbled down. Half fell into the moat and the other half into the outer bailey. My men all cheered. David and his archers managed to send arrows towards the men on the fighting platform as they were exposed. There were cries but we knew not if they had been killed or just wounded.

The success spurred my men on and they continued to shower the wall until it was too dark to see. We heard hammering which went on long into the night. Padraig came to me as I was about to retire. "Lord they are repairing the damage each night."

"I know but each day we grow closer to victory."

"They are using wood to shore up the damage."

"Aye." I could not see where Padraig was going with this.

"Wood burns. What if we made some incendiary missiles tomorrow, during the day. If we could fire the wood then that might be enough to bring down the wall."

"It is worth a try. Well done Padraig,"

He nodded, "We are keen to begone from here. The longer we stay the more chance those Welsh bastards have of slitting your throat! The sooner we get back to a civilised land the better."

My men took the threat to my life personally!

I told the King of our plan and he spent the afternoon with us. Each hit now brought down a stone. Some were larger than others. Dust filled the air. There was a small avalanche as a large stone tumbled to the moat and was followed by a flood of smaller infill stones. At the top of the wall, there was a gap of four paces. It narrowed to a hole the size of a man's head halfway down the wall. We would soon be in a position to assault the breach but only if they ceased repairing the wall. The last stone, as the sun was setting, was the most effective. It punched a hole in the wall and the gap at the top widened. While there was still a little light my archers sent arrow after arrow into the men trying to repair it.

The King was excited as my men brought out the ten missiles we had made. They were smaller stones than we usually used and they had been covered in material that would burn and bound with rope. They were soaked in oil and pig fat. He stood close to the machine. Padraig turned, "I would step back a little further, my lord. I would not have your whiskers singed."

The Archbishop was with us and I heard the intake of breath at the familiarity. Henry knew Padraig and he stepped back. Will Red Leg lit the soaked rope and even as it flamed Padraig sent it towards the castle. It struck the gap. There was an explosion of sparks and then flames. The second one was loaded and that arced its fiery way towards the wall. There was a scream when it hit. I guessed that a defender must have been trying to douse the flames of the first missile. Not all the fiery stones hit the same place but enough did to set fire to the timbers. The defenders might douse the flames but the timbers would be so damaged that our stones would breach them. I began to prepare my men for the assault.

Dawn brought a welcoming sight. There was a breach. The air was filled with the smell of smoke and tendrils still rose from the walls. I summoned David of Wales and Ridley the Giant. There was a tower to the right of the breach. That would cause us problems when we attacked.

"Aye, lord?"

"Ridley have the bridge we built brought up. David, I intend to make life unpleasant for those in the tower. Keep their heads down while we do so."

"Aye lord."

I had Padraig and Will realign their war machines. "I would have you aim for the tower. You have a bigger target and you know your machines. I want the fighting platform a charnel house. You do not need to bring this one down just make it impossible for them to use."

"Aye lord."

I gathered my knights and squires. "We have to protect Ridley and the men with the bridge. Find the pavise and we will act as shield bearers."

Sir Jocelyn said, "For men at arms?"

Sir Edward turned and growled, "For brothers in arms!" Sir Jocelyn recoiled from the ferocious gaze of Sir Edward.

Ridley had half of the men carrying the bridge. The other half of the men were with Will Red Leg. David of Wales' men sent arrows towards the tower. William handed me a pavise. They were heavier than a shield because they were larger but they were manageable. I went with Edward, Alfred and Peter to the front. The squires stood on the right-hand side and the other knights on the left. They would have the easiest task but they would have to carry the pavise on their left. It would be harder. I heard the crack of the mangonel.

Ridley said, "Lift!" There was the creak of wood and then he said, "Ready, my lord!"

I said, "March!" I lifted the pavise with two hands. It allowed me to see the ground for I did not want to walk into the moat. The bridge was awkward to carry and we did not hurry. Our journey was punctuated with the sound of the two war machines and arrows striking the battlements. Then the crossbows began to hit the pavise. In many ways, it was a reassuring noise for it told us that the pavise shields were protecting the men and that they were well made for no bolts came through.

I was almost taken by surprise when the moat loomed before my feet before I was expecting it. I barely managed to stop and cry, "Halt!" It was harder for those carrying the bridge and the front smacked into our calves. It hurt.

"Sorry, lord!"

"It was my fault."

I heard the crack of stones on stone. The mangonel and trebuchet were doing their job and we had almost finished ours. The next part would be the most dangerous. Edward, Alfred and Peter along with myself would have to shuffle right to allow the bridge to be lowered and then pushed across the moat. Sir Peter was on the right. "Petr move right!" As he shuffled we followed and when we reached the squires raised our pavise to form a roof. It was a relief for the squires' pavise were resting on the ground and took the weight. We were also safer. I watched the bridge as it was slid across the moat. Bolts thudded into the pavise.

"Done, lord!"

We now had to get back. "Men at arms, behind the pavise and we walk backwards." Roger of Hauxley joined me and he held the pavise with me. It was easier now for although we had to walk backwards there were two of us carrying the wooden board and we could move faster. We all reached the war machines without incident. Roger took away the pavise and I surveyed the tower. While there was little apparent damage I could not see any helmets there. The two machines could continue their assault while we attacked. The breach was a good thirty paces from the tower.

I turned, "Ridley have the men fed. We will attack at dusk. William, find the King and tell them that we have a breach and we are ready to attack." I knew that there were other breaches and the men who had broken through would also be ready to assault.

We returned to our tents and Egbert had ale and food ready for us. Sir Jocelyn asked, "How do we assault, Earl?"

"We use a formation favoured by the Romans. We make a column of knights and men at arms protected by our shields. It will be a smaller version of the one we just used. Once we reach the breach then the large warriors protect the smaller ones who can climb the rubble and then ascend to the fighting platform. The rest of us will follow."

"And that is it?"

"All that we will hold will be one small part of the wall. We then have to take the tower and that is never easy." I pointed to the wall and towers to the east of the breach. "Those men there will have to try to get back to the inner ward. David of Wales and our archers will follow us into the breach and when on the walls they can thin the numbers of those who flee."

251

William came rushing back. "Father, the King is with the men of Northampton. They have breached the east wall and they are attacking!"

"Fools! Dusk helps us. Is the breach a wide one?"

"Not as wide as this. It is but the width of a man and it is close to the eastern barbican!"

The eastern barbican was the main entrance to the castle and was the strongest defence apart from the keep. "Did you tell the King?"

William nodded glumly, "Aye, lord and he said to attack now!"

I looked over and saw that Ridley and his men had eaten. That was one positive thing. I was unhappy but we had little choice. The King commanded. Perhaps the Earl of Northampton thought to impress the King. "Sir Edward, have the men ready to attack."

"Aye lord. This will be bloody!"

I nodded. I went to the war machines. "Padraig, I need you and Will Red Leg to continue the attack right until we reach the breach. Then you can join us. Join me and my sons. Padraig, fetch an axe with you. Will, I will need your men for the attack. You help Padraig."

"Aye lord."

The crack of the war machines attacking the eastern wall had stopped. I had a feeling that they had forgotten the barbican. If so they would pay a terrible price. I reached my knights. "Sir Edward you take most of the knights and half of the men. Take and hold the tower. Sir Alfred and Sir Jocelyn, gather every spare man that you can. You will come with me and we will go to the aid of the men of Northampton." They nodded.

There was a corner tower at the junction of the north and east walls. We could not reach the barbican but we could reach the tower and, perhaps, alleviate some of the pressure on the men of Northampton. Even as we formed into a column I heard the sound of the assault on the east wall. Men would be dying. We were five men wide and twenty men deep. Not all were my men. There were some men at arms I did not know. I had Sam and Robert just behind me. We were a big target. Padraig would be bringing another ten to join us once they left their machines.

"Ready!"

"Aye, lord!" Their roaring words gave me confidence.

"We run and we sing!"

I began banging my shield and I started the chant which would help us stay together.

Men of Stockton
March from the north
Men of Stockton
Show what we are worth
Men of Stockton
Fear no foes
Men of Stockton
Add to your woes

The words themselves did not matter. It was the rhythm that we needed.

"March!"

Men of Stockton
March from the north
Men of Stockton
Show what we are worth
Men of Stockton
Fear no foes
Men of Stockton
Add to your woes

Crossbow bolts cracked into our shields. The stones from the trebuchet continued to smack into the battlements. I heard a cry from the rear of the column as a bolt found a leg. If it was one of my men at arms he would continue to march until we reached the wall. We all knew that if a man fell out then all were compromised.

We reached the bridge and began to tramp across. It vibrated. I remembered too late that we should not keep in step over the bridge and then I was across. We had been lucky. I saw, through the eyeholes of my helmet the rubble on the ground ahead of us. We were less than fifteen paces from the breach. I waited until the last men had left the bridge and then shouted, "Halt!" Bolts continued to hit us and I could hear the battle at the east wall. "Sir Fótr, lead your men!"

"Vanguard! With me!"

There was readjustment as men left the column. We closed ranks as Sir Fótr and his ten lithe warriors scurried across the rubble. I heard a cry as one was hit by a bolt and then I heard the rattle of arrows on the wall. I counted to ten and then shouted, "Now! Charge!" I did not have my sword drawn for I would need my right hand to help me clamber over the stones.

Alfred was to my side as we passed Ralph of Thorpe. He sheltered beneath his shield and I saw the bolt in his leg. "Give them hell, my lord!"

I heard, to my right, the clash of metal on metal as Sir Fótr and his men fought with those defending the base of the tower. Sir Edward and the rest of my men would soon be with him. As I slithered and fell down the blackened timbers and fallen masonry I looked to the stairs which led to the north wall. Amazingly no one was sending bolts our way. Those in the corner tower were too busy with the men of Northampton and the tower closest to us was under a ferocious attack from Sir Edward. I raced up the steps. Alfred and William were hard behind me and then the other squires. There were ten or so men at arms with us. Only Padraig, Will Red Leg, Sam and Robert were from my retinue. Sir Jocelyn brought up the rear.

The door to the north east tower was closed. I had expected that. When the assault had begun the defenders had cleared the fighting platform. We reached the door and I turned, "Padraig!"

Padraig and Will Red Leg both had axes. They ran to the door and began to hack furiously at it. "Shields!"

We held our shields up not a moment too soon. Stones and darts were hurled down from the fighting platform of the tower. Our shields held. My men at arms were strong and they knew where to strike. Padraig shouted, "It is ready to go, lord!"

"Stand clear!" I held my shield before me and Alfred and I ran at the door. The two men at arms had done well and the door fell inwards. The man at arms who had been behind it was thrown to the ground and Alfred's blade ended his life. The inside of the tower was dark. Sam and Robert tumbled beyond me to hack at the defenders who were barely visible. The only light came from the broken door and the hatch to the fighting platform. It was a confused maelstrom of men and blades. I hacked and sliced at the men before me. I heard Padraig roar as he led his men up to the fighting platform. Will Red Leg would follow him. I had a sudden, excruciating pain in my back. I had been stabbed. I continued to hack and stab at those before me. Suddenly there were no more enemies. They had fled.

"To the fighting platform!"

We raced up the steps to the top of the tower. I could feel the blood on my back. How had a blade penetrated my mail and gambeson? Padraig and his men had killed the crossbowmen on the tower. I looked to the breach which was being attacked by the Earl of Northampton and his men. Many men were lying dead within it and the men of Northampton had not yet gained the inner bailey. "Use the crossbows against the barbican!" We overlooked the barbican. They would be exposed. While my men at arms loaded the cumbersome weapons, I looked to the outer bailey. The survivors from the tower were flooding towards the keep. As soon as the bolts began to clear the barbican then it was as though the flood gates had been opened. The defenders left the barbican and raced across the inner bailey. The men of Northampton found that they could enter the castle and they ran after those who had been causing them so much grief.

We had done our part. I sheathed my sword. "Are any wounded?" I would keep my wound to myself until we reached our camp. The blood was flowing freely. How had someone managed to inflict such a deep wound? Was my mail damaged?

"No, lord, a few grazes for my lads."

I turned to speak to my men. They all looked hale. The ones who had accompanied us were also without wounds. "You did well, Padraig."

"Aye lord, but we were better led than those poor sods from Northampton." He pointed down and I saw dead knights and more than eighty dead men at arms and men of the fyrd.

It had been a costly breach. We could have saved many of those men had the Earl of Northampton waited until dark. I felt the blood seeping down my back. "Sir Jocelyn, ask the men of Northampton to take over this tower. We need to get back to our men."

"Aye, lord." He and his squire shouted commands to the men we had brought with us and they hurried through the gate to the breach.

Alfred was behind me and, as we neared the breach he said, "Father, you are wounded. There is blood."

"I know but I need to see that Sir Edward and the others are well."

My son snapped, "William, you, Sam and Robert take him to the doctor. There is much blood."

In truth, I felt a little weak and when Sam and Robert supported me I did not resist. They were both big men and they whisked me across the bridge to our camp. Egbert had seen my approach and the doctor was already at my tent. William took off my bloody surcoat and Sam and Robert my mail. The doctor, a small man said, "Earl, roll over."

William said, "Sam, Robert, guard the tent. Only my brother enters!"

"Aye Master William!"

"You have been stabbed, father, yet your mail is whole!"

"I felt something when we entered the tower. I thought it was a blow from one of the men at the door!"

I heard the doctor give a sharp intake of breath. "This is a long and deep wound. I have seen it before. The bandits of Lombardy use a weapon. It is a long narrow blade. They call it a stiletto. It is more of a spike than a knife. It can penetrate a mail link without breaking it. This could be a serious

256

wound. I dare not seal it yet in case there is some organ which is damaged within."

Alfred arrived. William said, "He was stabbed in the attack in the back. It was one of our men."

"Impossible!"

"Lie still, Earl."

William told Alfred what the doctor and I had said. "Sam and Robert were not behind him. Your squire and I were behind you brother. The rest were the men we led from the camp."

"And Sir Jocelyn and his squire."

Alfred nodded, "Aye. They were the only ones save our men and I trust all of our men as well as Sir Jocelyn and his squire. We must question the men who followed us."

William showed how much he had grown. "There is a killer out there. He may not be alone. From now on we keep our father here where he is safe."

"But the siege!" I felt myself weakening but I was still in command.

"We have taken the outer bailey. It will need machines inside the bailey to take the inner ward. You will not be needed for a day or two. I will go and speak with the King. William, you stay here and guard our father."

He left and the doctor said, "I fear you will not be able to move for at least three days. You are losing blood, lord." He hesitated, "Some Lombard bandits use poison. Your life hangs in the balance. Master William, I think we need a priest too."

I was about to protest when I suddenly felt incredibly sleepy. We had a killer loose in my camp. Despite the King's words, he was in as much danger as I was. A sudden thought came to me before I entered a black and bottomless world. Was I dying?

Chapter 17
Assassin's Blade

I found myself swirling in the bottom of a black lake and my mail was dragging me down. I felt as though my life was being sucked from me. Then I felt a heat I had never felt before. Was I drowning in a volcano? I looked up and saw my wife, her pale, long-fingered hand touched me and began to pull me to the surface.

"He is coming to!"

I opened my eyes. The doctor, my son and the King were there. All, especially the doctor, looked relieved. Alfred forced a smile, "We thought we had lost you. It has been three days."

"Three days?" It came out as a croak and the doctor said, "Give him some ale and do not crowd him so."

The King said, acidly, "You have a reprieve, leech. Let us hope he makes a full recovery or I shall make good on my promise." I saw Alfred shrug. I would discover the meaning of that later on.

William brought some ale and he cradled my head while I drank it. It tasted better than any ale I had ever drunk. "How goes the siege?"

Alfred shook his head, "The siege is unimportant. You nearly died. Tell him, doctor."

"The blade severed a blood vessel in your back. We had to enlarge the wound and cauterize the vessel or you would have bled to death. You were lucky it was such a narrow blade. We did not need to damage too much else. There is no putrefaction and the wound smells good. You should make a full recovery." He glanced nervously at the King, "But it will take another ten days to be certain of that."

"And the siege?"

The King sighed, "We lost seven knights in the attack by Northampton's men. He should have used your caution but I fear he was trying to impress me. If it had not been for your successful attack we would have lost even more. More than one hundred and fifty died before they closed their gates. We have miners digging beneath the cat. It will take time but we will bring down the wall. You have time to get well." He looked around. "I am concerned that one of the men we trusted could try to kill you."

I looked at Alfred. He shook his head. "The men who were with us when we attacked the tower have disappeared. No one remembers them arriving or which lord they served. When the column was formed they joined in! They could have been Welsh!"

"Or they could have been the men who served Sir Hugh. He seems to have inspired loyalty in his men." My worst fears appeared to have been realised.

"We are now scrutinising everyone. Sir Jocelyn was most concerned and he is as vigilant as any. We change the password each day. Your knights and the King are the only ones excused the rigour."

"And I am happy to give a password. You are worth more to me than any indignity I might suffer." The King rose. I stayed here until you woke to tell you that all is under control. I am still learning but I would rather you whole and leading us than leading and dead!"

When he had gone and a relieved doctor had departed I sat with my sons and Egbert. I could see that my loyal servant had been most concerned by the turn of events. "And our men?"

William laughed, "Any who approach our camp are given such a hard time that we are like a leper colony." His face lost its humour, "It is worrying, father. I did not know that there was a blade which could pierce mail "

Alfred nodded, "A sailmaker's bodkin can do the same. You have to be close to be able to kill. From now on there will be Sam and Robert at your back when you move… even when you pee!"

"And you found no such blade in the camp?"

"It would be easy to secrete. Do not worry that was their best chance. They failed! They will not catch us a second time."

I had had wounds before but this one took the most out of me. I felt as though I had no energy. Egbert proved to be a godsend. He sourced food which began to build me up. He served kidneys and calves' livers. The King was appalled when he heard that I was eating offal. Egbert was adamant. He knew what to serve me. He had the men at arms gather wild greens and cooked them with wild garlic and onions. Over the next week, I gained strength and energy. Alfred kept me apprised about the siege. The miners tunnelling under the cat were making progress beneath the wall of the inner bailey. Soon they would be ready to fire it. We had captured their supplies when we had taken the outer bailey. Already they would be suffering hunger.

When the fire was finally lit under the mine I was strong enough to go to the breach to view it. It was spectacular. The flames and the smoke erupted from the mine as though a dragon had breathed fire. The symbol of the Welsh was the dragon and it seemed apposite. As the fire burned the men on the outer wall fled to the keep. It was obvious that the wall would fall for the cracks appeared within a short time of the fire being lit. When the wall tumbled some of the men of Oxford raced through the breach. It was a mistake. Crossbow bolts cut them down.

The King took command and ordered all to stay in the outer bailey. He shouted, "We will do as the Earl of Cleveland did! Tomorrow we use shields to enter the bailey and secure the outer gate! We lose no more men to these traitors. Time and hunger are now on our side."

We sent men in at dawn and they opened the gate. It was a safer way to enter the inner bailey. We camped in the inner bailey and the garrison asked for a parley. Sir Jocelyn thought that the siege was over but Sir Edward and I knew better. "He is buying time. He has not enough supplies now and William thinks his brother Falkes is on the way. He is not. There are too many men twixt him and Bedford for that."

Sir Edward was right. The negotiations were for the safe passage of the females of the castle. The female members of the household, including Falkes' wife, and Henry de Braybrooke were released. The women were sent to the town while Henry de Braybrooke was held captive. After speaking with the King, we discovered that he was an innocent victim. He had been High Sheriff and Falkes de Breauté had held him captive. He became a valuable ally for he was able to tell us about the dispositions of the men within the keep. We discovered that there were just eighty knights who remained. Men at arms had been deserting over the walls and into the river. The thought passed through my mind that they could have been the assassins. Then I dismissed it. Deserting men just fled. William de Breauté would not surrender. De Braybrooke told us that he was certain his brother would come to his aid. The miners were set to build a mine beneath the keep. I knew why the knights did not surrender. They had been told they would be executed.

This time the mine was dug in two days. The garrison had neither bolts nor crossbows left and the miners were able to dig without hindrance. When the smoke began to pour from the keep the de Breauté standard was lowered and William de Breauté led out eighty men. They were paraded in the inner bailey so that the lords, barons, and men at arms could stand on the fighting platform and hear their trial. The Archbishop of Canterbury pleaded for leniency but we had lost over two hundred men and the King was in no mood to be merciful. Three men begged to be allowed to become Templars and go on crusade. They were the only ones who were not executed.

The King showed a new side to himself. He had been ruthless when dealing with the rebels and even while their bodies swung in the air he tasked Henry de Braybrooke with destroying the whole castle so that not a single stone remained. It was as draconian an act as I could ever remember. The churches and the roads in Bedford all benefitted. The treasure from the castle was distributed amongst all of us. King Henry showed that he understood the value of money. The siege had been expensive. It had cost him £1,311. That was a colossal sum and was seven times the annual income of William of Hartburn. It showed how committed he was to show the land that he was the ruler. The King wanted the bulk of the army to march back to London where Falkes de Breauté was said to be gathering men. I was happy to go but Alfred showed his new-found strength. He went to the King and told him, in no uncertain terms, that I was in no condition to go to war again. The King agreed and Sir Edward led my men south. He would command the men of Cleveland. Hindsight is wonderful. Vision when looking backwards is always perfect but I wonder what might have happened had I not headed north up the Great North Road with ten of my men at arms, my sons and servants and Sir Jocelyn de Braose with his men. I will never know but I do know that my dreams have been haunted by the King's decision ever since.

I was made to ride in a cart. Sam and Robert rode with me. Until we reached the Tees they would not relax their vigilance. Sir Alfred rode at one side, William at my other and Sir Jocelyn and his squire were the rear-guard. With Ridley the Giant and my men at arms before us, sniffing the air like hunting dogs, I felt sure that we would be safe. We did not relax. Each day we changed the password. One of my bodyguards slept outside my door and the other within. William shared my bed. Egbert slept at the foot. Alfred always had the room to my right and Sir Jocelyn to the left. I felt almost constricted. I confess that I felt better now. Egbert's diet appeared to have worked and I felt neither pain nor discomfort. It might have been different had I been riding but the cart was an easy and comfortable way to travel for I lay on furs and tents.

When we reached York I finally felt I could relax. Sir Ralph made us all welcome. We had good chambers and we spent two days there. I would only have Egbert and one of my bodyguards in the chamber with me. I was looking forward to a bed to myself. Alfred went to buy presents for his wife, child and mother. I sent William to buy something for his mother and sisters from me. Sir Jocelyn explored York. I spoke with the Sheriff.

"The King has grown then, lord?"

"He has," I told him of his actions.

"I am pleased. We need a good king who lives in England!" I nodded and sipped the wine he had provided. "I am more concerned about you. I fear, from what I have been told that these killers who seek you are not Welsh. They would have stood out and your men are no fools." The thought had crossed my mind. "I think it is the men who followed Sir Hugh and this mysterious son. We destroyed an empire. We both know how vacuous is the Earl of Chester. If we had not ended his reign then his empire would have grown. His men would know that. Perhaps they seek to return but to do so you must be out of the way."

He was right but I had not thought of it until then. "We should be safe here."

"No, Earl, just the opposite. York is a busy port. Ships leave here for Frisia, Denmark, Norway, France and Anjou not to mention every port in the east coast. My town is filled every day with strangers. My men are constantly rooting out those who would cause harm to my town. The obvious ones are easy but there are others who appear to be law-abiding. It is not until they commit a crime that you know they are evil. We have whores and doxies from all over the land serving those you use the river. I will be happier when you are in Stockton. There, strangers would stand out. The Lombard dagger is rare. It might be a foreigner who was hired to kill you."

"Then I will take care. We leave tomorrow and you will have to worry no more."

Sir Alfred, Sir Jocelyn and William were in high spirits when they returned. My sons had made good purchases and were looking forward to giving them to their mother and sisters. Sir Jocelyn just seemed in good humour. Sir Ralph gave us the best of feasts and we all drank well. It was Robert of Newton who would watch in the corridor while Sam Strong Arm would be behind the door. I had had a great deal to drink and I awoke in the dark of night. I needed to make water. I went to the garderobe and was about to return to bed when the handle on the door moved slightly. My senses had not been dulled by the drink. I drew my dagger and hissed, "There is danger."

Sam rose immediately and Egbert a heartbeat later. Egbert drew a dagger and Sam a sword. He hurled the door open and footsteps thundered down the corridor. Sam ran after the man and I knelt next to a dying Robert of Newton. "I am sorry lord but he gave the password. It was..." He said no more. Alfred appeared at his door. He had just a night tunic on but he had his sword in his hand. I pointed and rose. My son ran and his squire, Henry, followed. Behind me I heard William's door open. I ran down the corridor. This was the first real exercise I had had since the attempt on my life.

The noise had roused the hall and that was not a good thing. We had the chance to find the killer but if there were people around then it would muddy the waters. It soon became obvious that the killer was heading for the stables. There were guards there. Sir Ralph had been worried that a killer would need horses to flee. There were double guards at all the gates. The walls of York were as closely watched as anywhere. Only the river offered an avenue of escape. We had a chance. As we left the hall to race across the courtyard I saw Sam. He was fighting with two men at the door to the stables. He was struggling and was only saved from death by the intervention of my son, Alfred. Neither man wore mail. William was behind me and I only had a dagger but I did not hesitate. The alarm had been given and I heard Ridley the Giant leading my men from the nearby warrior hall. When I entered the stables, it was dark but I saw three men on horses. Their backs were to me. William appeared next to me. He had a sword in his hand.

"Surrender now and you will have justice. Fight and you die!" I tried to make my voice as forceful as possible.

They turned and I saw that it was Jocelyn de Braose, his squire, John, and another man. I was stunned but even as I stood, open-mouthed, many events suddenly made sense. "That is what you said to my father and yet you still

264

butchered him! Now you will die at the hand of his son!" He and his squire spurred their horses towards us. William stepped before me. It was brave but foolish.

A number of things all happened at once. I caught sight of movement to my right as Sam and Alfred, having despatched their opponents had raced in to the stables. They stood in the doorway to prevent them escaping. I saw that the squire, John, intended to ride William down and I grabbed my son and pulled him into one of the stalls. The third man rode at Alfred and Sam. Sam swung his sword at the leg of the man while Alfred lunged up at the middle of the squire, John. Sir Jocelyn was a little behind his squire and he swung his sword at Alfred who did not see him. The blade hacked into the skull of my son, Alfred. Even as his squire, Henry, ran to his lord's aid he too was cut down by the squire.

The evil knight turned and, as he spurred his horse shouted, "You took my father and now we are even for I have slain your son!" The knight and squire galloped from the stables.

I ran to Alfred. It was obvious that he was dead yet I still cradled his body in my arms and I hugged him as tightly as I had done when he was a bairn. "You died when it should have been me. I swear, my son, that I will have vengeance on Jocelyn de Braose."

I looked up as Ridley the Giant and my men appeared, "He shook his head, "They killed the sentries at the gate."

I rose, "Saddle our horses. We will follow him to the ends of the earth if needs be!"

I went to Sam. He was standing over the man he had wounded. I knelt and put my dagger at his throat, "Send for a priest." I pricked his neck with the dagger. "Answer my questions and you shall have confession before you die."

"I beg you, save my life!"

"Your life is forfeit but you may have absolution. Sam, bind the wound. Where has he gone?"

"He has a ship waiting on the river, lord. He will be long gone. He and his woman sail to France or Frisia, I know not which."

Ridley had been listening, "We will get to the river." He ran out.

"And who was his father?"

"The same man as was my lord too, Sir Hugh of Craven. I am now the last of them but we kept our oath."

The priest came in. I said, perfunctorily, "Hear his confession. William fetch my sword for I would execute this traitor myself!"

"No!"

"I promised you confession, no more!"

After I had ended the man's life I dressed and went, with the Sheriff to the river. My men had been too late. Five ships had all left at the same time. Sir Jocelyn's horse and his squire' mount were found wandering along the wharf. Despite our questions and the eagerness of those who lived along the river all that we knew was that the ship he had boarded had been bound for France. A woman had been with them. From the description of those who saw her she was Morag, One Eye Waller's woman. She had had her vengeance. When we returned to the gatehouse we saw that the men who were there had been poisoned and then stabbed in the heart with a small pointed weapon. Morag had been dogging us for some time. I guessed now that it had been she who had killed Harry son of John. A woman would not appear a threat. The passwords had been useless. Sir Jocelyn had been told them. We had only been safe when my sons had slept in my chamber. York would have been their last chance to murder me. Stockton was too well guarded.

My son's killer had escaped and a blackness came over me that was worse than the darkness of my wound. I felt it rise from within me. I felt angry and I felt foolish. I could now see all the clues which should have told me that Sir Jocelyn was the threat but I had been too concerned with the King. My son had paid the price for my negligence. I had almost lost William too! What was the point of securing a throne for a king if a man lost his children? I would follow Sir Jocelyn and I would kill him but first I had a son to bury.

Epilogue

My son never saw his own son grow nor did he know that he was an uncle. Rebekah had given birth to a boy while we were at York. He would be named Alfred after my son. Aunt Ruth aged twenty years in a moment. I swear that she began to die the day that I brought back the body of my son and the grim news. It was only that Matilda was even more distraught and needed my aunt. She used the strength of the loss of Ralph all those years ago to offer a few crumbs of comfort to the young widow.

I wept when he was buried in the church where his forebears lay. I sobbed for the loss. Had God offered me a trade, Alfred's life for mine, then I would have taken it. I looked at the tomb of the Warlord and my father. He was in good company and yet he had died before his life had begun. He had had so much to live for and now he was dead. Arsuf came back to me. Then I had been helpless to save my father. Thanks to my wound I had been helpless to save my son. I should have been the one to face Sir Jocelyn.

I knelt next to my son's body. My wife was with Aunt Ruth, Matilda, Rebekah, Isabelle and William. My son held his arms protectively around them. They stood and they wept. The body was still uncovered. Walter the Mason would carve an effigy to cover his body but for now his bandaged body awaited the stone lid which would cover him until Judgement Day. The bandages stopped his mother seeing the terrible wound which had ended our son's life. I put my lips close to where I knew the ear would be. He was dead and did not inhabit the body yet I spoke to him anyway. I had to. "I have failed you, Alfred. A father should protect his son and protect his family. I did not do that. Know that your family will want for nothing. Whatever was yours by birth will be your families by right. When we take ransom and treasure then your family will have your share. I will watch over your children and do a better job than I did with you. My family now takes precedence over the King and England! You would have been the greatest knight in Christendom. It may take me a lifetime but I swear I will hunt down your killer and end his worthless life." The candles in the church flickered as a rogue breath of breeze rustled down the aisle. Was my son speaking with me?

I stood and walked to the wet nurse who carried my grandson Henry Samuel. He was now more of a toddler and less of a child. I took him from the nurse. Matilda cuddled her newborn, Eleanor. "Henry, I make a solemn pledge to you here. Your father has gone but I will be as a father and a grandfather to you. I will be there to catch you when you fall and there to cheer you when you succeed." I looked at Matilda, "The curse that was Sir Hugh of Skipton continues to blight this land but at least you and my son had some happiness however briefly. You shall live here in Stockton. You will have your own quarters. We will make our home your home. When William and I return we shall have peace in our hearts as well as our land."

Margaret put her hand to her mouth, "No, husband! There have been enough deaths. Will you put our son in danger? Will you put yourself in harm's way again? And for what? He is a worthless knight who will come to a bad end. God will punish him"

I nodded, "Aye and it is I who will do God's work! We leave on the morning tide. The hunt begins!"

The End

Glossary

Bylnge -Billinge, near Wigan
Chevauchée- a raid by mounted men
Courts baron-dealt with the tenants' rights and duties, changes of occupancy, and disputes between tenants.
Fusil - A lozenge shape on a shield
Garth- a garth was a farm. Not to be confused with the name Garth
Groat- English coin worth four silver pennies
Hovel- a makeshift shelter used my warriors on campaign- similar to a '*bivvy*' tent
Luciaria-Lucerne (Switzerland)
Mêlée- a medieval fight between knights
Nissa- Nice (Provence)
Reeve- An official who ran a manor for a lord
Rote- An English version of a lyre (also called a crowd or crwth)
Vair- a heraldic term
Wrecsam- Wrexham
Wulfestun- Wolviston (Durham)

Historical Notes

This series of books follows the fortunes of the family of the Earl of Cleveland begun in the Anarchy series of novels. As with that series the characters in this book are, largely, fictional, but the events are all historically accurate.

The events in Scotland and Wales are largely fictitious. The Welsh King did try to take advantage of a boy King but he was defeated. Pembroke was attacked after the Earl Marshal died. The council of regents were in command until Henry reached the age of 20. The Charter of the Forests and the reissued Magna Carta helped to bring peace to England. Newark was held by a mercenary and was captured when a speedy attack took the town first. The siege of Bedford happened almost exactly the way I said. It marked the end of opposition to Henry. I have concentrated many sieges and battles for the purpose of the story.

The Charter of the Forests was issued by the Council of Regents and then endorsed, later, by the King to show his authority.

Carucage: Carucage was a medieval English land tax introduced by King Richard I in 1194, it was based on the size—variously calculated—of the estate owned by the taxpayer. It was a replacement for the danegeld, last imposed in 1162, which had become difficult to collect because of an increasing number of exemptions. Carucage was levied just six times: by Richard in 1194 and 1198; John, his brother and successor, in 1200; and John's son, Henry III, in 1217, 1220, and 1224, after which it was replaced by taxes on income and personal property.

Norham Castle

Two photographs taken by the author in 2018. They were taken from the inner ward. This is a modern bridge but you can see the gorge/ditch below. The river lies beyond the trees in the left-hand photograph. The gate house has gone but you can clearly see the foundations.

The story will continue when the Earl and his son seek the killers of Alfred.

Books used in the research:

- The Crusades-David Nicholle
- Norman Stone Castles- Gravett
- English Castles 1200-1300 -Gravett
- The Normans- David Nicolle
- Norman Knight AD 950-1204- Christopher Gravett
- The Norman Conquest of the North- William A Kappelle
- The Knight in History- Francis Gies
- The Norman Achievement- Richard F Cassady
- Knights- Constance Brittain Bouchard

- Knight Templar 1120-1312 -Helen Nicholson
- Feudal England: Historical Studies on the Eleventh and Twelfth Centuries- J. H. Round
- English Medieval Knight 1200-1300
- The Scandinavian Baltic Crusades 1100-1500
- The Scottish and Welsh Wars 1250-1400- Rothero
- Chronicles of the age of chivalry ed Hallam
- Lewes and Evesham- 1264-65- Richard Brooks
- Ordnance Survey Kelso and Coldstream Landranger map #74
- The Tower of London-Lapper and Parnell

Griff Hosker
September 2018

Other books by Griff Hosker

If you enjoyed reading this book, then why not read another one by the author?

Ancient History

The Sword of Cartimandua Series
(Germania and Britannia 50 A.D. – 128 A.D.)
Ulpius Felix- Roman Warrior (prequel)
The Sword of Cartimandua
The Horse Warriors
Invasion Caledonia
Roman Retreat
Revolt of the Red Witch
Druid's Gold
Trajan's Hunters
The Last Frontier
Hero of Rome
Roman Hawk
Roman Treachery
Roman Wall
Roman Courage

The Wolf Warrior series
(Britain in the late 6th Century)
Saxon Dawn
Saxon Revenge
Saxon England
Saxon Blood
Saxon Slayer
Saxon Slaughter
Saxon Bane
Saxon Fall: Rise of the Warlord
Saxon Throne
Saxon Sword

Medieval History

The Dragon Heart Series
Viking Slave
Viking Warrior
Viking Jarl
Viking Kingdom
Viking Wolf
Viking War
Viking Sword
Viking Wrath
Viking Raid
Viking Legend
Viking Vengeance
Viking Dragon
Viking Treasure
Viking Enemy
Viking Witch
Viking Blood
Viking Weregeld
Viking Storm
Viking Warband
Viking Shadow
Viking Legacy
Viking Clan
Viking Bravery

The Norman Genesis Series
Hrolf the Viking
Horseman
The Battle for a Home
Revenge of the Franks
The Land of the Northmen
Ragnvald Hrolfsson
Brothers in Blood
Lord of Rouen
Drekar in the Seine
Duke of Normandy
The Duke and the King

Danelaw
(England and Denmark in the 11th Century)
Dragon Sword
Oathsword

New World Series
Blood on the Blade
Across the Seas
The Savage Wilderness
The Bear and the Wolf
Erik The Navigator

The Vengeance Trail

The Reconquista Chronicles
Castilian Knight
El Campeador
The Lord of Valencia

The Aelfraed Series
(Britain and Byzantium 1050 A.D. - 1085 A.D.)
Housecarl
Outlaw
Varangian

**The Anarchy Series England
1120-1180**
English Knight
Knight of the Empress
Northern Knight
Baron of the North
Earl
King Henry's Champion
The King is Dead
Warlord of the North
Enemy at the Gate
The Fallen Crown
Warlord's War

Struggle for a Crown
1360- 1485
Blood on the Crown
To Murder a King
The Throne
King Henry IV
The Road to Agincourt
St Crispin's Day
The Battle for France
The Last Knight
Queen's Knight

Tales from the Sword I
(Short stories from the Medieval period)

Tudor Warrior series
England and Scotland in the late 14th and early 15th
century
Tudor Warrior

Conquistador
England and America in the 16th Century
Conquistador

Modern History

The Napoleonic Horseman Series
Chasseur à Cheval
Napoleon's Guard
British Light Dragoon
Soldier Spy
1808: The Road to Coruña
Talavera
The Lines of Torres Vedras
Bloody Badajoz
The Road to France
Waterloo

The Lucky Jack American Civil War series

Rebel Raiders
Confederate Rangers
The Road to Gettysburg

The British Ace Series
1914
1915 Fokker Scourge
1916 Angels over the Somme
1917 Eagles Fall
1918 We will remember them
From Arctic Snow to Desert Sand
Wings over Persia

Combined Operations series
1940-1945
Commando
Raider
Behind Enemy Lines
Dieppe
Toehold in Europe
Sword Beach
Breakout
The Battle for Antwerp
King Tiger
Beyond the Rhine
Korea
Korean Winter

Tales from the Sword II
(Short stories from the Modern period)

Other Books
Great Granny's Ghost (Aimed at 9-14-year-old young
people)

For more information on all of the books then please visit the
author's website at www.griffhosker.com where there is a
link to contact him or visit his Facebook page: GriffHosker
at Sword Books

Made in the USA
Monee, IL
14 May 2024

58476060R00163